"My apartm...
without you...
my bed," Ra...

"I sleep in the guest room."

"Not in my imagination."

His husky voice sent warning flares to her brain, the only part of her not affected by him—so far. His hand on her wrist was sending a stab of pleasure through her entire body.

"You've certainly changed from the impersonal stranger I first met." Lacey decided the best approach was a light one. "But it's no use being seductive. Your sister told me all about you."

His gaze sharpened. "What did she say?"

"That you're bad news to women."

"Could you be a little more specific?"

"I gather you have a rather short attention span. You tire easily."

His eyes sparkled with amusement. "My sister would scarcely be in a position to make that accusation. I can assure you, tiring easily is one complaint I've never received."

Dear Reader:

Romance readers have been enthusiastic about the Silhouette Special Editions for years. And that's not by accident: Special Editions were the first of their kind and continue to feature realistic stories with heightened romantic tension.

The longer stories, sophisticated style, greater sensual detail and variety that made Special Editions popular are the same elements that will make you want to read book after book.

We hope that you enjoy this Special Edition today, and will enjoy many more.

Please write to us:

Jane Nicholls
Silhouette Books
PO Box 236
Thornton Road
Croydon
Surrey
CR9 3RU

TRACY SINCLAIR
Champagne for Breakfast

Silhouette Special Edition

Originally Published by Silhouette Books
a division of
Harlequin Enterprises Ltd.

All the characters in this book have no existence outside the imagination of the Author, and have no relation whatsoever to anyone bearing the same name or names. They are not even distantly inspired by any individual known or unknown to the Author, and all the incidents are pure invention.

All rights reserved. The text of this publication or any part thereof may not be reproduced or transmitted in any form or by any means, electronic or mechanical, including photocopying, recording, storage in an information retrieval system, or otherwise, without the written permission of the publisher.

This book is sold subject to the condition that it shall not, by way of trade or otherwise, be lent, resold, hired out or otherwise circulated without the consent of the publisher in any form of binding or cover other than that in which it is published and without a similar condition including this condition being imposed on the subsequent purchaser.

First published in Great Britain in 1989 by Silhouette Books, Eton House, 18-24 Paradise Road, Richmond, Surrey TW9 1SR

© Tracy Sinclair 1988

Silhouette, Silhouette Special Edition and Colophon are Trade Marks of Harlequin Enterprises B.V.

ISBN 0 373 57500 9

23—8902

Made and printed in Great Britain

TRACY SINCLAIR

is the author of more than twenty Silhouette novels.
She also contributes to various magazines and news-
papers. She says her years as a photojournalist provided the most exciting adventures—and misad-
ventures—of her life. An extensive traveler—from
Alaska to South America and most places in between—and a dedicated volunteer worker—from
suicide-prevention programs to English-as-a-second-
language lessons—the California resident has accu-
mulated countless fascinating experiences, settings and
acquaintances to draw on in plotting her romances.

Other Silhouette Books by Tracy Sinclair

Silhouette Special Edition

Never Give Your Heart	Intrigue in Venice
Mixed Blessing	A Love So Tender
Designed for Love	Dream Girl
Castles in the Air	Preview of Paradise
Fair Exchange	Forgive and Forget
Winter of Love	Mandrego
The Tangled Web	No Room for Doubt
The Harvest Is Love	More Precious Than Jewels
Pride's Folly	

Silhouette Christmas Stories

Under the Mistletoe

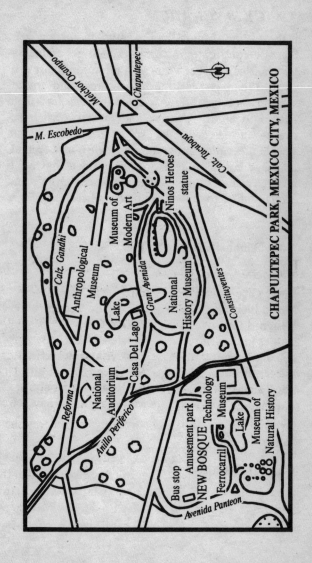

CHAPULTEPEC PARK, MEXICO CITY, MEXICO

Chapter One

Lacey Scott sank gratefully onto a vacant bench, putting her heavy shoulder bag on the seat with a sigh of relief. Chapultepec Park was beautiful but vast. She had walked for hours and covered only a fraction of the grounds.

It was foolish to try to see everything on the first day of her vacation. She wasn't even unpacked yet. That could wait, though. She hadn't come to Mexico City to waste her time in a hotel room. It was a pretty grim room anyway. So far, nothing was working out the way she'd planned.

Lacey's generous mouth drooped. It wasn't anyone's fault that her best friend, Mary Beth, dropped out at the last minute. Her whirlwind courtship was the stuff dreams are made of. When they'd planned this trip together, neither of them could have foreseen that Mary

Beth would wind up on her honeymoon in Acapulco instead.

Lacey stretched out her long legs, leaned her head back and closed her eyes briefly. A sudden rush of motion prompted her to open them. She uttered a strangled cry as she saw a ragged little boy running away with her purse.

"Stop! Come back here!" She leaped to her feet and started after him, colliding with a man who was walking by.

The encounter cost precious seconds. She stumbled and fell heavily against him as she tried to regain her balance. His muscular body absorbed her weight effortlessly, and his arms closed to steady her.

"Easy does it." His low, musical voice sounded amused.

She fought her way out of his embrace. "Let go of me! That boy stole my purse! I have to catch him."

The man's amusement vanished. He looked sharply down the path that held only a young couple strolling hand in hand. "Which way did he go?"

"Into those bushes." Lacey pointed at a dense stand of shrubbery behind a strip of grass.

The man plunged into the bushes with Lacey following. By the time she pushed her way through the tangled foliage he was on the other side, but the child was nowhere in sight.

"I'm afraid it's useless." He shook his head disgustedly. "Those little street urchins can disappear like magic."

"He *has* to be around here somewhere! Aren't there any police? How do I call them?"

"By the time they got here your little thief would be long gone—he is already. They have their escape routes picked out in advance."

Lacey looked frantically in every direction, unwilling to accept the fact that the boy was truly gone for good. "He can't be! Don't you understand? He stole my purse. All my money was in it!"

"Traveler's checks can be refunded," the man said soothingly. "I'll take you to the proper authorities."

Lacey started to tremble violently as the enormity of her loss sank in. She'd been carrying cash, not traveler's checks. This trip had been planned on a very tight budget. After she'd bought her airline tickets and prepaid the first night's rent at the hotel to be sure they'd hold her reservation, there wasn't that much left over. It had seemed foolish to go to the bother and expense of buying traveler's checks.

Her soft mouth trembled as she said, "I was carrying cash."

"Don't you watch your own television commercials?" he demanded. "Nobody in his right mind carries cash in this day of charge accounts and credit cards."

That was fine for people who could afford to pay the bills when they came in at the beginning of the month. Lacey didn't happen to be one of them. It wasn't something one told a stranger, however.

She looked so woebegone that his disapproving tone softened. "It's most unfortunate, but you mustn't let this spoil your vacation. Money can be wired in a matter of hours, and this time you'll know to be more careful."

If only it were that simple! The man acted as though she'd suffered only a minor inconvenience instead of a major tragedy. She was about to say so when she took a good look at him.

Lacey had been too upset to pay much attention to him before. After a comprehensive scrutiny, she realized that he wouldn't understand. He had money written all over him, from his elegant clothes to his thin gold watch and expensive haircut.

"Well, it's not your problem." She sighed.

"It's my city, though, so I feel a certain amount of blame." He smiled winningly, revealing even white teeth in a deeply tanned face. "I hope you won't judge all of my countrymen by this one regrettable incident."

At any other time Lacey would have been intrigued. He was strikingly handsome, besides being charming and sophisticated. Interesting, too. His dark eyes were kind now, but there was something faintly autocratic about the tilt of his head. The impression was reinforced by the kind of confident manner that was born in a person, not acquired. Who was this man? Someone important, no doubt. Well, it didn't matter. She'd never find out.

Lacey gathered her wandering thoughts and answered his remark. "It would be foolish to blame anyone for my own carelessness. I guess all big cities are the same. This could have happened anywhere."

"Sadly enough, that's true. I can only hope the fascinations of Mexico City will erase your bad first impression."

"I'm sure they would have," she answered politely. After all, he was trying to be nice.

He raised a dark eyebrow. "You're not willing to give us another chance?"

She shook her head regretfully. "I can't."

"Why don't we go across the street and have a drink at the El Presidente while I try to convince you that you're making a mistake."

"No, thank you." She slanted a dubious glance at him. No matter how helpful he'd been, the man was still a stranger. She had no reason to trust anyone here.

"It's a very respectable hotel, and the bar is on the lobby floor in full view of everybody," he coaxed, as though guessing the reason for her refusal.

She flushed slightly. "It isn't that."

"What is it, then?" His eyes lit with amusement. "I can assure you my intentions are honorable."

Lacey suddenly felt foolish. A man such as this didn't have to pick up women in the park. He could have his choice of glamorous females. Only kindness had prompted the offer, so it would be silly to refuse. The El Presidente was one of the top hotels in Mexico City, and this was her only chance to see the inside of it.

"I *would* like to sit down for a few minutes," she admitted.

She was further reassured by the fact that he seemed well-known. The doorman gave him a little salute, and several people called greetings in the lobby.

When they were seated at a table in the bar he said, "In all the excitement I didn't think to introduce myself. My name is Raoul Ruiz."

After she'd given her own name, Lacey said, "You seem to know everyone. Are you staying here?"

"No, I live down the block, but I come over often for lunch or a drink."

"This is a lovely neighborhood."

She wasn't merely being polite. The towering buildings adjacent to the hotel looked out over the park and the city beyond. The plush apartment houses were comparable to any in the United States, and undoubtedly just as costly.

"Where are you from?" Raoul asked.

"San Diego, which is a great deal smaller than Mexico City. I'm a little overwhelmed by all the people."

He smiled. "You'll get used to us."

"Maybe next time," she said wistfully.

"You're still determined to go home? That doesn't indicate a very forgiving nature." His voice was gently teasing.

Lacey didn't want to waste this brief time fending off his arguments. She decided to be honest. "I have no choice. There isn't anyone I can phone for more money."

"You don't want to tell your family?" he asked tentatively.

"I don't have any. I was an only child, and my parents died over two years ago."

"I'm sorry," he murmured, but he still looked puzzled. It was obvious that he couldn't conceive of anyone not having resources to fall back on.

Lacey had felt the same way before her parents were killed in a tragic auto accident. She had been the golden girl, bright, popular and adored by her mother and father. They had encouraged her to follow a fine-arts program in college, instead of taking anything practical. The interesting courses hadn't prepared her for a career, but her parents said she had plenty of time to experiment before settling into one profession.

Then, in her senior year, the bottom had fallen out of Lacey's world. In addition to her searing grief was the worry about money. Her father had taken out bank loans that were no problem while he was alive. His thriving business could pay them back. But that assumption ended with his death.

Lacey knew nothing about interstate trucking. With no one to run the business, the bank called in its loans. Her attorney had suggested bankruptcy proceedings to salvage some of the assets, but she wouldn't hear of it. She couldn't dishonor her father's memory for her own gain.

When all the bills were paid, Lacey was penniless and panicky. Her parents had always discouraged her from working. They had enjoyed pampering their only child, and she'd drifted along, following their wishes, planning on a vague career sometime in the future. The only jobs she'd held were temporary summer ones in boutiques, where she'd spent most of her salary on clothes.

After the ax fell, she had to drop out of college, before receiving her diploma. She got a job doing one of the few things she was suited for, modeling. Brazelton's, a local department store, hired her to wander from floor to floor displaying their couturier clothes. It was mindless work, but it paid the rent.

Raoul was eyeing her covertly, trying to figure her out. He'd bought enough costly gifts for beautiful women to recognize an expensive outfit when he saw one. Her blue and white knit suit hadn't come from any bargain basement, yet she claimed to be short of funds. He was too well bred to ask questions, however.

"Was your vacation almost over at least?" he asked.

"No, I just got here this morning."

"That's terrible!"

Lacey tried to smile. "At least I can truthfully say I've been to Mexico City. Not that I've seen it—just that I've been here."

"You can't possibly turn around and go home," he stated firmly.

"I can't do anything else. Your park is very pretty, but I wouldn't relish sleeping in it."

"Aren't you being a little foolish? I know it's embarrassing to admit you've been fleeced, but is it worth giving up your whole trip? Why don't you phone a friend to wire you some money?''

''That's the quickest way to break up a friendship,'' she answered lightly.

''Are you afraid to stay after what happened? Is that it?''

Annoyance rippled through her. Why couldn't he just let her enjoy this luxurious lounge? It was the only bit of glamour she was going to get out of this ill-fated trip.

''What do you do for a living?'' she asked abruptly.

He was clearly startled. ''I . . . well, I run my family business.''

''Which consists of what?''

''We own tin mines and real estate—farming property and a cattle ranch, that sort of thing.''

''You said it was a family business, therefore you have relatives,'' she continued crisply.

His perplexity was evident, but he answered readily enough. ''Yes, a large family. Besides my widowed mother and a married sister, I have numerous aunts, uncles and cousins.''

''You're very fortunate. I'm all alone in the world, and I wasn't equipped to carry on *my* family business. I support myself modeling clothes, and all my friends are in the same economic bracket. Now that you know why I can't stay on, can we just drop the subject?''

Chagrin was etched on his face. ''I'm sorry. I've been incredibly insensitive.''

After she'd vented her frustration, Lacey was the one who was sorry. ''It isn't your fault,'' she mumbled. ''You had no way of knowing.''

''In my own defense I have to say that's really true. You look so . . . elegant,'' he said helplessly.

Lacey smiled wryly. "The designer suit? Most of the women who can afford it aren't a size six. At the end of the season I'm allowed to buy things at a fraction of the cost. Which is a mixed blessing. I can't resist spending more than I should."

Raoul grinned. "Think of all the women who spend ten times as much for a size sixteen, hoping they'll look like you. You're dispensing dreams. The store should pay you handsomely."

She shook her head. "My kind of modeling doesn't pay much. The big money is in photographic work."

"Have you ever thought of doing that instead?"

His admiring gaze catalogued her long, shimmering blond hair, the slightly tilted, sapphire-blue eyes fringed by thick, curling lashes. Her skin was like cream, and her features were almost flawless. A perfectionist might find her straight nose a trifle too short and her mouth a little generous, but Raoul would have argued the point.

"I don't want to spend my life pouting in front of a camera, or assuming those weird poses for fashion magazines," Lacey answered.

"What do you want to do?"

"My immediate ambition is to be a buyer. I really think I know the kind of clothes women want."

"That shouldn't be a difficult field to move into. You're right there on the ground floor, so to speak."

She sighed. "That's what I thought. But I've been walking around like a plastic dummy for two years. No one takes me seriously. I'm tempted to buy some horn-rimmed glasses and gain twenty pounds."

Raoul smiled. "Isn't that a bit drastic?"

"You'd know what I'm talking about if you tried to sell somebody a ton of tin and he said, 'Hey, baby, how about dinner tonight?'"

"That would be a unique experience," he agreed with a chuckle.

"It isn't funny!"

"I'm sure it isn't," he soothed.

Lacey was once more remorseful. Why was she dumping on a perfect stranger? Especially one who couldn't possibly understand, anyway.

"Well, it's just something I'll have to live with," she said. "Tell me what to see if I ever get back here again."

"Where can I begin? The National Palace, the House of Tiles, the Pyramids of San Juan Teotihuacan."

"I'm sorry I asked," she answered ruefully.

"I'm giving you reasons to return."

"I'm sure I will one day."

Raoul stared at her thoughtfully. "Perhaps we can find a solution to your problem."

"You'd have to be a magician."

"I can't claim magical powers, but I do have an apartment. You're welcome to use it."

Lacey stared at him blankly. "You must be joking."

"Not at all. I have a large apartment, and you need a place to stay."

"As simple as that," she said dryly.

"Precisely."

She wasn't surprised, merely disappointed. Raoul had seemed genuinely concerned about her. She should have known better. "Do you always invite strangers to share your living arrangements?" she asked coolly.

The corners of his firm mouth twitched. "That wasn't my intention, but I'll be glad to reconsider."

She looked at him warily. "I don't understand."

"I was offering the use of my home—without my services thrown in."

She didn't believe him for a moment. "You mean I'd have my own bedroom?"

"Exactly."

"And you wouldn't expect ... visitation rights?"

"A right and a privilege are two different things. Now, if you were to issue an invitation, that would change matters."

Her ivory skin warmed becomingly. "I appreciate the delicacy of your proposition, but I'm not interested."

As she pushed back her chair, he said, "Where are you going?"

"Back to the hotel to get my luggage," she answered curtly.

"How do you intend to get there?" He leaned back in his chair, watching her as though he were a sleek cat contemplating a captive mouse.

Lacey's face reflected her dismay. That hadn't occurred to her. She'd be all right once she got to the hotel, thanks to the impulse that had led her to hide a twenty-dollar bill in her suitcase for an emergency. It would pay for transportation to the airport. The problem was getting to the other end of town, miles from here.

She swallowed her pride with difficulty. "Could you loan me bus fare?"

"You're admitting you need my help?"

"I'm not going to beg!" she said angrily.

Before she could stand up, Raoul's long fingers closed around her slim wrist. "Poor little Lacey, I shouldn't bait you after the bad experience you've been through, but I couldn't resist. You presented such a beguiling picture of outraged virtue."

"And you're not used to being turned down," she said stiffly.

"My offer didn't have any strings attached," he replied, sidestepping her allegation. "You would have discovered that if you hadn't jumped to conclusions. What I proposed to do was move to my sister's and allow you to occupy the apartment—alone."

Her mouth literally dropped open. "But you don't know anything about me! I . . . I could walk off with the silver. I could clean out your whole place!"

"The greatest loss would be my faith in human nature. I believe you're trustworthy."

"You're really serious, aren't you?" she asked incredulously.

"Completely. What's your answer?"

Uncertainty pervaded Lacey's thoughts. She'd have to be out of her mind to accept. In spite of his obvious wealth and breeding, this man could be a dangerous pervert. One thing didn't preclude the other. He might turn into a monster when he got her alone in his apartment.

As though he were clairvoyant, Raoul drew a bunch of keys out of his pocket. After detaching one, he handed it to her. "My building is around the corner. You can walk over there by yourself. I don't have another key," he said, anticipating her suspicion. "But you don't have to take my word for it. The front and back doors have bolts and chains."

Lacey stared at the key as though it might open Pandora's box. The urge to take it was powerful—like the lure of all forbidden fruit. But if Raoul's offer were sincere, it would be a blessing. She could salvage at least a few days of her vacation.

He kept his face carefully blank as he watched her wrestle with temptation. "Any other questions?"

Her eyes were troubled as she gazed at him, searching for the real man under the aristocratic features. Intelligence and compassion shone out of his steady eyes, but his high cheekbones, square jaw and uncompromising mouth held a hint of ruthlessness.

"Why are you really offering to do this for me?" she asked.

"Because you're a fellow human being in trouble," he answered simply. "If we can't help each other, what's it all about?"

"Would you be as generous if I were...well...fat and fifty?"

He grinned. "I hope so, yet I can't guarantee it. You're wise to be wary, but I assure you I have no ulterior motives. You'll have to decide that for yourself, however."

Lacey couldn't see any hidden traps. He'd been completely candid with her. It was an incredible offer that she couldn't refuse.

"I don't know how to thank you," she said breathlessly.

Something flickered in his dark eyes for a moment. "It isn't necessary. I just hope you enjoy your stay."

"Oh, I will! I'll appreciate it twice as much."

He glanced at his watch. "Good. As long as that's settled, I'd better inform my sister that she's to have a houseguest."

"What will she think when you tell her the reason?"

Raoul smiled. "She'll probably be wild with curiosity."

"That's understandable."

"I think I'll tell her you're fat and fifty," he said mischievously. "That way she'll lose interest."

"If she believes you."

"Rosa and I have a good relationship. She'll take me in even if she doesn't believe me."

"I hope it won't be an inconvenience."

Lacey realized that she was prolonging the conversation pointlessly. But once they parted today she'd never see Raoul again. They'd have no occasion to meet. When her stay was over she'd simply leave the key with the manager. And after she returned home she'd send him an effusive thank-you note and a small gift in appreciation of his hospitality.

That would be the end of it, as it should be. Yet she couldn't help feeling a tinge of regret that they'd never get to know each other. Even this small glimpse already showed her Raoul was the most fascinating man she'd ever met.

"Rosa and Edouard, her husband, have a large house staffed by more servants than they need," he was saying. "I won't be in the way."

"I'm glad I'm not disrupting more people."

"You aren't disrupting me, either," he assured her. "I won't even be there very long. I'm going up to the ranch toward the end of the week." He looked at her thoughtfully. "How long are you staying?"

"Would three days be all right?" she asked tentatively.

She wouldn't have to pay for a hotel room, but she did have to eat. If she bought food at a market instead of going to restaurants, the twenty should stretch that long.

Raoul was frowning. "Three days are nothing. You have to stay longer than that."

"Well, we'll see." She picked up the key from the table. "I know you must have things to do."

"A few," he admitted. "First I'll take you to your hotel so you can pack."

"I never *un*packed. But you're right, I have to pick up my suitcases. I forgot all about them."

"If you didn't unpack, there's no problem. I'll send someone for your luggage, and have it delivered to you."

When they parted outside the hotel she extended her hand. "I don't know what to say except thank you."

His handclasp was warm and firm. "Enjoy yourself. I'll call you in a couple of days to see how you're getting along."

Lacey's heart lifted unaccountably at the prospect of hearing from him again, even over the phone. As she prepared to leave he drew a well-stuffed wallet from his breast pocket. He took out a wad of bills and offered them to her.

"Here, take this," he said.

She looked at the money uncomprehendingly. "What's that for?"

"You have to eat."

She shook her head. "I have enough money to eat."

"How much?"

"Enough," she insisted.

"I can just imagine." When she put her arms behind her back, Raoul said impatiently, "My dear Lacey, contrary to what you might have heard, the best things in life are *not* free. I don't want you expiring on my living-room rug, so kindly take this. I'm beginning to see how difficult you are to convince, but I'm late for an appointment."

In spite of her determination not to accept any more from him, he stuffed the money into her hand and strode off before she could argue further. Lacey stared at the thick sheaf of bank notes in her hand. Even allowing for the difference in currency, the thousands of pesos she was holding amounted almost to the sum she'd budgeted for her entire trip!

She put her hand in her jacket pocket and started to walk to the address he'd given her, feeling like Alice in Wonderland. Raoul could wave his magic wand and make all kinds of marvelous things happen. It was probably a good thing they would never meet again. He could very easily change her whole life.

Not merely because of his money. He had a magnetism that was almost tangible, plus a forcefulness that didn't allow any dissent. He could get anything he wanted in life—or anybody.

Raoul's building was about what she expected, very posh, with a uniformed doorman haughtily guarding the portals.

She evidently passed inspection, because he touched his cap and said, *"Buenas tardes, señorita."*

"Good afternoon," she replied. "My name is Lacey Scott, and I'm going to be staying in Mr. Ruiz's apartment for a few days. *Alone,"* she added firmly as the man suppressed a leer. This was by no means a rare occurrence, evidently.

"Sí, señorita," he answered meekly, although it was obvious that he didn't believe her.

Lacey controlled her annoyance. What difference did it make what he thought? "My luggage will be arriving shortly. Please bring it up when it gets here," she instructed, matching his earlier hauteur. Holding her head high, she marched to the elevator.

Not even the building's lavish lobby and Raoul's undisputed wealth had prepared her for the interior of his apartment. The foyer opened onto a large room with glass windows that overlooked the metropolis. Thick beige carpeting deadened her footsteps as she walked down three steps to the sunken living room furnished in a mixture of modern and antique pieces.

The couches and chairs were large and comfortable, softening the starkness of their white leather upholstery. Some of the tables were glass, but others were intricately carved dark wood, like the huge armoire that held a fascinating collection of pre-Columbian artifacts.

Lacey was fascinated by the heads of animal gods, the pottery and mysterious fertility figures. In striking contrast were the modern paintings that adorned the walls, great slashes of color that invited long contemplation to decipher their meaning.

The dining room had a mirrored wall opposite the windows, so diners would be surrounded by the city lights. A crystal chandelier hanging over the black marble dining table added to the dazzle.

When Lacey switched it on briefly, she could visualize formal dinner parties peopled by elegant guests. This wasn't just a bachelor pad, it was a home. Surely Raoul invited more than girlfriends to this splendid place.

Intrigued by her glimpse into his life-style, Lacey walked down the hall to the bedrooms. The first door she opened was unmistakably a guest room. It had an anonymous feeling, although it was as luxurious as the rest of the apartment. The bed was covered with a quilted silk spread in a sapphire and white print. The carpeting and draperies were white, and the lamps had blue shades. After peeking into the well-appointed blue and white bathroom, she continued down the hall. She couldn't wait to see Raoul's bedroom.

The next room came as a shock, however. It was a child's room. The furniture was scaled down, and the bed was covered with stuffed animals. Every variety of toy imaginable was stacked in corners, and on tables and shelves. The organdy curtains and eyelet bedspread proclaimed it a little girl's room.

Lacey felt a curious letdown as she gazed around. Raoul hadn't thought to mention that he was married. But that couldn't be. He could scarcely loan out his apartment so casually if he had a wife. He once had, though. And obviously he still had at least partial custody of their child.

Lacey's mouth drooped for no reason as she proceeded to his bedroom. The master suite was as stunning as she expected, yet totally masculine. He must have done it over after his wife left. The king-size bed was covered by a tailored navy spread, and the massive highboy and dresser held only male implements. She glimpsed silver-backed brushes, a caddy for cuff links and an electric valet for pressing slacks.

A silver picture frame drew her eye. Lacey advanced into the room feeling like an intruder, but she had to see what kind of women he was attracted to. The photo didn't enlighten her. It was a picture of a beautiful dark-haired child about four years old. The family resemblance was immediately visible. This was Raoul's child.

Lacey walked slowly back to the guest room, wondering what the story was. You could tell he cared about his daughter. Hers had been the only photograph in his room. Also, the toys in her bedroom showed the indulgence he lavished on her.

Raoul was constantly confounding Lacey. She'd been so sure he was a bachelor playboy. It was difficult to picture him as a family man. What had caused his divorce, and which one of them had wanted it? The maddening thing was that she'd never find out.

Her luggage arrived in a surprisingly short time. After unpacking, Lacey set out to do some more sight-seeing.

She decided on the National Museum of Anthropology, because it was located on the other side of the El Presidente, within walking distance. It was getting too late for any lengthy excursions. Tomorrow she'd find out about group tours.

Her guidebook said this museum was the finest of its kind in the world, and Lacey felt it clearly deserved its reputation. The ground floor was filled with priceless artifacts dating back to prehistoric times. It was awesome to realize that many of these intricately designed pieces were made by people who lived more than two thousand years ago. Their art was a tangible link to the present, a reminder that they had worked and worshiped, loved and lived, with the same gusto as modern man.

After steeping herself in antiquity, Lacey visited the upper floors where modern-day Mexico was represented, complete with straw-covered huts, tape-recorded native songs and lifelike models of village activities.

The time passed so swiftly that she was surprised to find it was dusk when she finally left the museum. Fatigue overtook her suddenly. It had been a long, eventful day. She wanted to go back to the apartment and take off her shoes, but first she had to find a market.

The money Raoul had given her was enough for the most lavish restaurants, but she had no intention of using any more than she had to. It was money that would have to be paid back. Her original plan to eat frugally at home hadn't changed.

By the time she returned to the apartment with her bag of groceries, Lacey was drooping. She decided a warm bath would revitalize her, but when she almost fell asleep in the tub, she realized that was a mistake. Instead of getting dressed again she put on a long flowered robe, and decided to lie down for a few minutes.

The bedroom was in complete darkness when she awoke much later. A shocked glance at the clock told her it was after eight o'clock. How could she have slept so long? Now she'd never be able to go to sleep at a reasonable hour so she could get up bright and early. This whole day was off kilter.

The darkened apartment framed the brilliant lights of the city spread out below, and Lacey paused on her way to the kitchen to gaze out appreciatively. Bright automobile headlights resembled thousands of fireflies darting through the night in straight lines that bisected each other.

Everyone was going somewhere. The sprawling city hummed with vitality. Was Raoul out there, looking deeply into a glamorous woman's eyes, caressing her with his husky voice that was romantic even in broad daylight? Lacey sighed and continued on to the kitchen.

She couldn't imagine his wife doing anything so mundane as cooking, yet the kitchen was a gourmet's delight. The finest copper pots were stacked in cupboards, and every small appliance imaginable was handy on the long counters. The stove had a double oven, and alongside it sat a microwave.

It was a shame that nobody used all this superior equipment. Raoul evidently ate all his meals out. When Lacey had put her few things in the refrigerator, she found it almost empty. A couple of magnums of champagne were chilling, along with a bottle of white wine, but not much else.

She opened a can of spaghetti, spooned it into a pot and put it on one of the burners. Although she was hungry, it didn't seem worthwhile to go to the trouble of fixing anything else. After turning up the heat under the spaghetti, she went to her room to get a book to read while she ate.

As she was passing the front door she heard a scraping noise and male voices outside. Lacey stiffened. What else could happen today?

"Who's there?" she called sharply.

There was dead silence for a moment. Then Raoul, in a strangely muted voice, said, "I didn't expect you to be home."

So his offer *wasn't* altruistic! He'd lulled her into a false sense of security with every intention of sneaking back like a burglar! He'd outsmarted himself, though. She'd taken his advice about locking the doors.

Lacey was angry enough to confront him face to face. She turned the bolt, but was sensible enough to leave the chain in place. When she opened the door a wedge she was surprised to see the doorman was with Raoul. The man had a key in his hand and a confused expression on his face.

"What are you doing here?" she demanded irately.

"I didn't think you'd be home," Raoul said.

"I suppose you expect me to believe that, just like I believed you didn't have another key!"

"I don't. I asked Manuel to let me in because I thought you'd be out." He dismissed the doorman after noticing the avid look on his face. "You can go back to your post now, Manuel."

"You tricked me!" Lacey stormed.

"No, I didn't. I honestly thought you'd be out."

"How does that make it any better? You were going to wait here for me until I returned."

"No, I wasn't." Raoul sighed. "I needed a change of clothes, but I knew if I suggested coming back with you,

you'd get the wrong impression. I decided to stop by while you were out to dinner. I expected to be in and out without your ever knowing.''

Her anger collapsed abruptly. Of course he would need his things—a razor, pajamas, a clean shirt. As she looked at him remorsefully, Raoul lifted his chin and sniffed the air with a slight frown.

''Do you smell something burning?'' he asked.

''My spaghetti!''

Lacey raced into the kitchen and snatched the smoking pot off the burner. She only hoped the pot wasn't ruined.

''Lacey! Are you all right?'' Raoul's urgent voice drifted in from the hall.

She ran back and took the chain off the door. ''Don't worry, I'll clean up the mess.''

''What happened?''

''I was heating some spaghetti, and it sort of burned a little.''

''Why were you doing that?''

''For dinner.''

''*That's* what you were going to have for dinner?'' He looked at her incredulously. ''With all the wonderful restaurants in Mexico City?''

''Well, I . . . uh . . . I didn't feel like going out.''

''That's not the reason. Tell me the real one.''

''It is, really. I . . . I don't like to eat alone.''

''You're alone here,'' he pointed out.

''It's different,'' she mumbled. ''Besides, this place is so beautiful. I was going to take a tray onto the terrace and look out at the view.''

''You didn't want to spend the money I gave you,'' he said quietly.

"Not on food," she admitted. "But I'm going to use part of it. I want to take some bus tours."

"That's no way to see Mexico City! With a bunch of tourists."

A dimple showed enchantingly at the corner of her mouth. "That's what I am."

"You deserve better after what you've been through. I'll arrange for a car and driver to pick you up tomorrow morning."

"Please, Raoul, I can't get any further in to your debt."

His dark eyes held a glow, but his voice was mild. "Have I asked for payment?"

"No, but you've done enough."

"We'll discuss it over dinner," he said.

"Haven't you eaten?"

"No one dines here before nine or ten."

Lacey's objections to dinner were half-hearted. Besides the fact that she was ravenous by now, the prospect of spending the evening with Raoul was irresistible.

"While you're getting dressed I'll throw a few things into a suitcase," he said.

Everything was turning out differently than she expected. As Lacey hurried to her room to get dressed, she was too excited to wonder if all of this wasn't just a little too pat.

Chapter Two

The restaurant Raoul selected was in Chapultepec Park, the last place Lacey would have expected the elegance that greeted her. The dining area's subdued lighting provided an intimate atmosphere for quiet conversation, although a dance floor indicated there would be music later.

They were shown to a choice table looking out at a lighted waterfall that cascaded into a pool filled with lilies. The floor-to-ceiling windows also allowed a stunning view of the park beyond.

Lacey glanced admiringly around the half-empty restaurant. "What a charming place. I'll bet it's filled on the weekends."

"It will be crowded tonight, too," Raoul assured her. "As I told you, we dine late, although perhaps not as late as they do in Spain. Their restaurants don't fill up until eleven o'clock or later."

"Have you been to Spain?"

"Many times. We have family there."

"I'd love to go to Europe some day, especially Spain because the language wouldn't present as big a barrier as that of other foreign countries."

He looked surprised. "You speak Spanish?"

"Not very well, but I understand quite a bit from living in San Diego, so near the border."

"We'll have to converse in Spanish."

"No way! Not when you speak such perfect English. How did you get to be so fluent?"

"Your language is taught in our schools, and I do a lot of business in the United States. Becoming fluent is merely a matter of practice, that's why we should speak Spanish. By the time you go home you'll sound like a native."

"In three days?" she asked skeptically.

He raised a dark eyebrow. "I don't understand the hurry. Aren't you happy with your accommodations?"

"Your apartment is glorious! Do you live there all alone?" she asked artlessly, hoping her curiosity wasn't too transparent.

Raoul's smile was faintly mocking. "Are you inquiring about my love life?"

"No, of course not! I was just…I mean, it's such a big place for one person. The rooms are tremendous. You could put my whole apartment in your living room." Lacey's cheeks were warm as she heard herself babble on. Did he guess that she'd made a thorough inspection?

"Then you shouldn't be anxious to go home," he said smoothly.

"You must be awfully comfortable at your sister's."

He shrugged. "I'm comfortable wherever I am."

That was certainly true. She'd never met a man so completely in command of himself and every situation. Raoul appeared to be only in his middle thirties, but he had the poise and authority of a man twice his age. There was also a steely quality under the urbane exterior. She got the distinct impression that it would be a mistake ever to cross him.

"Would you care to dance?" His deep voice broke in on her rather apprehensive appraisal.

As she preceded him to the dance floor, Lacey realized that he had neatly avoided answering any personal questions. Who was the child in the picture—and what had happened between Raoul and her mother?

All the questions were forgotten when he took her in his arms. He held her in a loose embrace, but Lacey was instantly aware of his intense masculinity. She wouldn't have believed that his shoulders were actually that broad, not merely the product of an excellent tailor. His whole body was lean and muscular, she discovered when they brushed against each other. The contact sent a strange tingle up her spine.

"You're a very good dancer," he said after a few moments.

"Thank you. It's one of the pluses of being a model, I suppose. We're taught to glide around with a haughty look on our faces. The snobby look is one of the minuses."

"It must be difficult for you. You have a very expressive face."

She smiled wryly. "You've only seen the down side—shock, despair, anger."

"I've also seen some very positive emotions." Tiny pinpoints of light glittered in his dark eyes. "They make me wonder what you would look like . . . under the happiest of circumstances.''

His remark was innocent on the surface, but Lacey sensed the hidden meaning. ''I haven't had many of those lately,'' she replied coolly.

''We'll have to change all that.'' He drew her closer.

She stiffened instinctively. ''You aren't responsible for my happiness.''

''But I'd like to contribute to it,'' he murmured.

''You've done as much as I'm going to permit,'' she stated firmly.

Raoul's chuckle had a deep male sound. ''Are you afraid of me, little one?''

''No, just cautious.''

''And rightly so. You're a strikingly beautiful woman. But haven't I proved that I'm harmless?''

That wasn't a word she would have used to describe him. Not that Raoul would ever force himself on a woman—he wouldn't have to. His powers of seduction were awesome. Just the touch of his fingertips stroking the nape of her neck was incredibly suggestive. Harmless? Raoul? Scarcely!

His white teeth flashed when she didn't answer immediately. ''You don't agree? Don't tell me you're wondering if I'm going to pounce when I take you home.''

''I know you wouldn't do that,'' she replied hastily.

''You're right. I'd like nothing better than to coax you into my bed, but you have me at a disadvantage. It would be very bad form for a host to make a pass at his guest.''

''I'm glad you were taught etiquette,'' she answered lightly.

''Because you don't think I could please you?'' His warm breath stirred the fine hair at her temple.

Lacey had a swift vision of what a superb lover Raoul would be. He would arouse her with his husky voice, his knowing touch, taking his time until her desire rose to match his. Then he would—

She drew a deep breath. "Because I don't indulge in casual affairs."

He examined her delicate features before replying, lingering on her generously curved mouth. "Any man fortunate enough to make love to you would never take the experience casually."

"Is that calculated to reassure me?"

"I was just being truthful."

"Well, if you don't mind, I'd rather you went back to making polite conversation."

"Does it bother you to talk of making love?" he asked.

"It isn't something I usually discuss."

"Poets have been writing about it for centuries."

"I think we're talking about something quite different, and I'd like to change the subject," she said grimly.

"All right, *cara*." He gave her a little hug. "I shouldn't tease you, but you're enchanting when your cheeks turn that lovely shade of pink."

Lacey was glad that the music stopped so she didn't have to answer. She turned to walk off the dance floor, wondering if Raoul had, indeed, been teasing.

A long table facing the bandstand that had been empty when they started to dance was filling up now with elegantly dressed couples. As Lacey started up the few steps from the sunken dance floor, an attractive dark-haired young woman called to Raoul.

"So there you are! Where did you disappear to? I didn't hear you go out."

His frown came and went instantly. "Rosa! What a coincidence seeing you here." He guided Lacey over to the large table.

"What do you mean?" Raoul's sister had watched their approach, inspecting Lacey covertly. "You knew we were all coming here for Delores's debut."

He clapped himself on the forehead. "Is that *tonight*? I thought it was *next* Monday."

"What you need is a social secretary. But at least you're here. Delores would have been really tiresome if you hadn't shown up." Rosa slanted an avid glance at Lacey.

Raoul was aware of it, but he made the introductions smoothly. Then Lacey was introduced to Edouard, Rosa's husband, and to the rest of the party in such quick succession that she couldn't remember all the names.

"I'll have them set two more places," Rosa said.

"That won't be necessary," Raoul answered. "We already have a table."

"I think it would be better if you joined us." Rosa gave him a significant look.

Raoul was clearly torn. He hesitated in a most uncharacteristic manner.

Lacey had only a glimmering of what was going on, but she gathered he'd forgotten a previous date. In the general confusion, she drew him aside.

"If there's been some kind of mix-up, don't worry about it. I can get a cab and go back."

"You'll do no such thing," he said firmly. "I asked you to have dinner with me."

"You also seem to have a date with someone else."

"It wasn't a date. A friend of ours is making her debut here tonight. She's a singer."

Lacey's curiosity was aroused. Was this the special woman in Raoul's life? No, that could hardly be if he forgot her opening. But she must mean *something* to him. His sister was acting very peculiarly.

"I'm afraid we'll have to join Rosa's group," he said apologetically. "She's never learned to take no for an answer."

"I don't mind," Lacey said.

"But I do." He sighed. "However, it can't be helped. This evening is turning into a comedy of errors."

"Not for me." She grinned. "It's a lot better than burned spaghetti."

He smiled faintly. "Well, I hope at least the dinner lives up to expectations."

Lacey was seated between Raoul and Edouard, a pleasant man who was easy to talk to. He knew about her mishap, and didn't consider it titillating that Raoul had loaned her his apartment. Rosa also appeared to accept the story.

"It must have been a terrible experience, having your purse stolen," she said. "That happened to me once, and it took weeks to notify all the right people."

"My wife confuses credit cards with playing cards," Edouard teased her. "She thinks you have to have fifty-two of them."

Raoul smiled. "You knew she was extravagant when you married her."

"I thought shopping was only a hobby," his brother-in-law replied in mock complaint. "I didn't realize it was a full-time career."

"If I had a real career, I wouldn't have time for shopping," Rosa answered.

"I have terrible news for you, *cara*," Edouard said to his wife. "The business day does not begin at noon, nor does it end at the cocktail hour. A job would interfere seriously with your social life.''

The banter between them was good-natured, with a strong undercurrent of affection. The same sentiment was evident in Raoul's relationship with them. They were a happy family, Lacey thought wistfully. More than ever she was aware of her own solitary state.

''You'll give Lacey the impression that I'm completely useless,'' Rosa protested. ''She probably has a marvelous job.''

''No, I just work in a department store,'' Lacey answered candidly.

Raoul covered her hand with his. ''Lacey is a model. I'm sure the finest one they have.''

''How fascinating!'' Rosa exclaimed. ''Oh, how I envy you. Imagine being paid to wear beautiful clothes!''

Edouard laughed. ''I think you've finally found your calling.''

Lacey had felt slightly defensive about her work, but she discovered that these privileged people weren't snobs. Rosa's interest was genuine, and Raoul's compliment hadn't been an empty one.

''We must have lunch tomorrow,'' Rosa was saying. ''You can tell me what the latest fashions are for fall.''

''Please tell her this year's styles are the same as last year's,'' Edouard begged.

His wife ignored him. ''Will one-thirty be all right? I'll pick you up.''

''Well, I really intended to go sight-seeing, since I'm going to be here for only a few days,'' Lacey said reluctantly. If time weren't so short, she'd love to have had lunch with Raoul's sister.

''I thought you just arrived,'' the other woman remarked.

"Lacey is afraid I'm imposing on your hospitality," Raoul answered for her.

"We scarcely know he's around," Rosa said reassuringly.

"Does that take care of your objections?" Raoul asked Lacey.

"I suppose so," she answered slowly. Should she reconsider?

"How long were you planning to stay?" Rosa asked.

"Ten days," Lacey replied hesitantly.

"Wonderful! We can get to know each other, and you can give me pointers on how to walk. I'd love to look professional when I model in the Assistance League fashion show next month. Who knows what it might lead to."

"You're making a one-time-only appearance," Edouard said firmly.

"Never marry a Latin," Rosa told Lacey with a sigh. "They're impossibly macho! What's wrong with having a career?" she asked her husband. "Delores has one."

Pablo, the man across the table, joined the conversation. "She doesn't have a husband," he said.

"She'd gladly give up her career for one." Edouard chuckled, glancing at Raoul. His amusement was replaced by discomfort when he became aware of Lacey's attentive ears. "I suppose that makes me the male chauvinist my wife accuses me of being," he added weakly.

"You all heard him admit it," Rosa announced.

"As you've gathered, Latin men frown on their wives working," Raoul said.

Was that what had broken up his marriage? Lacey filed the thought away for future examination. At the moment she was more interested in the mysterious Delores.

"I'd heard that about Latin men, but having a friend with a glamorous career would provide your sister with an incentive. What's Delores's last name?" she asked innocently. "I wonder if I've heard of her."

"I doubt it. This is her first singing engagement. Before that she dabbled in the theater—only local things here in Mexico City."

"I've always thought acting was her forte." Rosa's voice held a slight edge. "She's an excellent mimic."

"But not always a kind one," Edouard agreed sympathetically.

An elusive picture of a strong-willed, self-indulgent, perhaps even thoughtless woman was emerging. Lacey could scarcely wait to see Delores in the flesh. A short time later the lights dimmed, and she got her wish.

A man walked out to the spotlight, accompanied by a drumroll. After adjusting the microphone he announced the debut of that stellar performer, Delores Carvalho, in her premiere local appearance. The introduction was in Spanish, but Lacey got the gist of it, barring a flowery adjective here or there.

A stunningly beautiful woman walked onstage to spirited applause. She wore a tight red sequined gown that showcased her full breasts and rounded hips to advantage. Her face was as sensual as her lush figure, with pouting lips and bold dark eyes under provocatively lowered lids.

Delores Carvalho had remarkable poise, considering this was her first singing engagement. She took the microphone confidently, flashing a big smile at the audience. The only thing she lacked was a pleasing voice. Her performance was more theatrical than musical. She acted out the songs, suffering through unrequited love and other assorted emotions.

Lacey considered her act embarrassing. Without influence, the woman couldn't have gotten a job calling out train stations. How did Raoul feel about it? A glance out of the corner of her eye didn't tell her anything. His attention was focused on the singer, but his face was devoid of expression.

A burst of applause broke out at the end of Delores's act. She must have a lot of friends, Lacey thought cynically as she dutifully joined in the clapping. A few men even stood up as Delores was presented with a huge bouquet of red roses.

When the lights came up Rosa said, "I think she should stick to acting."

Edouard looked at her in amusement. "Your claws are showing, *querida*."

"Not at all. I'll leave it up to a disinterested party. What did you think of Delores's voice, Lacey?"

Lacey was caught off guard. "I can't really...that is, I'd say her act is quite...unusual." She turned hurriedly to Raoul. "What did you think?"

He smiled. "I'd agree that you described it perfectly."

Edouard chuckled. "I never knew there were so many ways to say someone was terrible."

"Hush!" Rosa warned. "Here she comes."

No matter what anyone else thought, Delores felt she'd scored a triumph. Her face was animated as she stopped at various tables to greet friends. By the time she reached their table, her excitement climaxed.

"My darling friends!" She threw her arms wide. "How good of you to come."

Murmurs of congratulations rippled through the group, but Delores zeroed in on Raoul. He and the other men had stood politely. She threw her arms around his neck and pulled his head down for a passionate kiss.

After a seemingly endless moment, Raoul reached up and unclasped her arms. With unruffled poise he said, "If you don't mind, I'd prefer not to be part of the show."

She smiled up at him through long lashes, not at all abashed. "Don't pretend you're inhibited, *mi amor*—not with *me*."

Aware of how Lacey must feel, Rosa tried to distract Delores. "I was so impressed. You didn't seem a bit nervous out there."

"Why should I be?" Delores answered carelessly.

"I can think of one reason," Edouard murmured, too low for her to hear.

"I'll go and change." Delores linked her arm through Raoul's. "After that we'll celebrate."

Raoul turned to include Lacey, who was listening to their exchange with both embarrassment and apprehension. What would the volatile singer do when she discovered Raoul wasn't alone?

"Before you go I'd like you to meet Lacey Scott, our guest from San Diego," he said.

Delores acknowledged the introduction with disinterest before turning back to Raoul. "Tonight is very special to me," she said in a throaty voice.

Rosa came to the rescue again. "We'll all help you celebrate."

Delores gave her an amused look. "You were never very perceptive, darling." Without waiting for an answer, she patted Raoul's cheek. "I'll be right back. Have them bring your car around."

"Don't you think you owe it to your public to stay for a while?" he asked. "They did come to see you."

She pouted for a moment before heaving a theatrical sigh. "I suppose you're right. Be a dear and order me a drink. I won't be long."

"That was fast thinking," Edouard murmured.

"What do I do for the second show?" Raoul asked sardonically.

Lacey had overheard the low-voiced exchange between the two men. She picked up her purse and stood up with a fixed smile on her face.

"Thank you for a lovely evening," she said to Raoul. And to Edouard, "It was so nice meeting you."

Raoul put his hands on her arms, preventing her from leaving. "I'm sorry about the misunderstanding with Delores. I'll clear everything up when she returns."

"Don't do that. This is her night, and she wants to spend it with you." Lacey's color rose. "I mean, she expects you to be part of it."

"Believe me, there was no understanding between us."

"I know." She pretended to believe the fiction. "But it will be better all around this way."

"I won't hear of it," he said firmly.

He took her purse from her resisting fingers, and placed it on the table. An insistent arm around her shoulders urged her onto the dance floor.

"Raoul, this is a big mistake," Lacey said earnestly. "Whether you think so or not, Delores thinks you have a date. I just met her for a second, but I can tell she's not the type to shrug off the mix-up with a great big chuckle."

"Delores happens to be a very spoiled young woman. She believes what she wants to believe. I agreed to come to her opening, along with numerous other people. We had no further commitment."

"You don't have to explain anything to me," Lacey said primly.

Raoul's smile lit up his face. "You have much to learn about Latin men. We can be led, but not driven. I *want* to explain."

"Why?"

His arm tightened around her waist as he stared into her wide blue eyes. "Because I don't want you to leave."

Lacey bit her lip. What had she gotten herself into? Was Raoul targeting her for his next romance? Or was he just using her to break up an old one?

"Delores has many admirers here this evening." He brushed a pale lock of hair off her forehead. "She doesn't need me."

Another possibility occurred to Lacey. Was he using her to make the other woman jealous? That didn't seem too likely, judging from Delores's passionate kiss. But they might have had a lover's quarrel and he was getting even.

"I'm sorry the evening turned out this way. I intend to make it up to you if you'll let me," he said softly.

"It's been a delightful evening," she answered quickly. "I enjoyed meeting your sister and brother-in-law. They're quite charming."

"Yes, they're good people. If they weren't family, I'd want them for friends."

"That's probably the nicest compliment you could pay a relative."

"I hope you'll have lunch with Rosa tomorrow. Although it will probably turn into a busman's holiday." He laughed. "She'll undoubtedly take you shopping afterward."

"It was kind of her to invite me. You're all so hospitable."

"We want to be sure you enjoy your visit and take back happy memories," he answered in a deep velvet voice.

"You can be certain of that!" Lacey knew she would never forget this vital, charismatic man.

Delores was at the table when they returned. She had changed to a slinky, low-cut gown with a gorgeous diamond brooch at the plunging neckline. She was surrounded by people, but her earlier animation had been replaced by a sulky expression. Lacey braced herself for the coming explosion. She tried to distance herself from Raoul, but his hand closed around her wrist.

Delores's eyes narrowed at the gesture. She examined Lacey carefully this time, assessing her shining blond hair, ivory skin and willowy figure. The summation didn't please her.

After they were seated at the table she fired her opening salvo. "I don't recall ever hearing your name before, Miss Scott. Are you a friend of the Ruiz family?"

"Not exactly," Lacey answered reluctantly.

"I thought Raoul said you were their guest."

"That's correct." Raoul answered for Lacey.

Delores continued to address her questions to Lacey. "Are you staying with Rosa or Mama Ruiz?"

"Lacey is staying in my apartment," Raoul said calmly.

"Is this some kind of joke?" she asked ominously.

"Not at all. You asked a question, and I answered it."

"Is he telling the truth?" she demanded of Lacey.

"Well, yes, but—"

Delores's eyes flashed black fire as she confronted Raoul. "And you *dared* bring her here tonight? To *my* opening?"

"It's not what you're thinking," Lacey said hastily. "Raoul just—"

"I'll handle this." His voice cracked like a whip when he turned to Delores. "First of all, lower your voice," he commanded.

Edouard moved unobtrusively to Lacey's side. "May I have this dance?" he asked.

She stood up gratefully.

When they were on the dance floor he said, "You mustn't let Delores bother you."

"You didn't by any chance see someone off on the *Titanic*, did you?"

He smiled sympathetically. "She can be quite formidable, but Raoul is a match for her."

"I don't want to cause trouble between them."

"Raoul is not her lover, if that's what you're thinking."

She was surprised at his frankness, also a little annoyed that he thought her that gullible. Lacey decided to be just as frank. "She seemed very sure of his response when she kissed him. A woman usually doesn't imagine these things."

"I didn't say there was never anything between them. It's none of my business. I can only assure you that Raoul is a free agent."

"Too bad nobody told Delores," Lacey answered dryly.

"Raoul has tried in every way imaginable, but she's a woman who doesn't give up easily."

"That's pretty obvious. I wouldn't want to stand in the way of something she wanted." Lacey shivered slightly.

"No, I imagine she would be quite ruthless." Edouard gave her back a reassuring little pat. "But don't worry, I told you Raoul could handle her. You mustn't let Delores spoil your evening." He smiled engagingly. "The entertainment was a bit amateurish, but did you at least enjoy your dinner?"

"Very much! This restaurant is so lovely. I can't believe we're in a public park."

"Is that so unusual? You have a famous park in San Diego."

"Yes, but it isn't noted for haute cuisine like this place."

"Chapultepec is unique," he agreed. "Perhaps the only city park that houses four museums and a castle, among other attractions."

"I was exploring some of them when my purse was stolen," Lacey remarked ruefully.

"A most regrettable occurrence, but I hope it won't keep you from continuing your exploration."

"Oh, no," she assured him. "I hadn't gotten to Chapultepec Castle yet."

"It's well worth seeing. The furnishings are the original ones brought from Europe by the Emperor Maximillian."

"I can't wait to see everything," Lacey exclaimed. "You don't know how grateful I am to Raoul. If it hadn't been for him, I'd be back home right now."

"So actually, that little street urchin did you a favor."

She returned his smile. "Isn't that stretching things a bit?"

"Not at all. You were here alone, a sad way to enjoy the beauties of Mexico City. Now you have friends."

"It's still quite unbelievable," she marveled.

"Perhaps it was destiny. Look at it that way."

Edouard had relaxed her, but Lacey's nerves tightened as they started back to the table. She needn't have worried, because Delores was gone.

Raoul greeted her with a smile. "I was afraid you and Edouard had run away together."

"Don't make trouble," he said. "I'm a happily married man."

"Would you remember if I didn't keep reminding you?" Rosa asked her husband, but it was obvious that she wasn't worried.

"What happened to Delores?" Lacey whispered to Raoul as soon as she had a chance.

"She's making the rounds of her adoring fans," he answered.

"Did you explain about me?"

"No explanations were necessary."

His imperious tone indicated the matter was closed, but Lacey couldn't leave it at that. "I hope you told her the truth. I wouldn't want her to draw the wrong conclusions."

"Why does it matter?"

"Because she thinks we . . . that you and I . . ."

He grinned. "It's an interesting thought. I've dwelt on it myself."

Lacey knew he was baiting her again. "Be serious, Raoul," she said crossly. "What's the point of making a big thing out of this when you could clear up everything in a few words?"

When he saw she was really upset, he said soothingly, "Your reputation is safe, *cara*. I told Delores what happened."

"That's a relief!"

"I'm hurt." He didn't look it. His eyes glinted mischievously. "Is the idea of having an affair with me so repulsive?"

"That's not what I came to Mexico for," she answered curtly.

"You should be more flexible," he teased.

"I'll keep it in mind the next time I meet a passionate stranger."

After the awkwardness over Delores was resolved, they slipped into an easy relationship. When he wasn't making her uneasy, Raoul was a delightful companion. The evening passed quickly. Lacey could hardly believe it was after two o'clock when the party finally broke up.

As they clustered at the entry, waiting for their cars to be brought around, Rosa said to her, "Remember, we have a luncheon date tomorrow."

She took it for granted that Lacey had accepted. In some ways Rosa was very like her brother. They were both high-handed, yet too charming to refuse.

The drive through the park was scenic but brief, since Raoul's apartment was just on the other side of the broad boulevard called Paseo de la Reforma.

"I had no idea it was so late," Lacey remarked. "Do you have to work tomorrow?"

He nodded. "I have a breakfast appointment."

"It's too bad I dispossessed you," she said as they pulled up in front of his building. "You'd be home now."

He raised a dark eyebrow. "Is that an invitation?"

"No, just an observation. Do Rosa and Edouard live far from here?"

"Just a few blocks." He got out of the driver's seat and came around to open her door.

At the entrance she said, "You don't have to go up with me."

"I'd like to come in and get some cuff links. I forgot them when I packed a bag earlier."

Lacey was instantly on the alert. Was that just a convenient excuse? Raoul had said some very suggestive things to her during the evening. She rejected the suspicion as unwarranted. For one thing, he didn't have to overpower a woman; his problem was just the opposite. For another thing, he'd had an opportunity earlier, if that's what he had in mind.

Since she knew he'd be amused by even a hint of wariness, Lacey forced herself to reply casually. "It's hard to remember everything when you pack. I always forget at least one thing."

"Fortunately you can usually buy what you need wherever you go."

"Unless you're on safari in Africa."

"In which case, you probably don't need it anyway."

They reached the door of his apartment, chatting idly like old friends. As soon as they were inside, Raoul went down the hall to his bedroom. He returned almost immediately.

"Have a good time with Rosa tomorrow," he said pleasantly.

Lacey was suddenly reluctant to see him go. It had been a wonderful evening, and she didn't know when—or if—she'd see him again.

"Would you like a nightcap?" She laughed self-consciously. "That's kind of funny. I'm offering you your own hospitality."

"I appreciate the offer, but I think I'd better leave."

"Yes, I guess it is late, and you have to get up in the morning."

"That's not the reason." His hand curled around the nape of her neck, under the spill of silky hair. "I've spent all this time assuring you that I'm no threat. If I stay, I might go back on my word."

He was so close that one step would have put her in his arms. She had been there before, but this time would be different. This time Raoul would mold her to his hard length and caress her knowledgeably. She would feel the passion leashed in his lean body.

She moistened her lips nervously. "I trust you."

He cupped her chin in his hand and lifted her face to his. "A woman as lovely as you shouldn't trust any man."

His mouth touched hers gently, savoring the sweetness. It was almost a chaste kiss, yet subtly seductive, promising infinitely more. The promise was reinforced by his lithe body, just inches away.

Lacey felt a thrill of awareness race through her. She wanted to put her arms around his neck and run her fingers through his thick hair, to trace the rippling muscles in his broad shoulders. The unexpectedness of the urge kept her rooted to the spot.

Raoul lifted his head reluctantly. He smiled down into her dazzled eyes. "Will you have dinner with me tomorrow night? Just the two of us, the way it was supposed to be tonight."

She nodded, not trusting herself to speak.

"Splendid. I'll pick you up at nine. Sleep well, little one."

Lacey remained staring at the door after he left. How was she supposed to sleep when every nerve in her body was vibrating?

Raoul was without a doubt the sexiest man in the whole world! He was also one of the most experienced. He could create desire with just one kiss and that smoky, caressing voice. She didn't allow herself to think what he could do when he wasn't holding back!

Would he continue to practice restraint? Could *she*? Lacey pushed the ridiculous thought out of her mind. She wasn't some love-starved teenager. Raoul was a very handsome and charming man, but he would be merely a pleasant memory once she returned home.

Chapter Three

The restaurant Rosa selected for lunch was as elegant as the one the night before had been. Though they were late and the restaurant was crowded, her reservation had been held. As they followed the headwaiter to their table, Rosa stopped frequently to greet friends.

"This seems to be a popular place," Lacey remarked when they were finally seated.

"The food is decent, and you run across everyone you know," Rosa answered carelessly. "You must have the same sort of place at home."

Lacey smiled faintly. "I wouldn't know. I'm not one of the ladies who lunch."

"How I envy you! You've no idea how boring life can be sometimes."

"Would you really like to have a career?"

"I don't know," Rosa replied frankly. "I don't have any special talent. I just feel as though I don't have enough to do."

"You have a husband and children to take care of. And a big home to run."

Rosa waved an airy hand weighed down with a large, square-cut emerald. "The servants do that. Do you know what it's like to wake up in the morning and have absolutely nothing you have to do?"

"It sounds like heaven to me."

"It isn't, take my word for it. When I look at women like you, I get frustrated."

"Your trouble is, you don't know how the other half lives," Lacey remarked dryly.

"Pretty well, if you consider yourself one of them."

Rosa looked at Lacey's chic, white silk suit accented by a sapphire-blue blouse that matched her eyes. Her blond beauty had drawn a lot of attention as they walked through the restaurant.

"I buy my clothes at a discount, and I do my own hair," Lacey said. "I also scrabble around to pay the rent on occasion, when unexpected bills come in. I have to save for things that you consider necessities. Believe me, it isn't a glamorous life," she continued, surprised by her own defensive tone.

"I didn't mean to sound condescending." Rosa's face was troubled.

"You didn't." Lacey smiled reassuringly. "You can't be expected to know what it's like."

"I know I have more than most people," Rosa said apologetically. "I do appreciate the fact. It's just that sometimes I have the feeling life is passing me by."

"Then do something about it! You don't have to hold down a job to be fulfilled. With your money and influence, you could be a real force in Mexico City."

"Doing what?"

"Any number of useful things."

"I belong to a dozen charitable organizations. All we do is go to luncheons and sit around and gossip."

"Why not be one of the people who organize the luncheons and decide where the money goes?"

"I wouldn't know how," Rosa said helplessly.

"You could learn. Or you could try something entirely different. What you have to do is find a need and fill it. People have made millions doing that."

Rosa gazed at her doubtfully. "You mean start a business?"

"No, you don't need the money or the aggravation. I was thinking more about being the power behind someone's throne."

"You mean like in politics?"

"Why not?"

Rosa looked reflective. "It might be very interesting."

"Right. Find out which lawmakers are doing the things you approve of. If they're running for election, volunteer to help with their campaign. Anyone would turn somersaults to have your backing."

"There *is* a young man we've heard good things about," Rosa said slowly. "He doesn't have party support, but he's honest and sincere. I think he could be very effective if he were elected."

"Then get the word out. Organize rallies, and solicit funds from your friends. Offer to work at his headquarters."

Rosa's face lit with dawning interest. "It *would* be exciting."

"And rewarding. If he wins you'll be courted by more politicians than you can handle. And if he loses, you'll still be known in political circles as a mover and shaker."

"That's a wonderful idea! You've been so helpful. Oh, Lacey, I wish you lived here. I'd like you to tackle this with me."

"You don't need anyone. You're going to find out how competent you are."

"I'd feel a lot more confident if we were a team."

Lacey smiled. "I can't afford to volunteer my services. I have to work for a living."

Rosa clapped her hands. "I have a brilliant idea! Move down here and I'll find you a rich husband."

Lacey raised a delicate eyebrow. "Didn't someone once say the hardest way to earn money is to marry it?"

"Only if you're talking about some crotchety old man. With your looks you can get someone young and dashing."

"I hope you don't have your brother in mind," Lacey said, in what she hoped was a joking voice.

Rosa answered seriously. "No, I'm afraid Raoul is a lost cause."

"His first marriage soured him on the institution?"

"Raoul was never married."

Lacey was thrown into confusion. "Oh, I'm sorry. I just assumed . . ."

"Why would—" Rosa's puzzled expression was replaced by one of comprehension. "Of course. You saw Carlotta's room."

"I just happened . . . I didn't mean to pry."

"It's understandable."

Lacey knew she should let the subject drop when Rosa didn't pursue it, but this was her only chance to solve the mystery. "I was quite surprised to see a child's room. Raoul isn't exactly the parental type."

Rosa's face held unaccountable sadness. "He's a very devoted father."

It was true then. The girl in the picture was his child. But Rosa said he had never been married. That didn't jibe with Lacey's conception of Raoul. She couldn't imagine him deserting a woman who was bearing his child. Then why hadn't he married her? Was it conceivable that she was the one who refused?

Lacey hurriedly filled the silence that had fallen. "I didn't mean to imply that Raoul wouldn't be a good father. He's a very kind man."

Rosa nodded. "He's determined to devote his life to Carlotta."

"She doesn't live with him," Lacey said tentatively.

"Only because he feels the ranch is a better environment until she's ready to go to school. He goes up there every weekend."

"I see," Lacey said, not seeing at all. She remembered, though, that Raoul had mentioned going up to the ranch.

Before she could explore the subject further, Elena Rodriguez appeared, apologizing for her tardiness. Rosa had asked her to join them for lunch. Elena and her husband, Pablo, had been at the restaurant the evening before, but Lacey hadn't had much opportunity to talk to her.

"Wasn't Delores dreadful last night?" Elena asked happily, after they had exchanged amenities.

Rosa shrugged. "She doesn't know it, so it doesn't make any difference. I only wish I had her confidence."

"Raoul shook it a bit," Elena observed smugly. "He's the only one she can't push around."

Lacey was a bit puzzled. "If you don't care for her, why did you go to her opening?"

"We've known each other all our lives," Rosa said simply.

"We're used to her antics," Elena explained. "They don't usually bother us, but someday she's going to go too far."

"She almost did last night," Rosa commented. "Raoul was not amused, to put it mildly."

"I'm sorry if I was the cause of any unpleasantness," Lacey said.

"It was more entertaining than Delores's act," Elena assured her. "I'll always treasure the way Raoul cut her down to size."

"In front of everyone?" Lacey was surprised. That didn't seem like Raoul's style.

Elena laughed. "He kept his voice so low I had trouble hearing, but Delores was more cooperative."

"It's her own fault if she was embarrassed," Rosa agreed.

"The whole thing was an unfortunate misunderstanding," Lacey said. "Raoul isn't interested in me. I'm sure he made that clear to her."

The two women looked at her appraisingly, then exchanged a glance. "Raoul is as spoiled in his way as Delores is," Rosa said. "He isn't used to accounting for his actions."

"He told me he *did*," Lacey insisted.

"I suppose he must have, or she would have been waiting to claw your eyes out."

Lacey hesitated. "Edouard said Delores and Raoul aren't . . . they don't . . ." She didn't know how to put it politely, especially to his sister.

Rosa took pity on her. "They aren't having an affair, but not because of any unwillingness on her part. She can't accept the fact that whatever there was between them is over."

"Her heart wasn't broken," Elena said scornfully. "She just liked the idea of snaring the most eligible bachelor in town. It would have been quite a feather in her cap if she'd managed to lead him to the altar."

Rosa raised her eyebrows. "She has two chances—little and none. Can you see her as Carlotta's mother?"

"I'm afraid nobody can fill that role, especially not Delores. She doesn't have time for children."

"I should think she'd make an exception for Raoul's daughter," Lacey said slowly.

"He isn't going to give her—or any other woman—that chance," Rosa said. "Delores refuses to believe it, though. She sees every female as a threat. That's why she was so unpleasant to you last night."

"I'm just an innocent bystander," Lacey protested.

"You'd have to wear thick glasses and sensible shoes to convince her of that."

"It's a good thing you don't live here," Elena said. "Delores has an unpleasant way of getting even with people she has a grudge against."

"Doesn't she have *any* good qualities?" Lacey asked.

The two women laughed unexpectedly. "Oh, sure. We just get carried away when we start carving her up," Rosa said. "Delores can be difficult, but she can also be a lot of fun. She's remarkably generous, too."

Elena smiled. "That's true. She'll give you anything except one of her men."

The subject of Delores appeared to be exhausted, and the conversation shifted. When lunch was over, Rosa suggested they go shopping—as Raoul had predicted.

The restaurant was in a section of the city called the Zona Rosa, which had the finest shops. Their merchandise was comparable to any in the world. In fact, much of it was imported. Different stores carried designer clothes from France and Italy, English porcelain, pearls from the Orient. The selection was impressive.

When they came to an elegant china shop, Rosa said, "Do you mind stopping in here for a minute? I have to order some glasses."

The carpeted interior had the hushed atmosphere of a museum. It resembled one in many ways, too. Exquisite Steuben and Lalique figures were displayed in lighted niches along the walls, and tables the length of the room held countless other beautiful objects.

A well-groomed salesman greeted Rosa with an air of deference. *"Buenas tardes, Señora Portola. Como está?"*

"I'm fine, José."

"What may I do to help you this fine afternoon?"

When Rosa answered him in English, the man switched to that language immediately. Everyone Lacey had encountered was fluent in English, and considerate about speaking it in front of her.

"I need some water glasses," Rosa said. "You have my pattern on record. This is the one." She picked up a beautiful Waterford goblet. "Send me a dozen."

"I suppose I might as well order more champagne glasses while I'm here," Elena remarked. "Some are bound to get broken tomorrow night. The Shelby pattern, José."

"Will a dozen be sufficient?" he asked.

"I certainly hope so. I'm not anticipating a drunken brawl." She turned to Lacey. "We're having a little party tomorrow night. I'd like you to come."

"That reminds me," Rosa said. "I must order the invitations for the foreign trade delegate's reception next month. Edouard does a lot of business entertaining," she explained to Lacey.

"Rosa is wonderful at it," Elena said. "She's had as many as two hundred people at a garden party."

"And you were complaining about not having enough to do?" Lacey exclaimed.

"That's just being an extension of my husband. I want to do my own thing like you do."

"You don't give yourself enough credit. It takes executive ability to run a big house, take care of a family and manage a staff of servants. I could never do it."

"Sure you could. I'll teach you. I'm going to find Lacey a husband so we can keep her here," Rosa said to Elena with a smile.

"What a marvelous idea!" Elena agreed. "How about Juan? He'd adore her."

Rosa shook her head. "He's a terrible bore, and his mother is a dragon. Lacey doesn't need a mother-in-law like that."

"True. Well, what about Domingo?"

"That womanizer?" Rosa said scornfully. "He'd be flirting with the bridesmaids during the ceremony."

"Are you sure I can't snare Raoul?" Lacey joked. "Then we'd be relatives."

Rosa sighed. "I only wish you could, but he isn't a prospect. Don't waste your energies on him."

"I was only joking. I'm not looking for a husband."

Rosa was suddenly serious. "Don't get tangled up with him in any way, Lacey. You'll only get hurt."

Lacey smiled. "That's hardly likely in ten days—only eight and a half by now, actually."

"Raoul is a fast worker. He can be very...persuasive," Rosa said delicately.

"He's been a perfect gentleman with me," Lacey assured her, ignoring the small incident the night before. It had been only a good-night kiss. He'd left right afterward.

"I hope so." Rosa clearly wasn't convinced. "He's my brother and I love him, but he's lethal to women. I want you to know where you stand."

The salesman reappeared with their receipts, ending the discussion.

Rosa didn't elaborate her warning afterward as they browsed through a number of small boutiques, looking at clothes with astronomical price tags. Neither woman bought anything, but Lacey had a feeling it was because of her. They knew she couldn't afford to. With all their money, Rosa and Elena were remarkably sensitive, yet not patronizing. Lacey felt almost as comfortable with them as she did with her friends from home.

When they parted, Elena said, "Remember, you're coming to my party tomorrow night."

"I'm looking forward to it," Lacey answered truthfully.

Although it was late when Rosa dropped her off, she had hours to get ready for her date with Raoul. The difference in customs between their two countries was marked. At home, a date would both begin and end earlier. These people lived at a different, more exciting tempo.

Lacey went onto the balcony to look out over the sprawling city. Chapultepec Park was a long green oasis in the frenzied activity that surrounded it. The snarl of traffic was so horrendous that the noise reached her even high in her tower, yet the vitality of the place was stirring. A thought came unbidden. She could live here happily.

Sure, in the lap of luxury like this, a tiny voice mocked. What would it be like to have unlimited money? To spend hundreds of dollars on Steuben stemware for everyday use? One thing she'd learned from Rosa and Elena and, of course, Raoul was that it didn't necessarily change a person.

Raoul rang the bell promptly at nine.

"This must be a new experience for you," Lacey said as she opened the door.

"I could get used to coming home to a beautiful woman," he answered, gazing at her admiringly.

"I meant being a guest in your own home."

"It has a certain piquancy. Are you going to offer me a drink?"

"I don't know where you keep things."

"Then allow me to take over as host."

He opened doors in a paneled wall to reveal a built-in bar. A refrigerator under the counter provided ice and mixes.

"Did you have a good time with Rosa today?" Raoul asked once they were seated on the couch with their drinks.

"I had a great time! She's a super person."

He smiled indulgently. "Yes, Rosa is unique. If someone could leash her energy, he could light up the city."

"I sort of got her interested in politics," Lacey said tentatively.

His smile turned into a grin. "What's she going to do, run for president?"

Lacey's dimple showed. "Maybe next year. I suggested she start by backing a candidate of her choice. It sounds to me as though she has plenty to do, but she doesn't agree, so I kind of gave her a suggestion. I hope you don't mind.''

"Edouard might, but I think it's a fine idea. Rosa has a lot to offer."

"You're certainly different from other Latin men."

"Maybe uniqueness runs in the family."

"Also, she's not your wife," Lacey commented cynically.

"That has nothing to do with it." Raoul was abruptly serious. "If I did have a wife I'd want her to be a partner, someone I could discuss things with—business, politics, whatever."

"I'll bet your views aren't popular."

He shrugged. "It's academic since I'm not married."

"Maybe you'll change your mind when you are."

"Possibly. Shall we go do dinner?" he asked, deftly putting an end to the subject.

The restaurant was in one of the choice hotels. The room was softly lit, with flowers on every table and a platoon of waiters to ensure faultless service. The place was undeniably plush, but Lacey couldn't help thinking with a twinge of wryness that she seemed destined to spend her entire vacation in restaurants.

Yet how could she complain? She looked across the candlelit table at Raoul's patrician profile as he conferred with the wine steward, knowing she wouldn't choose to be anywhere else.

After the wine was selected he devoted his entire attention to her. "You look happy," he said softly. "Are you finally enjoying your vacation?"

"Very much—thanks to you."

"I wasn't looking for thanks," he protested.

"I know that. You're a very nice man."

He smiled ruefully. "You're constantly thwarting my advances. How can I seduce you when you look at me with those beautiful, trusting eyes?"

"You wouldn't want to spoil a budding friendship," she joked. "This way we can write each other long chatty letters after I go home. You can tell me about your girl-friends, and I'll tell you about the men in my life."

He took her hand and ran his thumb over the soft skin of her wrist. "I don't think I want to hear about the men in your life."

"Okay, I'll think of some other way to be interesting."

"That wouldn't be difficult." His eyes gleamed as they ranged over her shining hair and angelic features. "My apartment will never be the same. I keep picturing you in my bed."

"I'm sleeping in the guest room," she reminded him.

"Not in my imagination."

His husky voice sent warning flares to her brain, the only part of her not affected by him—so far. His hand on her wrist was a small gesture, but it was sending a stab of pleasure through her entire body.

Lacey sat back in her chair. "You've certainly changed from the impersonal stranger I first met."

"I found you just as desirable then, but I didn't think you were in any mood to hear about it."

"What makes you think I am now?"

He chuckled. "It never hurts to find out."

She was never sure when he was serious, so the best approach seemed to be a light one. "It's no use being seductive. Rosa and Elena told me all about you."

His gaze sharpened. "What did they say?"

"They indicated that you're bad news to women."

That was evidently not what he was worried about. Raoul's smile returned. "Could you be a little more specific?"

"I gather you have a rather short attention span. You tire easily."

His eyes sparkled with merriment. "My sister would scarcely be in a position to make that accusation. I don't claim to be the world's greatest lover, but I can assure you that's one complaint I've never received."

"You know that's not what I meant," Lacey muttered.

"I had to be sure. I wouldn't want you to be hesitant because you thought I couldn't satisfy you."

Lacey didn't permit herself to imagine the ways. She regained her light tone. "I've always heard practice makes perfect. But you're too much in demand. Rosa has more available bachelors lined up for me."

"Who does she have in mind?"

"Juan and Domingo were mentioned."

"They're not for you," Raoul said confidently.

"Why not?"

"Let me put it this way. Domingo is the better of the two. He's known as the Spanish sleeping pill. Juan isn't quite as stimulating."

Lacey repressed a smile. "That's not very kind."

"I'm just trying to save you from disaster. One of Juan's dates was so starved for excitement after an evening with him that she joined the circus."

"And Domingo's date?"

"She entered a convent."

"You've made quite a case against them. But are you sure you're protecting my interests and not your own?"

"I was hoping they were the same," he said meltingly.

"Rosa warned me that you could be very persuasive," Lacey answered.

"My little sister is bent on sabotage." He sighed. "Sometimes I can see the merit in being an only child."

"You don't have any other brothers or sisters?"

It was an innocent enough question, but it produced a strange result. A curtain seemed to descend behind Raoul's eyes. His expression was hard to define.

"No, there are just the two of us," he answered without inflection. Before she could comment, he signaled to the waiter.

Lacey decided she must have been imagining things, because Raoul was his normal, urbane self after he'd paid the check.

"I didn't mean to rush you, but I thought we might go to the late performance of the Ballet Folklorico. If that's all right with you," he added.

"I'd love to!" she answered, forgetting her momentary curiosity. At last she was going to see some of Mexico City's culture.

The ballet was a charming mixture of cancan, pantomime, comedy and religious ceremony. The costumes were colorful, and the music had a lilting rhythm.

Petticoats flashed and high heels pounded a staccato beat as the dancers performed agricultural dances from Jalisco, an Aztec ritual ceremony and a fiesta from Veracruz.

Lacey was entranced by the intricate choreography, the beauty and sheer energy of the ensemble. She watched the stage with shining eyes, unaware that Raoul was gazing at her with equal appreciation.

She bubbled with enthusiasm on the ride home. "I thought they did the Aztec ritual dance especially well, didn't you?" she asked. "I had goose bumps when the high priest held that huge knife over the victim on the altar. For all their advanced civilization, the Aztecs were remarkably bloodthirsty—much more than the Mayas. Their human sacrifices don't bear thinking about.''

"You're very well versed in pre-Columbian cultures," Raoul remarked.

"I took a course in college—when I should have been learning something useful." She laughed.

"Knowledge is never wasted. It prepared you for your visit here."

"True, but a little practical knowledge would have been better—like how to hang onto your purse."

His hand covered hers on the seat between them. "Do you regret it, Lacey?"

"No," she answered softly. How could she? Had anyone ever had such a wonderful adventure? "Not any more."

He turned his head to look at her for a moment, and his hand tightened. "Maybe we were destined to meet."

Edouard had voiced the same sentiment. *Was* it fate? And if so, for what purpose? To show her there were men like Raoul in the world? A lot of good *that* was going to do her!

When they reached the apartment, Lacey thought it only polite to ask him in for a drink. But he declined.

"We did have quite a lot of wine with dinner," she said. "I noticed some cocoa and a package of marshmallows in the cupboard. Would you like a cup of hot chocolate instead?" She was as bad as Delores, Lacey thought disgustedly. Why hadn't she taken no for an answer?

After hesitating a moment, Raoul accepted her alternate suggestion, which threw her into confusion. She'd been so sure he'd refuse again.

As soon as they entered the apartment she headed straight for the kitchen, to show him the offer was a valid one. Raoul trailed after her.

"Do you need some help?" he asked.

He looked as out of place in the kitchen as a tiger at a tea party. Lacey smiled. "Would you know what to do?"

"No," he admitted. "But you could tell me."

"It's a one-person job." She took a tin of cocoa from the pantry, and milk from the refrigerator. "You obviously don't use this beautiful kitchen. Do you eat all your meals out?"

"Most of them. Although I do have dinner parties now and then. I hire a caterer," he added needlessly.

"Don't you even have breakfast at home?" She hadn't seen eggs or bacon in the refrigerator, not even milk. She'd bought some herself at the market.

He smiled slowly. "If it's an occasion, I might have champagne."

Lacey got the picture. Well, at least his girlfriends weren't expected to cook for him. A picture of Delores flashed through her mind. *She* wouldn't know how!

From his place at the kitchen table, Raoul watched her move gracefully around the room. "Do you like champagne?" His voice was a velvet purr.

"Not for breakfast," Lacey answered curtly.

"Ah, *cara*, you're missing one of life's pleasures. There is nothing like lying in bed and sipping a glass of sparkling wine while watching the sun come up over the park."

"My room doesn't look out on the park."

"I know," he murmured.

Her blue eyes glittered with annoyance as she turned their full power on him. "Some women like champagne in the bedroom, and others prefer hot chocolate in the kitchen. I'm one of the latter. And if you don't behave yourself, you won't even get that!''

He laughed. ''Has anyone ever told you you're adorable when you hiss like a kitten?''

''Don't be deceived,'' she answered coolly. ''I have grown-up claws. What's it going to be, chocolate for one or two?''

His white teeth flashed in a grin. ''You win. From now on, I'll pretend to be a eunuch.''

Raoul's long-limbed body made the idea laughable. Every muscle and sinew gave a promise of virility. No one would ever pick *him* to guard a harem!

''That's better.'' She opened a package of marshmallows and held them up questioningly. ''How many?''

''I'll have what you're having.''

''I always have two.''

His gaze roamed admiringly over her slender figure. ''I'm glad you're not one of those women who's forever dieting.''

''I've never had to. But after that delectable dinner, I probably shouldn't be doing this.''

''I gather all of your sins are minor ones,'' he observed sardonically, getting to his feet. ''Put everything on a tray, and I'll carry it out to the terrace. I just want to get something from the bedroom before I forget.''

Lacey poured the steaming cocoa into thin china cups, and put them on a tray along with spoons and napkins. After washing the pot she decided to take the tray out herself. After all, it wasn't heavy.

As she reached the swinging door, Raoul pushed it open from the dining room. They collided, and the tray tipped, spilling the contents all over him.

He gave a sharp yelp as the steaming cocoa soaked his shirt front and ran down his slacks. Some of it spattered Lacey, too, but her concern was for Raoul.

"Did you get burned?" she asked anxiously.

"No, it was just hot, not scalding." He gingerly pushed the wet shirt away from his chest and looked down at his trousers. "How could such a small amount of milk cover so much territory?"

"Your beautiful suit! It's a mess!"

"No problem. The cleaner will take care of it."

"I'm afraid the stains will set if they're allowed to dry," she fretted. "Take off your clothes and I'll try to wash out the worst part."

"Don't worry about it. Accidents happen. I'll just change clothes—after I take a shower." He smiled. "I smell like a nursery school."

Lacey picked up the broken china and mopped up the spilled milk before going to retrieve Raoul's discarded clothes. She stopped in her own room first and hurriedly changed to her flowered eyelet-lace robe. The chocolate spots had to be rinsed out of her dress, too.

The shower was running, so Lacey felt free to enter his bedroom. She never expected to find the bathroom door open. Her cheeks flamed as she got a comprehensive view through the clear glass shower door.

Raoul's body was deeply tanned, except for a narrow white strip around his loins. A mat of dark hair tapered down to his navel and crowned his thighs. Lacey stared at his muscular flanks, knowing she should turn her head, yet unable to.

His eyes were closed as he lifted his face to the spray, but Lacey realized she was on borrowed time. Wrenching her fascinated gaze away, she grabbed the heap of clothes off the floor and slipped out of the room.

At first, she thought she'd imagined hearing the doorbell. But when she turned off the water in the kitchen, it pealed again. She went to the door, wondering who it could be at that hour.

Delores Carvalho stood in the hallway. "I hope I didn't wake you," she said, looking at Lacey's robe.

"No, I . . . I wasn't asleep."

"May I come in?" the other woman asked.

"Oh . . . of course."

Lacey opened the door wider, feeling a ripple of apprehension. Delores sounded pleasant enough, but she'd seen her dark side. Besides, what did she want?

"My friends tell me I made a bit of a scene last night." She smiled appealingly, as though sharing a joke.

"Not really," Lacey murmured. "It was just a little misunderstanding."

Delores nodded approvingly. "Everyone said you're very *simpático*. That's why I thought we should get to know each other." She walked uninvited into the living room.

Lacey followed reluctantly. She didn't trust this sudden show of friendship. What would this hot-tempered seductress do if she knew Raoul was just down the hall? If only he'd stay there!

"Are you planning to be here long?" Delores continued, sinking gracefully down on the couch and crossing her slim legs.

"Only about a week."

"I suppose you have someone special waiting for you at home." The veiled question was accompanied by a conspiratorial smile.

"No, I just have to get back to work." Lacey could have agreed and made her happy, but she didn't see any reason to lie.

"I can't believe an attractive woman like you doesn't have a lot of men on the string," Delores persisted.

"Not really, but I'm sure *you* do," Lacey remarked with an air of innocence.

The other woman's eyes narrowed. "There is only one man for me."

"That sounds very romantic."

"It is. I've been in love with Raoul for years." Delores's expression was suddenly ominous. "No one's going to take him away from me."

Lacey stood up, hoping she would take the hint. "If that's a warning, it's unnecessary. I have no designs on Raoul."

"I'm glad to hear it, because you would have had a fight on your hands. And I warn you, I fight dirty."

Lacey's face reflected her distaste. "I'll keep it in mind."

"As long as we understand each other, I'll be going."

She had almost reached the door when Raoul came down the hall wearing a short, black satin robe. He was rubbing his hair briskly with a towel.

"Did you take my clothes? I told you—" He broke off abruptly when he saw the other woman. "Delores!"

"So there's nothing going on between you," she hissed, her gaze raking him up and down. It was obvious that he was naked under the robe.

"There isn't, really!" Lacey said distractedly. "This isn't what it looks like."

"Do you take me for a fool?" Delores swung back to Raoul, her face a mask of rage. "You lied to me!"

"I don't lie." His voice was icy. "I don't have to."

"You told me she was staying here alone."

"I *am*!" Lacey said.

"You little slut. If I'd come a few minutes sooner, I'd have found you two in bed."

Raoul's mouth was compressed in a straight line. "You'd better leave," he ordered.

"So you can go back to bed with this little tramp you picked up in the park? I'm really disappointed in you, Raoul. You never used to go in for cheap thrills."

He took her arm in a punishing grip. "I've never struck a woman yet, but I'm perilously tempted to break that rule. Out!"

She wrenched her arm away and turned for a parting shot at Lacey. "I warned you. I'll get even with both of you!"

Lacey's face was pale. She'd never been the object of such hatred. Her slender body was still rigid after Delores had gone.

Raoul held out his hands helplessly. "I'm so sorry, *querida*. What can I say?"

"She's really rather frightening, isn't she?"

"No more than a child with a temper tantrum. She can't harm you," he said soothingly.

"I'm not afraid. It was just so...unpleasant." Lacey started to tremble as reaction to the nasty scene set in.

Raoul gathered her in his arms and smoothed her hair, murmuring reassuring words.

She relaxed against him, absorbing his strength. In spite of her denial, Lacey was shaken by the force of the other woman's hostility.

"I wouldn't have had this happen for the world," Raoul said regretfully.

He kissed her temple and stroked her back, trying in every way possible to atone for something that wasn't his fault. Lacey told him so when her composure returned.

She tilted her head back to look up into his concerned face. "You aren't responsible for Delores's behavior."

"You're very generous." His expression changed as he gazed down into her flowerlike face, only inches away.

Lacey caught her breath as she recognized the lambent desire in his eyes. Raoul's attempt to reassure her had been innocent, but the circumstances made restraint difficult. He was nude under the brief silk robe, and she wasn't wearing much more.

A slow warmth crept through her as she felt all the hard angles and taut muscles she'd glimpsed through the shower door. Raoul was molding her body to his, making her totally aware of him.

Before she could move away, his lips touched hers. The kiss was different from the first time. He parted her lips for a slow male exploration that aroused all her senses. She was powerless to resist as his mouth awakened sleeping passions. When his hand cupped her breast, Lacey gave a breathy little sound of pleasure.

He parted her robe and bent his head to string a line of tiny kisses along the top of her breasts. "You're so enchanting, *cara*. I want to make love to you. I want to hold your beautiful body in my arms and make you part of me."

"Raoul, Raoul," she murmured helplessly as his fingertips slipped inside the waistband of her bikini panties, tantalizing her with the promise of imminent joy.

"Tell me what you want so I can please you, *mi amor*." His husky voice was a siren song of seduction, fanning the embers of her desire into a white-hot flame. "I want to know everything about you, my beautiful little stranger."

His words were like a cold breath of reason in a fantasy world. Was she out of her mind? She'd known this man exactly a day and a half! How could she even consider letting him make love to her? She wrenched herself out of his arms and pulled her robe together hurriedly.

"What is it, *cara*? What did I do?" he asked.

He hadn't done anything without her willing cooperation, Lacey was forced to admit. "I'd appreciate it if you'd leave now," she said in a muted voice.

He gripped her shoulders. "Why? Tell me what I've done?"

"It was my fault as much as yours," she mumbled. "I should have stopped you."

A ghost of a smile lightened his intensity. "You did. What I want to know is, why?"

Her cheeks were very pink, but she met his eyes. "I meant it when I told you I don't have casual affairs. I'm not denying that I'm attracted to you. That's pretty obvious. But without any emotional involvement, it would just be meaningless sex."

"I see." Raoul's hands dropped to his sides. "Your principles are admirable. I'm sorry I can't give you what you're looking for."

"I don't expect anything from you," she said earnestly. "I'm just explaining."

He stared at her for a long moment, then touched her cheek gently. "I have a feeling it would have been wonderful between us." Before she could respond he said, "I'll get dressed and leave."

Lacey drifted onto the terrace after he left, trying to sort out her chaotic thoughts. Her feelings toward Raoul bothered her the most. She was admittedly attracted to him sexually, but was it becoming deeper than that?

He was everything she'd always hoped for in a man. With continued association, she might easily fall in love with him. But Raoul had made it very clear that he wasn't interested in any kind of commitment.

Should she pack up and go home? Lacey sighed. That would be rather foolish. Raoul wanted only one thing from her. After turning him down tonight, she wasn't likely to see him again.

Chapter Four

Lacey overslept the next morning, exhausted by the emotion-charged experience of the night before. She'd meant to get out early, just in case something happened to cut her visit short. Life had held one surprise after another lately. As she was about to leave the apartment, the telephone rang.

She hesitated before answering it. Suppose it was one of Raoul's girlfriends? She didn't want to cause any more problems. But what if it was Rosa wanting to chat? They'd struck up an immediate rapport that Lacey wanted to continue for the time she had left in Mexico.

She picked up the phone. "Hello," she said tentatively.

"I was beginning to think you'd gone out," Raoul's deep voice answered. "Did I get you out of the tub or something?"

"No, I was just about to leave. I...uh...I didn't know if I should answer the phone."

"Why not?" He sounded surprised.

"Well...you know. I didn't want a recurrence of last night's unpleasantness. With Delores, I mean," she added hurriedly, in case Raoul thought she was referring to what had occurred between them. The encounter had been many things, but not unpleasant.

"You can put her out of your mind completely. The whole thing was deplorable, but I guarantee she won't bother you again."

"If you say so," Lacey answered doubtfully, remembering the other woman's parting shot.

"You're not really worried, are you?"

"I guess not. It's unlikely that we'll ever meet again."

Raoul hesitated. "I can't promise you *that*. She might very possibly be at Elena's and Pablo's tonight."

"Oh." Lacey's heart sank. She'd been looking forward to the party until then. Would Delores continue her vendetta? It wasn't likely that Raoul's volatile ex-mistress had cooled off overnight. "Couldn't you call and explain what happened? Everyone got so excited last night."

"Do you really think she'd believe me?"

"If you told her calmly."

"You have a remarkably trusting nature. In fairness to Delores, I must admit appearances were against us. No one else would believe we hadn't been making love either."

"But that's so unfair!"

"Yes, isn't it?" he asked sardonically.

She was glad he couldn't see her heightened color. "Do you think she'll tell everyone?" Lacey asked apprehensively.

"I'd be very surprised. Delores would never admit that another woman was more desirable than she."

"But I wasn't . . . er, I didn't . . . I'm not!"

"Do you want me to describe the ways?" His voice was honeyed enough to spread on biscuits.

"We settled all that last night, Raoul," she said firmly.

"No, we merely agreed not to make love. That doesn't mean I don't still desire you."

"At ten o'clock in the morning?"

His chuckle had a rich masculine sound. "I didn't realize you were such an innocent."

Lacey tried to regain control of the conversation. "I have other things on my mind at the moment. I'd like to go sightseeing—if I ever get out of here," she added curtly. "Did you have some purpose in calling?"

"I was concerned about you. You were upset last night."

And he was part of the reason! But Lacey couldn't help unbending. Raoul was remarkably thoughtful. "I'm fine. You don't have to worry about me."

"I do worry about you, little one. You seem so defenseless."

"I've been fighting my own battles for a couple of years, and I've managed to survive," she assured him. "I do a few boneheaded things every now and then, like not buying traveler's checks, but even that worked out— thanks to you."

"No more gratitude, please."

"I . . . I wanted to mention it one last time, in case we don't see each other again."

"Is that what you want, Lacey?"

She knew her answer should be yes, but she couldn't bear to make the parting final. "Don't you think it's for the best?"

"I'd be sad to think I lost a friend."

"I would, too," she said earnestly.

"Then why don't we settle for friendship? I also called to ask if I could take you to the party tonight."

Lacey's heart lightened. This wasn't the end of the road! But then a thought occurred to her. Was Raoul asking because he knew Delores was going to be there and he wanted her to act as a buffer? If the other woman intended to stage another spectacle, it wouldn't be fair to Elena.

"I might be too tired to go at all after running around all day," she hedged.

"You don't have to make excuses," he said quietly.

"I'm just trying to do what's right for everybody," she explained carefully. "You've all been so good to me. But if my presence is going to present a problem, maybe I should stay away."

"If that's your only reason, it isn't good enough. I intend to escort you tonight, unless you say you don't want to see me."

How could she honestly do that? "If you're really sure, Raoul. I seem to get you into trouble every time we're together."

He laughed. "What are friends for? See you this evening, *cara*."

Lacey's thoughts weren't on sight-seeing as she left the apartment house and walked slowly toward the el Presidente where she intended to take a bus tour.

Last night Raoul had made it clear that he did not want to become involved. He was willing to deny his very real desire, if she expected more than a passionate night of sex. Lacey had to admire his honesty. Not many men played that straight. So why the turnabout?

She hadn't expected to see him again. The strong sexual attraction between them seemed to preclude mere friendship. Yet that was what Raoul said he wanted. Did he really mean it? Or was this some male ploy? But if down deep he was interested in a purely physical relationship, he wouldn't have given up so easily the night before. Lacey was thoroughly confused by the time she boarded the tour bus.

Her personal problems were pushed to the background as the large vehicle pulled out into traffic. Who could think of anything else while cars hurtled at them like bugs bent on destruction against a light bulb? The collisions were always miraculously averted, but Lacey couldn't help gasping a couple of times.

"They do drive like maniacs, don't they?" an older woman next to her remarked. "I'm from New York City, and these fellows would make a New York cabbie look like a little old lady from Great Neck."

"The amazing thing is that they don't kill each other."

"That seems to be the one traffic law they obey," the woman agreed.

The wondrous sights soon took precedence over the traffic. Lacey trooped through cathedrals and museums with the other tourists, trying to assimilate the vast amount of information fed to them. The history behind all these imposing monuments was staggering.

"The early inhabitants had a really impressive culture, didn't they?" she asked her seatmate.

The woman nodded. "It hasn't changed much through the years, either. The rich are still rich, and the poor are still poor," she said cynically.

"You could say that about any country," Lacey protested.

"Not like here. I understand the aristocracy live in mansions staffed by an army of servants who wait on them hand and foot. Can you imagine, in this day and age? My once-a-week cleaning girl tells *me* what she'll do and won't do."

"It's a different way of life," Lacey had to agree.

"I wonder how you get to be a member of the club?" the woman joked.

"You're born into it," Lacey said somberly.

The tour was interesting, yet slightly disappointing. They were whisked from place to place much too fast, with no time to absorb what they saw. Lacey arrived home in the late afternoon with a head crammed with facts and figures, and a determination to go exploring alone the next day.

As she examined her wardrobe much later, she was struck by an uneasy thought. What if the party that night was formal? Surely Elena would have mentioned it, yet perhaps not. She might simply have taken it for granted that one would know what to wear for the occasion. These people were accustomed to elegance.

Lacey hadn't brought anything really dressy. Who would have believed she'd need it? She was sure no matter what she wore, all the Rodriguezes' guests would be very polite, but it would still be embarrassing. Rather than worry needlessly, she phoned Rosa.

"You'll see everything," Rosa assured her. "Some of our friends are conservative, and others, like Delores, dress really far out."

"Will she be there?" Lacey asked with trepidation. Raoul had only said it was a possibility.

Rosa confirmed her fears. "Probably. She hates to miss anything, especially a party."

"Isn't she still singing at the dinner club?"

"If you can call it that. Yes, she's still torturing the paying customers, but there's all that time between shows. She'll undoubtedly pop in at Elena's, even if it's just for a short time."

"I see."

Rosa wasn't deceived by Lacey's expressionless tone. "You don't have to worry about Delores making another scene. That brother of mine is awesome. He has her eating out of his hand."

Not if he wanted to retain the normal number of fingers. Raoul's sister obviously didn't know what had taken place the night before.

Rosa had a more interesting subject than Delores to discuss. "Guess what? I took your advice and went down to Manuel Salizar's headquarters," she said eagerly. "You were right. They were very receptive."

Lacey smiled. "You didn't waste any time, did you?"

"I only wish I'd done this ages ago. It's so exciting! I have a million ideas for fund-raisers."

"How did Edouard take the news?" Lacey asked cautiously.

"I haven't exactly told him yet," Rosa admitted.

"Oh, boy! Do me a favor and wait till I'm safely back home before you do."

"Don't be silly. Edouard will be delighted." Rosa laughed. "He just isn't aware of it yet."

"If I hear of another earthquake in Mexico City, I'll know his delight is running over."

Rosa wasn't worried about her husband's possible wrath. "I have to rush now, but we'll talk later. I want your advice on one of my ideas."

Lacey was smiling indulgently as she turned on the water in the sunken tub. With Rosa behind him, Manuel Salizar could go right to the top.

After her bath, Lacey skillfully applied makeup. The eye shadow that deepened her blue eyes wasn't obvious; nor was the blusher she applied to her high cheekbones. When she was finished, her face had a natural look—if nature had blessed all women with glowing skin, luxurious lashes and provocatively curved mouths.

Lacey's training had made her adept at creating glamorous hairdos, too. In a matter of minutes she had braided part of her hair into a coronet at the crown of her head, and had combed the rest into a swirl of ringlets and waves.

The pale-yellow silk dress she selected was deceptively simple. It had been designed to enhance every curve of a body as slender as hers. From head to toe, she looked as though she'd stepped out of the pages of a fashion magazine.

Raoul seemed stunned when he came to call for her. His gaze was that of a man regarding a work of art.

"You're exquisite," he murmured deeply. "What have you done to yourself?"

"Just applied my working face. This is the way I look every day at the store," she answered carelessly, hiding her pleasure at his reaction.

"How many men do you have to fight off in a day?"

"It hasn't been a problem."

"American men must practice a lot of restraint." He reached out to trail a forefinger very gently along the curve of her ear.

Lacey caught her breath. The small caress was more sensuous than a kiss. She tried not to show it. "We encourage restraint,'' she remarked lightly. "No one is permitted to handle the merchandise."

"Is that a warning?" Something flickered in his eyes.

"Just a statement of policy. I wasn't trying to be provocative," she assured him hastily. The last thing Lacey wanted was to challenge his male ego.

"Why are you so nervous with me, *cara*?" he asked softly. "I've never forced myself on a woman."

"I know that, Raoul," she murmured.

"Of course I might make an exception in your case." The primitive expression that crossed his face was chilling somehow, although it was gone in an instant.

His voice was joking, but she felt a little tremor shiver up her spine. Had she gotten a glimpse of the real Raoul? The one who would take what he wanted without compunction?

The quiet in the luxurious apartment seemed suddenly oppressive. Lacey picked up her purse. "Hadn't we better be leaving?"

"Whenever you say," he answered promptly.

She felt slightly foolish. The mystery surrounding Raoul was making her imagine things. He did have a very autocratic nature, but he was certainly no threat.

The Rodriguez house was a mansion by any standards. It sat in the middle of a lush green lawn enclosed by a tall grillwork fence. Inside were spacious, beautifully furnished rooms with high ceilings. Music and the laughter of many stylishly dressed guests filled the house.

Raoul and Lacey made their way through the throng to greet their host and hostess. They found Elena with Rosa and Edouard.

The women immediately enthused over Lacey's hairdo, her makeup, her dress.

"That gown is divine!" Rosa exclaimed. "It's French, isn't it?" She correctly named the designer.

"I love what they did with your hair," Elena said. "Who did you go to?"

"I told you, I do my own," Lacey answered.

"I can't believe it! My hairdresser never managed anything that glamorous. Can you teach me how?"

The two men were completely ignored. As they edged away, Edouard turned to Raoul with amusement. "I sometimes feel our main function in life is to act as escorts. When three ladies get together, they don't need a man."

Raoul chuckled. "You're getting old if you believe that, my friend."

"Wouldn't you like to be appreciated in the living room as well as the bedroom?" Edouard asked dryly.

"Are you asking me to choose?" Raoul's eyes swung to Lacey's lovely face.

Edouard frowned slightly as he followed his brother-in-law's example. "I don't know if you're aware of it, but Rosa is quite taken with your little friend."

"She's captivating," Raoul agreed.

"You don't quite get my drift. This is none of my business, of course, but your sister would be most annoyed if you . . . um . . . took advantage of the girl."

Raoul's expression chilled. "I pride myself on never having taken advantage of *any* woman—even before I was faced with a bitter example," he added with controlled ferocity.

Edouard gripped his shoulder. "I wasn't implying anything like that. You know my feelings toward you." He sighed deeply. "I was only trying to keep peace in the family. Your sister can be very vocal."

Raoul was mollified, but still slightly resentful. "She has nothing to worry about where Lacey is concerned. I've never seduced a woman, nor have I ever misrepresented my intentions."

"I'm sure that's true," Edouard soothed. He glanced over his shoulder at Lacey. "*I* understand, but are you sure the little American does? Something may have suffered in the translation."

"It didn't."

"The attraction between you is visible," Edouard said delicately.

"I haven't made love to her," Raoul answered curtly.

Edouard's gaze was a mixture of sympathy and cynicism. "At the risk of interfering again, I suggest you keep it that way. Come, let's join the ladies and insist they notice us this time."

Waiters circulated among the guests, pouring champagne, while waitresses offered trays of canapés. The bite-size morsels were vastly different from the onion dip and hot dogs on a toothpick that Lacey was used to at parties.

There were olives stuffed with smoked oysters, mushrooms mounded with a spicy sausage filling, small crepes rolled around thin asparagus spears, and much more.

Lacey sampled everything. "This food is fantastic!" she said.

Raoul smiled indulgently as she took a tiny cream puff filled with curried chicken from the tray of a passing waitress. "Elena will be happy to hear that."

"My friends will be so impressed when I tell them about this party—and this house. Is Rosa's house like this?"

"Somewhat similar."

"It must be like living in a hotel," she marveled.

He chuckled. "Not exactly. There's no magazine stand in the foyer."

"That's *all* that's missing. You're certainly cushioned from life's hard knocks."

Raoul's smile faded. "You think money guarantees happiness?"

"No, but it can sure make you comfortable while you're miserable."

His jaw tightened. "I'm glad you think so."

Lacey sensed that her joking had touched some invisible nerve. Did Raoul think she resented him for being rich? She cast about for a safe topic of conversation, but the one she chose was no improvement.

"You mentioned going up to your ranch. Will you be leaving soon?"

"Not until the weekend." His austerity deepened rather than lightened.

"Will I . . . that is, if I go home while you're gone, should I leave the key in the apartment or give it to the doorman?"

"I thought you'd decided to stay for ten days."

"I did, but Sunday will be a week. I don't know how long you'll be away."

As he was about to answer, Raoul became aware of an undercurrent in the conversations around them. He glanced up and froze.

The expression on his face was so unusual that Lacey followed the direction of his eyes. When she saw what he was staring at, she, too, tensed.

Delores was standing in the doorway, her head thrown back challengingly. She was smiling, but her smile reminded Lacey of a cobra's hiss. A tall man was standing next to her.

"Did everyone miss me?" she called. When no one answered she started toward Raoul.

A sudden hush fell over the room as the guests moved aside, creating a path. Raoul stood rigid, never taking his eyes off her.

She took her time, enjoying the spotlight. When she reached him her eyes were glittering with excitement. "Look who's here," she drawled, with a quick glance at her escort. "Carlos has returned."

"You bitch!" Raoul ground out through clenched teeth.

"I told you I'd get even, *mi amor*." She cast a look of amusement at the shocked faces of the little groups surrounding them. "Isn't someone going to bring me a glass of champagne?"

Everyone turned away hurriedly, pretending to resume broken-off conversations as their hostess rushed over.

"This is absolutely unforgivable!" Elena stormed.

"Why the fuss? I did receive an invitation," Delores answered carelessly.

"The *last* one! This time you've gone too far."

Rosa joined them with equal fury on her face. "You must be out of your mind!"

"I don't know what you're all raving about. Did you expect me to sit home alone just because Raoul chooses to flaunt this woman in my face?" Delores included Lacey in her malice.

"I *expected* you to show some sense of decency, but I should have known better," Rosa fumed. "We're leaving, Elena. I'm sure you understand. Come, Raoul."

His face might have been carved out of stone, but he'd gained control of himself. "I have some unfinished business here."

"Please, Raoul," Rosa begged. "Nothing will be gained by violence."

A nerve throbbed at his temple. "That's what I should have used in the first place," he said grimly.

"You enjoy hurting people, but it's different when the shoe is on the other foot, isn't it?" Delores taunted.

Rosa grasped Raoul's arm. At the same time, Elena grabbed Delores and hustled her away.

"Leave it alone," Rosa said urgently. "She isn't worth it."

"Someone should teach her the error of her ways," he muttered.

"Not you! This episode will cost her dearly. I guarantee it."

His eyes narrowed dangerously. "I can fight my own battles."

"No one doubts that. But do you really want to stir up all the talk again?" When he hesitated, Rosa pressed her advantage. "Come away with me now. Don't let her trick you into making a scene."

Lacey was totally confused. This couldn't have anything to do with her, except indirectly. Delores was getting even for the night before, but how? As far as she could see, Delores hadn't done anything to provoke this violent reaction from everyone. To a lesser degree, even the other guests were aghast. What were they expecting to happen? And what gossip did Rosa want to avert?

While she was deeply grateful that the scene didn't center around her this time, the evening was clearly spoiled. Lacey decided to cast her vote with Rosa's. Raoul seemed to have forgotten she was alive, so she approached him diffidently.

"I'm ready to leave anytime you are."

He stared at her blankly for a moment, then frowned as her words registered. "It's early yet."

She laughed nervously. "Maybe for you people, but I'm not used to these late hours."

He glanced pointedly at his watch. "Eleven-thirty?"

Lacey exchanged a helpless glance with Rosa, who gave an imperceptible nod of approval. "Is that all it is?" She pretended surprise. "I guess I overdid the sight-seeing today. I'm really bushed."

"We'll leave shortly." His curt tone didn't invite further discussion.

Rosa wasn't intimidated. "Lacey is your guest. If she wants to leave, it's your obligation to take her."

"Don't treat me like a child!" he lashed out.

"I really would like to go," Lacey said hesitantly.

"Stay out of this," he ordered. "I know what you're trying to do, but the matter doesn't concern you."

She paled. Raoul was like a stranger—a hostile one. She'd glimpsed the imperious side of his character, but it had never been directed against her. What had brought out this primitive response in such a civilized man? How had Delores managed to get to him?

Lacey's curiosity was stronger than her hurt and bewilderment. Pride urged her to walk out and keep on going, but then she'd never solve the mystery. One thing she did know. Raoul must be under great pressure to act as he did. She moved away, deeply troubled.

The whole atmosphere of the party changed after Delores's arrival. Lacey could see it in the earnest way groups of people were conversing in lowered voices. Those who hadn't witnessed the encounter between Delores and Raoul were being supplied with details.

Lacey received her share of attention, too. She was uncomfortably aware of the avid glances cast her way.

Edouard was a friendly face in a sea of strangers. She gratefully went to join him.

He greeted her with his customary smile, although he seemed preoccupied. "Can I get you something to drink?"

"Not right now, thanks." She didn't want him to leave her.

"We haven't had a chance to talk. Did you manage to visit some of our attractions today?" he asked pleasantly.

"Yes, I took a tour. Raoul told me that was no way to see the city, and I'm afraid he was right. They attempt to cover too much territory."

"I suppose they try to hit the high spots."

"Yes, I guess that's all they can do."

Lacey didn't want to make small talk. She wanted information. Edouard had been quite frank with her before, but she couldn't come right out and ask what was going on.

"If there's anyplace special you'd like to see, perhaps Rosa could take you," he was saying. "She's always looking for interesting things to do."

Lacey couldn't very well tell him his wife had found something to do. It was one more strand in the web of intrigue entangling them—herself included.

"She's already been more than generous with her time, especially since I'm a virtual stranger."

"Any friend of Raoul's comes with a built-in recommendation." He smiled.

"You're a very close family."

"Yes, extremely. I'm as fond of Raoul as if he were a blood brother. He's a true gentleman in every sense of the word."

"He certainly has been to me. The only time I've ever seen him upset has been with Delores," Lacey remarked innocently.

"That one!" The way Edouard bit off the words made them sound like an epithet. "She ought to be quarantined as a deadly virus!"

"She certainly created a stir here tonight. Maybe she was inspired by having a bigger audience," Lacey commented acidly.

"The one at the restaurant was extensive enough."

"I was referring to last night. She threw a tantrum when she came to Raoul's apartment and found...I mean, we'd come home from the ballet, and he hadn't left yet. I'm afraid she got a totally erroneous impression."

"Ah, that explains it," he murmured.

"Not to me. Why was Raoul almost shocked to see her? He told me himself that she was likely to be here."

Edouard's eyes were chilly. "This is a mistake she'll live to regret."

"But she was invited," Lacey persisted. "What did she do to upset him?"

"It's nothing to concern yourself about." He was as remote as Raoul. "If you'll excuse me, I must speak to my wife."

Lacey stared after him, feeling resentment rise. She'd just been told again to mind her own business. Edouard hadn't been as blunt as Raoul, but the meaning was the same. Since she'd been the object of Delores's wrath on so many occasions, they might have the decency to tell her what this was all about.

Lacey gravitated toward a man standing alone. He was gazing sardonically at the nearest guests who had left a small area of space around him. Maybe *he'd* welcome her company, she thought resentfully.

"Hello, I'm Lacey Scott," she said.

"Carlos Mendes, at your service." He raised her hand to his lips and kissed it.

"What a charming custom," she commented. "I've seen it in the movies, but I didn't know men really did that."

"Latin men are very affectionate."

"I thought hand kissing was a mark of respect."

He laughed. "It depends on the circumstances. You're an American, aren't you?"

She nodded. "From California."

"Really? I never would have guessed."

"Why?"

"Your skin is so creamy, not baked to a crisp from the sun." The compliment was conventional enough, but the expression in his bold dark eyes wasn't.

"I don't get out in the sun much," she answered.

"I prefer the nights, too." His voice dropped in pitch. "They're more romantic."

"I never really thought about it that way."

"When I look at you I can't help myself," he murmured.

Lacey raised her eyebrows. "Your nickname isn't Speedy, is it?"

He chuckled. "I arrived late. The other men have had all evening to romance you, so I must make up for lost time."

It suddenly occurred to her that this was the man who had been standing next to Delores. She hadn't paid enough attention at the time to recognize him until now. A more careful scrutiny revealed a handsome man with an easy charm. He was a little overly familiar for Lacey's tastes, however, and his slightly satiric manner didn't appeal to her. Raoul was sophisticated; this man seemed jaded. Still, she could see how he would be attractive to many women.

"Who was the man lucky enough to escort you?" he asked.

"I'm here with Raoul Ruiz," she answered apprehensively, wondering if he was going to take up Delores's feud.

Carlos's reaction was exactly the opposite. His eyes glowed with an inner excitement. "You are the girl in his apartment?"

"Good lord, that sounds terrible!"

"We're all adults here." His appraising gaze swept over her curved figure.

"It's nothing like that! Raoul merely loaned me his apartment. We're not—he isn't staying there."

"He must care for you a great deal," Carlos murmured.

"No! Delores got that into her head, but it isn't like that. I wish someone could convince her."

"I'd be happy to try. Why don't you tell me the whole story?"

Lacey sighed. "I'd do anything if you could straighten her out."

"That might be arranged. Let's go someplace quieter where we can talk."

"You mean now? I couldn't leave with you. I came with Raoul."

"The man deserves to be dumped if he left you alone like this."

She privately agreed, but it would be a lapse of good manners. Besides, she wanted to be with Raoul, not

Carlos. Raoul's temperament was mercurial. Maybe everything would blow over and he'd be his old self.

"The biggest favor you could do for me would be to take Delores out of here," she said.

As he was about to answer, his expression changed. A wary look replaced the former playful seductiveness. Lacey glanced over her shoulder to see what had caused the abrupt transformation. Her pulse quickened as she saw Raoul. His mood hadn't changed. If possible, it had worsened. There was something frightening about his steely control.

The two men stared at each other for a seemingly endless moment before Carlos broke the silence. "Hello, Raoul. It's been a long time."

Raoul's eyes were like splinters of ice. "Not long enough."

"I was hoping you were ready to let bygones be bygones."

"You were wrong," Raoul answered tautly.

"Haven't I paid enough?" Carlos asked plaintively.

"How much is enough? What price do you put on human suffering?"

"I made a mistake," Carlos muttered. "Everybody makes mistakes."

"The difference is that most people take responsibility."

"It would have been a disaster! Everyone was so emotional. I was only trying to do what was best for everybody in the long run."

"Just a bighearted humanitarian, aren't you?" Raoul sneered.

Carlos's face was sulky. "I couldn't know how it would turn out. I agreed to all your terms. What more do you want?"

"I want you out of my sight for the rest of your miserable life."

"I could make some pretty valid demands myself," Carlos blustered.

Raoul started toward him, then restrained himself with an effort. "Don't push your luck. If you know what's good for you, you'll get out and stay out."

Lacey was standing on the sidelines, trying to make sense out of what was going on. She'd figured out that Raoul's fury at Delores was for bringing Carlos to the party. Delores had known his presence there would be unacceptable to everybody. Edouard had implied as much. Carlos admitted to having done something wrong, so Raoul's anger was justified, but what had Carlos done? What could be this serious?

His face was defiant as he faced Raoul. "I'll go where I damn well please! You can't do any more to me than you've already done."

"Don't count on it," Raoul grated. He turned away, motioning to Lacey. "Come on, we're leaving," he stated, striding away.

"You don't have to go with him," Carlos said urgently. "I'll take you home."

Lacey didn't even consider it. She followed Raoul without a word, leaving Carlos to stare after them with the expression of a frustrated jackal.

Raoul's grim face didn't invite questions as he drove swiftly yet competently through the traffic. They rode in silence for most of the distance until Lacey's curiosity overcame her better judgment.

"Is Carlos a friend of Delores's?" she asked tentatively.

"Carlos isn't a friend of anyone's," he bit out.

"You must be right. No one at the party seemed glad to see him. I wonder why he came."

Raoul smiled without humor. "He likes to live dangerously."

A small silence fell as she looked for another opening. "Have you two had business dealings?"

"No."

"I thought that might be why you didn't care for each other. It's unfortunate, but sometimes even good friends can have a falling out over business. You hear it all the time." She realized she was talking too much, but Raoul's rigid profile was making her nervous.

"Leave it alone, Lacey," he said tersely.

"I'm sorry," she murmured. "I can't help seeing that you're upset. I just thought maybe you'd like a sympathetic ear."

He pulled up in front of the apartment house and waited for the doorman to open her door instead of getting out to do it himself. It was obvious that the evening was over.

"Good night, Lacey." His voice and expression were devoid of emotion.

Indignation accompanied her up in the elevator and into the apartment. Raoul had no right to dismiss her in that curt manner. She'd only been inviting him to unburden himself. He didn't have to act as though she'd been prying.

Lacey found it hard to sustain her resentment. She had to admit that was exactly what she was doing. Not through idle curiosity, though. She was really concerned about Raoul. He'd shown her too many good qualities to suddenly turn into a villain. Whatever Carlos had done must have been horrendous.

Would she ever find out? Lacey sighed. Once more she wondered if she would see Raoul again. He always kept her dangling, but tonight's farewell had seemed pretty final. The prospect hurt even more than she had imagined.

Chapter Five

Lacey dressed the next morning without her usual enthusiasm for the day ahead. Raoul occupied her thoughts more than the tourist sights she'd been so anxious to see. Would he even remember she was alive this morning? Or was he still consumed with some blood feud over who knew what?

If only time weren't so short. It scarcely seemed possible, but it was Thursday already. Raoul said he was going to the ranch for the weekend, so that left today and tomorrow if he intended to see her again. Maybe only part of tomorrow. If the ranch was any distance away, he might leave in the early afternoon.

Lacey dawdled over dressing, irrationally hoping the phone would ring. A few days ago she hadn't known Raoul existed. Now he was dominating her mind and governing her actions. Even knowing how incongruous that was, she couldn't help herself.

After she'd eaten breakfast, cleaned up the kitchen and made her bed, there was nothing else to do. Still, she hesitated. Should she call Rosa to find out how Raoul was? After all he'd done for her, it might be considered heartless to ignore his obvious distress.

But even as she tried to convince herself, Lacey knew she was looking for an excuse. What really deterred her was the fear of being met with the same coldness Raoul and Edouard had shown.

How about Elena, then? It was only good manners to thank one's hostess after a party. Besides, she might be a more willing source of information since she wasn't a member of the family.

When Elena answered the phone, Lacey acted as though nothing unusual had happened the night before. "Your party was lovely," she said. "It will stand out as one of the high points of my vacation."

"We were so happy you could come," Elena replied politely, with no hint that anything had gone wrong.

"Your home is really beautiful."

"It's nice of you to say so."

Elena's noncommittal answers weren't promising. Lacey's expectations began to dim, yet she persevered. "I was really sorry to leave so early, but I think Raoul's been overdoing the late hours. I've never seen him like that."

A moment of silence fell before Elena said, "Raoul was under a great deal of stress last night, as you must know."

"Well, yes. I couldn't help noticing, but I don't know why."

"He didn't say anything to you?"

"No, not a word!"

Elena sighed. "I guess that doesn't surprise me. Raoul is a very proud man."

"I'm not trying to pry into his private affairs. I'm just concerned about him," Lacey said earnestly. "Under all that anger, I could tell he was hurting last night."

"Poor Raoul. I'm afraid the scars will never heal."

"*What* scars? I gather this involves Carlos, but what happened between them?"

Could Raoul's injury be physical? Lacey couldn't conceive of him being the loser at anything, yet it was possible.

"It's not my story to tell," Elena replied. "If Raoul had wanted you to know, he would have told you." Elena's voice was quietly implacable. "It was nice of you to call, but I really must go now."

Lacey put the phone down with a feeling of frustration. They had all closed ranks against her. She was the outsider.

She went over her meager conversation with Elena, looking for clues. All she'd learned was that Raoul had been scarred, possibly for life. Lacey's mind raced on wildly. Suddenly she turned cold. Could he be incapacitated sexually?

Her blood started to circulate again when she remembered the passionate interlude in his arms. The man who'd been on the verge of making love to her was a normal, healthy male. She had been the one who'd called a halt.

No, his injuries had to be psychological—and those were the most difficult to cure. Lacey sighed. Raoul was the strongest man she'd ever met. If he couldn't solve his problems, she certainly couldn't. He'd made it clear that he didn't want her help anyway.

The zoo in Chapultepec Park was just a short walk away. Lacey didn't have much enthusiasm for sight-seeing, but she thought animals would distract her more than ancient monuments.

The Mexico City Zoo was famous for its two panda bears. A pair of the rare animals had drawn huge crowds when they toured the United States. People stood in long lines for a brief glimpse. Lacey hadn't had an opportunity at home, so she welcomed the chance now.

One bear was lumbering around his compound, looking like a huge stuffed toy. The black circles around his eyes gave him a startled, comic expression, and his clumsy movements added to the clown effect.

The other bear was lying on her back, contemplating a sprig of bamboo held expertly in a back foot that functioned as well as a hand. She plucked off a leaf and chewed on it daintily, like a fat lady eating a bonbon. Lacey was enchanted. In spite of their size, the black and white pandas looked as cuddly as teddy bears.

After finally tearing herself away she visited the rest of the animals. Everything was an anticlimax after the main attraction, however.

A bus on Paseo de la Reforma took her down to the old section of town where the run-down hotel she'd intended to stay at was located. That wasn't something she wanted to revisit, but many historic sites were located nearby.

She got off at the Zócala, the central plaza built by the Spaniards in the heart of the Aztec city they conquered. The huge square was modeled after the one in their native Spain. Around it they built a cathedral and the ornate building that was now called the National Palace.

The colonial buildings were interesting, but Lacey was more intrigued by the ancient Aztec city, Tenochtitlan, that had been there before. She knew all the myths and legends surrounding it. The Aztec kings chose the site after a prophecy told them to build where they saw an eagle with a snake in its mouth alight on a cactus. The spot was on an island in the middle of a lake.

Lacey squinted her eyes, trying to visualize the glittery city that arose, filled with great pyramids and temples faced with gold. It was no use. The conquistadors had torn down the buildings and filled in the lake.

She wandered through the narrow streets surrounding the square, passing small *tiendas* offering everything from pottery to piñatas. The vendors coaxed her to buy, with friendly smiles and soft words. A purple and yellow piñata was a temptation, but, at the thought of carrying it home on the plane, she regretfully turned it down.

The hollow, animal shapes were made out of loops of bright crepe paper, the more colorful the better. At Christmas time they were traditionally filled with toys and hung from the ceiling. Children broke the piñatas with sticks and scrambled for the prizes that showered down.

Christmas must be a very happy time in Mexico, Lacey reflected. Did Raoul fill a piñata for his daughter? She hadn't thought about him for hours, and didn't welcome the intrusion.

To take her mind off Raoul, Lacey decided to go shopping. She wanted to bring back little remembrances to several of her friends, and time was growing short. But that was something else she didn't want to think about.

By chance, she stumbled onto one of the largest markets in Mexico City. A huge building housed a multitude of small shops filled mostly with native handicrafts, exactly what she was looking for.

It was hard to choose from all the appealing treasures displayed. Some were impractical because they were either breakable or too big to be transported home. Like the lovely pottery candle holders decorated with stylized native figures, or the gaily colored straw baskets large enough to use as clothes hampers.

Finally Lacey settled on some silver rings and pendants set with turquoise and amethyst. The semiprecious stones were mined in Mexico. The items originally cost more than she wanted to spend, but when she shook her head and started to walk away, the shopkeeper lowered his price sharply.

All the guidebooks advised bargaining, but Lacey would have felt uncomfortable. She even felt guilty accepting the drastic reduction, except that the man seemed too happy to have taken a loss. Evidently the books were right. She'd bargained without knowing it.

After her gifts were taken care of, she browsed through the little shops just for fun. Many of the items were puzzling, such as a cluster of little sticks topped by small, colored pebbles.

"What are these?" she asked the woman behind the counter.

"*Mondadientes, señorita.* You like?" At Lacey's uncomprehending expression she said, "*Por los dientes.*" When that wasn't any clearer, she tapped her teeth.

"Oh, toothpicks!"

"*Sí, sí.*" The woman joined her in laughter.

She'd certainly have to buy some of those, Lacey decided. They'd give a touch of class to the hot dogs at her next get-together.

Her smile faded as she made the inevitable comparison to Elena's elegant party fare. The whole way of life was better forgotten. She'd received a brief look at a place where she didn't belong.

It was late afternoon before she returned to the apartment. The bus had been jammed, and she'd had to stand up the whole way. Her feet hurt, and she was hot and rumpled. A cool bath was going to feel heavenly.

A man was standing with his back to her, talking to the doorman in front of the building.

Manuel hastened to open the door for her, saying, "*Buenas tardes, Señorita* Scott."

When the other man turned around, Lacey was surprised to see it was Carlos Mendes. After last night he was the last person she would have expected to see there. He was smiling, but his eyes were watchful.

It would have been rude to walk right by him. He hadn't really done anything to her—except spoil her relationship with Raoul, Lacey reflected wryly.

Some of that resentment colored her voice as she said, "Hello, Carlos."

He stopped her before she could continue inside. "I was hoping to see you again."

"Why?" she asked bluntly.

His smile wavered slightly, but he was undeterred. "Surely you know the answer to that."

"Look, Carlos, I don't want to be rude, but we're practically strangers—and I'd like to keep it that way."

"Why do you say that?"

"For one thing, because I don't want any more trouble with Delores." If the other woman thought she was poaching on her property again, who knew what she might do?

"Delores means nothing to me," he declared.

"It seems I've heard that song before," Lacey replied ironically. "Either you Latins are shockingly forgetful, or she has the imagination of a fiction writer."

"We're friends, nothing more," he protested.

"Your choice of friends is perilous to my peace of mind," she said curtly. "See you around, Carlos."

"Lacey, wait!" He followed her to the door. "I want to talk to you," he said urgently.

"You'll have to make it fast. I'm tired, and I want to get out of these clothes."

"Not here. Have a drink with me," he coaxed. "There's a little place right around the corner."

"If you really have something to say to me, you'll have to do it here."

"Raoul has turned you against me, hasn't he?"

"Raoul didn't have to," she answered coolly. "Between you and Delores, you ruined a perfectly lovely evening."

"It wasn't my fault! I tried to be civil." His voice took on a slight whine. "You heard me apologize."

Lacey didn't remember an apology, but it suddenly occurred to her that Carlos could tell her what none of the others would.

"You might at least listen to my side of the story before believing everything Raoul told you." His face was sulky.

"What's your version?"

"What did *he* say?" Carlos countered craftily.

Lacey could see that he wasn't going to divulge anything without a trade-off. "Raoul didn't tell me anything."

His eyes narrowed. "You mean he didn't say what he's planning to do."

"I never know *what* Raoul is going to do," she replied a trifle bitterly. "Or any of the rest of you, for that matter. I didn't have the faintest idea what was going on last night."

Carlos stared at her in disbelief. When the frustration on her face sank in, his expression changed. But the look of exultation was quickly masked.

"It wasn't as serious as it sounded." He smiled.

"You must think I'm simpleminded! Raoul was about to take you apart and scatter the pieces on different continents!"

He spread his hands deprecatingly. "We Latins have hot tempers."

If he wasn't going to tell her any more than the others, she was wasting her time. "Okay, Carlos, I get the message. You and Delores and Raoul are really the best of friends. And I'm the tooth fairy," she added sardonically. "Excuse me while I go upstairs and rinse out my wings."

He put his hand over hers when she reached for the door. "You're right, I wasn't being candid with you. But only because I didn't want to speak badly about Raoul."

"When are you going to start telling the truth?" she asked impatiently.

He sighed. "It's such a long story. I can't relate it standing here. Come with me for that drink, and I'll explain everything."

Lacey hesitated. This might be her one chance to learn the truth. But how did she know Carlos would give it to her? He hadn't been exactly forthright so far. The mire of intrigue got muddier by the moment.

"I've been out all day. I'd really like to get cleaned up," she said indecisively.

"I understand. Why don't we meet in an hour? Will that give you enough time?"

"I suppose so."

Lacey heard herself agreeing, although she had very real reservations. She didn't know what the grievance was about, but her loyalties were with Raoul—in spite of his defection.

"Take all the time you need," Carlos was saying. "I'll wait for you." He strode off quickly, before she could change her mind.

Lacey didn't even know whether she wanted to or not. It had become increasingly important to find out why Raoul rejected her. Or was it all of her sex? The scars he carried had to have been put there by a woman. Not Delores, certainly. Perhaps someone so wonderful that he could never love again? That was a hurtful thought. But what part had Carlos played in the tragedy?

Lacey turned on the shower with a feeling of dread. She was about to find out.

She felt better after changing to fresh clothes, but the reluctance to face unpleasant facts was still there. What if Raoul wasn't the titan she thought him to be? Suppose he had feet of clay like any other mortal?

Carlos met her at the door of the intimate cocktail lounge and led her to a booth in the back.

"You look ravishing," he said. "Most women would take all day to accomplish what you've done in an hour."

"Did I look that bad before?" she asked cynically.

"No! Most assuredly not. I merely meant that you're radiant."

"You must have excellent eyesight. This place is dark enough to develop film in."

"Would you rather go somewhere else?" he asked quickly.

"No, this is fine."

If Carlos had chosen this discreet spot so no one would see them together, that was *her* fervent wish, also. Running into Delores would be bad enough; having Raoul find out would be a disaster! The mere thought made

Lacey nervous. He'd take a very dim view of her consorting with the enemy, and she didn't want to be included in his wrath. Her soft mouth drooped unconsciously. His indifference was bad enough.

"I'm so glad you changed your mind about meeting me." Carlo's lowered voice was intimate. "Our conversation was cut much too short last night."

"The whole evening ended abruptly," she answered tersely. "Or did the party go on as usual?"

"I don't know. Delores and I left right after you did."

"When all the fireworks were over it must have been dull for her. She thrives on attention. But didn't it bother you to be part of that three-ring circus?"

"Raoul was the one who started it!"

"If you want to get technical, it was Delores. She knew exactly what would happen when she brought you there—and you must have, too. Why did you come?"

His face hardened. "Raoul thinks he's God. But he can't have it his way forever."

"That's no answer," she said impatiently. "When are you going to stop being evasive? I agreed to meet you because you said you'd tell me what happened between you and Raoul."

"Was that the only reason?" He reached for her hand across the table. "Surely you felt the same spark I did when we met. Like that beautiful song—you sought me out across a crowded room."

She pulled her hand away. "I sought you out, as you put it, because I didn't have anyone else to talk to."

"I don't think so. I believe a magnetic current brought us together, the magnetism of our attraction for each other." His voice was deep and melodious.

"Get real, Carlos! That line is enough to get you drummed out of the Latin lover corps."

"I'm sorry if I'm not as romantic as Raoul," he answered sulkily.

Lacey stared at him through narrowed eyes. "So that's it! I'm beginning to get a glimmering now. You're not interested in me. You think Raoul is, and you're trying to get back at him."

"That's ridiculous!" Although he denied the allegation, he couldn't hold her intent gaze.

"Did he take someone away from *you* once?" Lacey's brow wrinkled. She'd thought it was the other way around.

"Raoul fancies himself a great lover, but I've forgotten more women than he'll ever know!"

"I'm not interested in your credentials. Just tell me this. Is that bad feeling between you and Raoul because of a woman?"

"Yes," he answered reluctantly.

"Well, finally! What happened?"

He looked at her silently for a moment, as though making up his mind. Then he began slowly. "It was a long time ago, almost five years. We were both in love with the same girl, as you've guessed. She was young and beautiful . . . and innocent." He sighed.

When he didn't continue, Lacey prodded him. "Which one of you was she in love with?"

"At first she couldn't make up her mind. She enjoyed the excitement of having two older men vying for her attention. The balance could have tipped either way. But then I was called out of town on business, leaving the field open for Raoul. He took advantage of the fact."

"Well, naturally he'd see more of her if you weren't around."

"If only he'd settled for that. But Raoul didn't trust his own attractions. He made up lies about me."

Lacey remembered Raoul's icy contempt when Delores accused him of lying. His firm denial of that particular fault had held the ring of truth.

"That doesn't sound like Raoul," she said slowly.

"You're like all women," Carlos answered bitterly. "None of you can see through that smooth charm. Take my word for it, you don't know the real Raoul. He's utterly ruthless when he wants something badly enough."

Lacey was uncomfortably aware of having had the same thought. "Aren't you being a little unfair? Even if he did disparage you a bit, she didn't have to believe him."

"I told you she was unsophisticated. After he got through telling her about all the women I was supposedly involved with, she wouldn't even talk to me on the telephone. I never had a chance to clear myself."

"I don't understand. You're saying Raoul double-crossed you. But if he got the girl, why is *he* angry at *you*?"

"The story doesn't end there. In light of what happened, I wish to God it did," Carlos said somberly. "When I heard of their plans to marry, I was heartbroken. I redoubled my efforts to see her, but it was no use. Raoul had done his work well. As their wedding day grew near I went a little crazy. I knew I'd lost her, but at least I wanted to clear up the misunderstanding between us, to let her know I wasn't the lying cheat Raoul had painted me to be."

Lacey felt a chill of foreboding. She almost told him not to go on. But she didn't.

"The night before the wedding, I climbed through her window in the middle of the night," he continued. "I told her I knew it was too late for us, but I wanted her to know I'd always love her. She cried and confessed that she loved me, too, that she'd only chosen Raoul after discovering I had several other women on the string. Once we were face to face, I was able to convince her that it was all a pack of lies.''

"Did you make love to her?" Lacey asked in a muted voice.

"No! I asked her to postpone the wedding, to give me a chance to win her back. But the idea frightened her. She said all the arrangements had been made, it would be a terrible scandal, and what would her parents say?''

"She does sound young," Lacey murmured.

"We argued for hours. When I couldn't persuade her, I said I was going to Taxco in the morning. I couldn't bear the thought of being in the same city while she married another man. We kissed—desperately—and that's the last time I ever saw her," he concluded heavily.

"But she didn't go through with the wedding! Rosa said Raoul's never been married.''

"I was more persuasive than I realized," Carlos said tonelessly. "After thinking about it the rest of the night, she changed her mind. She must have tried to call me, but I never went home. After I left her, I went from bar to bar trying to drown my sorrows. Then I went directly to the airport. When she couldn't reach me at home, she decided to follow me. Her plane crashed on takeoff.''

"Oh, no," Lacey whispered.

"Raoul never forgave me.''

"What a tragedy for everybody.''

"Exactly! But he held *me* responsible. He set out to destroy me, and he succeeded.''

Carlos didn't look down and out. His suit was tailor-made, and his nails were manicured. "In what way?" she asked.

"Raoul and I both managed our family businesses, although his was larger by far. We were competitors, but I was no threat to him. He didn't have to ruin me."

"He caused your business to fail?"

"He might as well have. He forced me out of it." Carlos's face was a mask of hatred and frustration. "He spread false rumors that I'd been gambling."

Lacey looked at him blankly. "Is that all? I'm not saying it's a noble thing to do, but why would anyone care what you did in your personal life?"

"A few times our shipments were late. That happens sometimes in business. Nobody can anticipate everything," he insisted, as though she'd been arguing the point. "But Raoul put out the word that our machinery was outdated, that we'd continue to be unreliable because we couldn't afford new parts. He said I'd been siphoning off all the working capital to support my high-flying life-style."

Lacey gazed at him speculatively. "You didn't, I suppose?"

"As God is my judge!"

"I'm not doubting your word," she said slowly. "I just can't see Raoul retaliating in that manner. He strikes me as the kind of man who'd be more apt to pound you to a pulp, or maybe challenge you to a duel."

She could almost see Raoul in tight black pants and a flowing white silk shirt unbuttoned halfway down his broad chest. The dawn light would illuminate his patrician features as he selected a pistol from his second.

"A very romantic picture," Carlos sneered, correctly interpreting her fantasy. "That's the way *gentlemen* settle their differences. Unfortunately for me, Raoul is the lowest kind of street fighter. The dirtier it gets, the better he likes it."

"Oh, come on, Carlos. You're getting carried away."

"Am I? What do you call a man who would take away the livelihood of an entire family just to get revenge on one member of it? The company supported all my relatives, but do you think that bothered him? No! As long as he could drag me down, that was all that mattered."

"Businessmen don't take sides in a grudge match. Couldn't you have gone to your customers and assured them you'd make deliveries on time? I don't know much about industry, but wouldn't a performance bond or something like that have proved you were a responsible company?"

"Raoul took care to plug that loophole. He lowered his price on unrefined ore until there wasn't any profit in it. I would have had to be competitive to stay in the game, but I couldn't afford to take even a short-term loss. He could."

It did seem as though Raoul had held all the cards. Even though he'd been deeply hurt, there was something distasteful about one man destroying another cold-bloodedly. It was such a ruthless, compassionless thing to do.

"What happened to your company?" she asked. "Did you have to declare bankruptcy?"

Carlos's black eyes flashed. "That would have dishonored my family name!"

"But you said he ruined you."

"When I told him I was prepared to fight back, to pawn my mother's jewels if necessary to keep the business afloat, he did the sneakiest thing of all. He went to my younger brother behind my back and offered him a loan if Raymond would force me out. The family held a secret meeting and decided to accept Raoul's offer."

"Your own family?"

"I don't blame *them*. They would have been destitute if the company failed. Raoul is the culprit. He used his money to seduce them in the vilest kind of treachery."

"They could have gone out and gotten jobs," Lacey said impatiently. "Why does everything have to be handed down from father to son in this country? If you people hadn't had grandfathers, you'd *all* be destitute!"

"You don't understand our traditions," Carlos answered stiffly.

"Maybe not, but where I come from, families stick together."

"No one can win against Raoul. I did the honorable thing and stepped down. I even left town to ease the tensions."

"What have you been doing?"

"Surviving," he said grimly.

"Why did you come back?" she asked curiously.

"I decided it was time to end my exile. I hoped Raoul might have softened after all this time."

"You should have picked a less public place to find out. Was it Delores's idea to show up at Elena's party?"

"She suggested it," he admitted.

"With friends like her, you don't need any enemies. She could have told you what your reception would be."

"All those people were once my friends," he said sadly. "I had no idea the whole world had turned against me."

Lacey felt an unexpected rush of sympathy. She didn't find Carlos wildly appealing, but he'd certainly suffered a lot. Who could blame him if he came on a little too strong? Maybe deep down he was looking for affection. Losing his real love and having his family turn their backs on him, too, must have been traumatic.

"The whole world isn't against you," she said gently. "You've had more than your share of hard knocks, but things change."

He grasped both of her hands. "I knew at first glance you were *simpático*. That's why I wanted to tell you my side of the story before Raoul could fill your head with lies."

"I told you he didn't say anything about you."

"He will. And when he does, perhaps you can say a word on my behalf."

So that was the reason for his rendezvous. Carlos wasn't trying to take her away from Raoul; he wanted a friend in court. It was a more honorable motive in a way, but just as futile. She had as much influence with Raoul as a lamb had over a wolf.

She tried to tell him so. "I don't even know if I'll see Raoul again before I leave."

"Delores said—" he stopped abruptly.

"If you're taking lessons from Delores, you'll have to go to school twice as long," Lacey said acidly. "In spite of what she told you, Raoul and I are not making mad, passionate love in his apartment. If we were, why would he be staying at his sister's house?"

"I wasn't implying anything...improper."

"That's good, because the true story is fit for your maiden aunt's ears."

"I always knew Raoul wasn't a real man," Carlos said contemptuously.

That was another of his misconceptions. Would she ever forget the masculinity of Raoul's hard body, or the probing seductiveness of his warm mouth? Just thinking about that heated episode in his arms brought the inflaming moments alive. She ducked her head to hide the guilty evidence.

But her heightened color gave her away, along with her failure to meet his eyes. "I wouldn't know about that," she murmured. "He's always been a perfect gentleman with me."

Carlos correctly guessed there had been lapses in Raoul's good conduct. "He never tried to make love to you?" he asked softly. "The man's a fool as well as a villain."

"The circumstances of our meeting make it sound romantic, but I can assure you our relationship is nothing like that," she said firmly. "Raoul befriended me when I was in trouble, in spite of the fact that I was a total stranger. That's why your story shocks me so. He's shown me only kindness."

"It makes him feel good to play lord of the manor," Carlos sneered. "After all, what does it cost him? You're grateful, and everyone says what a splendid fellow he is. Just don't cross him or you'll see a different Raoul. He can turn on you in a minute."

"It's pointless to argue about it, because I'll never find out," she said. Loyalty prevented her from admitting that he had done exactly that the night before. "Raoul is going to his ranch, and I'm leaving in a few days. I'll most likely be gone before he gets back."

"Does he know that?"

"Yes." She suddenly realized that Carlos could solve the rest of the mystery. "Raoul's daughter lives on the ranch," she remarked innocently. When he didn't comment, she said, "Did you know he had a child?"

"I heard he'd adopted one."

Lacey's conscience hurt, but that didn't stop her. "I've seen her picture. She looks just like him."

"They say that happens sometimes," Carlos answered noncommittally.

"Do you know who the mother is?"

"I've been out of touch for some time."

His evasiveness indicated that Carlos knew more than he was telling. But why would he hold anything back? He hadn't been shy about blackening Raoul's character before. Maybe she was wrong about the little girl being Raoul's.

"It seems strange for a bachelor to adopt a child," she said slowly.

"Even a man like Raoul needs love, I suppose." His mouth twisted sardonically.

"There are more conventional ways of getting it."

"I'm sure he uses those, too."

Lacey's color rose. "I meant getting married and having your own children."

Carlos shrugged. "Why should he get married? He has the best of both worlds."

"It's nice to know the value you put on women," she remarked coolly.

"I didn't mean it that way!" He was swift to make amends. "I was merely saying that with his money, Raoul can afford to have a family, even if he doesn't choose to marry."

"I would have thought he'd want a son to carry on the family name."

"Even Raoul can't have everything he wants."

She was repelled by the satisfaction on his face. "None of us can," she responded sharply.

Carlos was instantly aware of having lost her sympathy. "Don't be angry with me, *cara*. I can't help being resentful. Raoul and I have both suffered, but I'm willing to forgive and forget. I extended an olive branch and he struck it down—publicly."

"Maybe it was the shock of seeing you so unexpectedly. That wasn't really wise. If I were you, I wouldn't take Delores's advice again."

"You're right. She was just using me," he said sadly. "Delores is as vicious as Raoul when someone crosses her."

"Even when she just *thinks* they have," Lacey muttered.

"She and Raoul would make a good pair."

"Were they ever as close as she claims?"

"Only in her own mind."

"Does he...um...is he involved with any other woman?"

"Raoul's involvement ends in the morning," Carlos said cynically.

She was sorry she'd asked. "Well, from what I've heard, he's a good father, anyway."

"Yes, Carlotta is his life."

Lacey slanted a speculative glance at him. Carlos professed to know nothing about Raoul's child, yet he knew the little girl's name. "Maybe that's how you can get back in his good graces. By making friends with his daughter."

He sighed. "I don't think anything would help, but I feel better after getting it all off my chest. You were kind to listen."

It was a story Lacey could have gone without knowing, but she had only herself to blame. Nothing good ever came from opening Pandora's box. It was a lesson to remember.

"Will you have dinner with me tonight?" Carlos asked.

"I can't," she answered promptly.

"You said you weren't seeing Raoul."

"That's true, but I . . . well, I have some things to do."

"Nothing I've said has made any difference, has it?" he asked sadly. "You despise me, like all the rest."

"I don't, Carlos! Honestly I don't. It's just . . . this whole story has been so depressing. I simply don't feel up to going anywhere tonight."

"Does that mean you'd be willing to go out with me some other time?"

"I won't be here much longer," she hedged.

His smile was twisted. "I guess you've answered my question."

"You're wrong. I'd be happy to have dinner with you another time."

She didn't really want to, but he looked so vulnerable. It would be cruel to kick a man when he was down. Even his friends had deserted him.

He gathered both her hands in his. "I'm going to hold you to that."

"It's a deal." She extricated herself and slid out of the booth. "Take care, Carlos. Better times are coming."

A little smile played around his rather weak mouth. "That's what I'm counting on."

Chapter Six

After leaving Carlos, Lacey tried to put the whole sordid story out of her mind. None of this had anything to do with her. Her life had touched Raoul's for a brief moment, nothing more.

If she dared to dream a little, it was only romantic fantasizing. He would be incredulous if he knew. Raoul had made his intentions perfectly clear—including the fact that he didn't even have those anymore.

Lacey puttered around the apartment all evening, unconsciously waiting for the phone to ring. It didn't. She tried to focus on her plans for the next day, but they didn't seem very interesting. Finally she went to bed.

The phone woke her from a deep sleep the next morning. She returned to consciousness reluctantly. In a stirring dream, Raoul had been gazing deeply into her eyes, saying something vitally important. An irritating noise prevented her from hearing what it was. The dream shattered as she realized it was the telephone.

"Hello." Her voice was grumpy.

"Did I wake you?" Raoul's voice chased away the last shreds of sleep.

"No, I . . . I was just about to get up."

"You're still in bed?" His voice deepened.

"Yes, but I probably shouldn't be. What time is it?"

"It's early, but I wanted to catch you before you went out."

He sounded the way he had when she'd first met him. The disastrous evening at Elena's might never have occurred. Lacey thought maybe she was still a little foggy.

"What did you want?" she asked cautiously.

"I wondered if you'd like to visit the pyramids today."

"I'd love to, but I don't want you to send a car and driver." She remembered his previous offer. If this was Raoul's way of making amends for the other night, she wasn't interested.

"Not even if the car is mine and I'm the driver?"

"I thought you were going up to your ranch," she said warily.

"Not until tomorrow morning. How about it?"

Her spirits rose like a soufflé. "It sounds wonderful! How long do I have to get ready?"

"Don't rush. I have some business to take care of this morning. Suppose I pick you up about eleven?"

Lacey felt as though she'd received a shot of vitamins. She jumped out of bed and raced into the shower, although she had hours to get dressed. What had brought about this transformation in Raoul? It didn't matter. The only important thing was, he was back to normal. She was going to see him one more time before she left.

Lacey couldn't help feeling a little tense when she went to answer the door some time later, but Raoul's attitude left nothing to be desired. His eyes held the special glow that made even her toes tingle.

"All set?" he asked brightly.

"And raring to go. It's very nice of you to do this for me."

He smiled. "My motives aren't entirely unselfish."

She slanted a dubious glance at him. "What do you mean?"

"Would you believe I have a burning desire to climb a pyramid?"

"I'd doubt it rather seriously."

"Then you must be the attraction." Putting his arm around her shoulders, he led her out the door.

"The trip takes about an hour on the main highway, or considerably more if we take the two-lane road that winds through a lot of little villages," he said as they drove away from the apartment house. "Which would you prefer?"

"The one through the villages, definitely. If you have the time, that is."

He turned his head to gaze at her. "I don't have a thing to do until tomorrow."

Lacey looked away hastily. "You don't really get to see anything on a throughway except other cars."

"That's true." His face wore a look of amusement.

The drive was slow because the narrow road was often clogged with wagons and trucks. Lacey didn't mind, since it gave her a chance to get more than a quick glimpse of the picturesque little villages they passed through.

She was fascinated by the contrast to the modern city they'd just left. The countryside still had the flavor of old Mexico. Goats and horses grazed beside the road, and bales of hay were stacked high on thatched farmhouse roofs.

She saw women scrubbing their clothes in a small brook, while others were spreading garments on the ground or on trees and shrubs to dry. This was the rural equivalent of a laundromat, she supposed.

"It's like going back in time," Lacey exclaimed.

When they reached the Pyramids of San Juan Teoti-huacan, the impression deepened. The entire area of ruined temples, houses and pyramids had a brooding atmosphere, as though the land itself was remembering its past glory.

"The largest one is the Pyramid of the Sun," Raoul told her. "The base is bigger than the famous tomb of Cheops in Egypt. It faces the Pyramid of the Moon at the end of this broad avenue."

A series of steps was cut into the stone tiers, broad at the base, then narrowing toward the top. The steps were dotted with tourists toiling upward like ants. The summit held a cluster of people who had persevered to the top.

"Can we climb up?" Lacey asked eagerly.

"If you like. There are two hundred and forty-eight steps," Raoul warned. "Why don't we save it till last and see how you feel?"

They wandered through the ruins to a large courtyard fronting the temple of Quetzalcoatl, named for the Tol-tec serpent god. A passageway in the back was lined with fabulous carvings of mythical feathered snakes and a goggle-eyed being who represented the rain god.

Lacey was tireless. She led Raoul all around the quad-rangle, inspected the houses adjacent to it and walked along the entire half-mile Avenue of the Dead. But if he thought she'd be too tired to climb the pyramid, he was mistaken.

"I don't want to miss a single thing," she coaxed.

"Next time I come here I'm bringing a woman who isn't in such good shape," he grumbled good-naturedly.

Even Raoul had to admit the view from the top was worth the breathless climb. The valley spread out on all sides, and was dotted with the charming villages they'd passed through.

"It's mind-boggling to realize this stone altar we're standing on was built two thousand years ago." Lacey's voice was filled with awe.

Raoul nodded. "Except that it wasn't as stark then. The pyramids were originally covered with white plaster decorated with bright-red designs along the base."

"I did learn that in my history course. They must have really sparkled in the sunshine." The breeze ruffled her long hair as she lifted her head to gaze at the clear blue sky. "It's so peaceful up here. How could they use this lovely spot to make living sacrifices?"

"They weren't being deliberately cruel, only misguided. *We* know that thunder and lightning, for instance, are natural phenomena. They thought they meant angry gods were demanding tribute."

"It's strange that their religion was so primitive when the rest of their culture was so advanced. Did you know that a thousand years before Christ, the Olmecs farmed by using irrigation ducts and figured out a calendar of three hundred sixty-five days?"

Raoul grinned. "Which one of us is the native here? I'm supposed to be instructing *you*."

"I'm sorry. Of course you know the history of your own country," she said remorsefully.

"Not as well as you do, I'll wager." He gently removed a windblown strand of hair from her cheek. "I'll just have to find another field to excel in."

His husky voice and the caressing gesture subtly changed the atmosphere between them. The warmth Lacey felt wasn't solely from the sun. She could think of one field he had probably mastered completely. Raoul could be effortlessly arousing even under circumstances that weren't the slightest bit erotic. Now, for instance, she thought with some trepidation.

"From what I've seen, you excel at everything you do," she murmured.

He laughed. "If I have you that brainwashed, perhaps I'd better quit while I'm ahead."

That was good advice for both of them. The strong sexual attraction that flared so readily could only lead to complications at best—or heartbreak at worst.

She drew away. "Shall we start back? It shouldn't be as difficult going down."

When they reached the car Raoul said, "The one thing this place lacks is a good restaurant. We missed lunch completely."

"I didn't even notice. Are you terribly hungry?"

"Mildly so." He consulted his watch. "The trouble with eating lunch now is that it will spoil our dinner."

He seemed to assume they were having dinner together, but Lacey didn't take anything for granted with Raoul. "Do you have plans for tonight?" she asked cautiously.

"I thought I'd leave it up to you. What would you like to do?"

She was filled with a lilting happiness. "Whatever you'd like."

He grinned mischievously. "That's a dangerous offer."

"Within reason, then."

"I knew it was too good to be true. Okay, let's start over. Where would you like to eat?"

She didn't really feel like getting dressed up and going somewhere fancy after the strenuous day. Besides, they'd both be ravenous long before the fashionable restaurants began serving.

"I have an idea. Why don't we go back to the apartment and I'll cook dinner," she suggested. "That way we won't have to wait until ten o'clock."

"I don't want you to go to all that trouble," he protested.

"Are you afraid I can't cook?"

"You *did* burn the spaghetti," he reminded her with a smile. "Not to mention what happened with the hot chocolate."

"You're right, let's not mention it," she said hastily.

"Why don't we just go to a nice quiet restaurant?" Laughter glinted in his dark eyes.

"No, my reputation is at stake. Anyway, the third time has to be a charm."

"I'll bet that's what Zsa Zsa Gabor said when she married her third husband."

"Now you've issued a challenge! I'm going to cook you the best dinner you've ever eaten."

"If I live through it, that is."

"Just say your prayers, and stop at the nearest market."

Raoul carried the bags of groceries into the kitchen and lounged against a counter, watching as Lacey unpacked them. They'd decided on coq au vin.

"I'll make a little snack to tide us over while the chicken is cooking," she said.

"*Tapas*, you mean."

Her brow wrinkled. "Did we buy those?"

"*Tapas* are the Spanish version of what you call hors d'oeuvres."

"Oh. Well, your stomach better be adaptable," she warned. "You're about to be introduced to American fast-food cuisine."

After mixing a carton of sour cream with a package of dried onion-soup mix, she spooned it into a bowl and filled a larger bowl with potato chips.

"You scoop up the dip with a potato chip," she explained.

"I'm not exactly new to this. We do the same thing with taco chips and salsa."

"Really? I didn't think you ate anything without a knife and fork."

"Are you making fun of me, young lady?"

"No, you're just so dauntingly elegant, that's all. It wouldn't surprise me if you dined every night on Wedgwood, and went to sleep on monogrammed silk sheets."

"Doesn't everyone? Sleep between silk sheets, I mean. They feel so good on your bare skin. Or are you one of those inhibited women who wears nightgowns to bed?" He watched with derision as the telltale color rose in her fair skin.

Raoul was obviously getting even with her for kidding him about his life-style. "Can't you take a joke?" she asked plaintively.

"Certainly. But I'd still like an answer to my question."

"What difference does it make?" she muttered.

4

IRRESISTIBLY CAPTIVATING NOVELS

FREE!

PLUS!
2 Glass Oyster Dishes
AND
a Surprise Mystery Gift

Silhouette Desire romances bring you all the heartbreak and ecstasy of
fulfilling and contemporary relationships as they are lived today.

**And to introduce you to this powerful, highly-charged series,
we'll send you 4 Silhouette Desire titles, a beautiful pair of Oyster
Dishes plus a Surprise Mystery Gift, absolutely FREE when you
complete and return this card**

We'll also reserve a subscription for you to our
Reader Service, which means you'll enjoy:

- **6 WONDERFUL NOVELS -** sent direct to you every month.
- **FREE POSTAGE & PACKING -** we pay all the extras.
- **FREE REGULAR NEWSLETTER -** packed with competitions, author news and much, much more.
- **SPECIAL OFFERS -** selected exclusively for our readers.

CLAIM YOUR FREE GIFTS OVERLEAF

A DELIGHTFUL INTRODUCTORY OFFER FREE!

FREE BOOKS CERTIFICATE

Yes! Please send me my **4 Free Silhouette Desires** together with my **Free Gifts**. Please also reserve a special Reader Service Subscription for me. If I decide to subscribe, I shall receive 6 Superb new titles every month for just £7.80 post and packing free. If I decide not to subscribe I shall write to you within 10 days. The free books and gift will be mine to keep in any case. I understand that I am under no obligation whatsoever – I can cancel or suspend my subscription at any time simply by writing to you. *I am over 18 years of age*

2S9SD

NAME _____

ADDRESS _____

_____

_____

POSTCODE _____

FREE GIFT

Return this card now and we'll also send you this beautiful set of 2 glass oyster dishes absolutely Free together with...

A SURPRISE MYSTERY GIFT.

We all love surprises, so as well as the FREE books and glass dishes, there's an intriguing mystery gift especially for you.

POST TODAY!

Reader Service
FREEPOST
P.O. Box 236
Croydon
CR9 9EL

NO
STAMP
NEEDED

The right is reserved to refuse an application and change the terms of this offer. Offer expires June 30th 1989. You may be mailed with other offers as a result of this application. Readers in Southern Africa write to: Independent Book Services Pty. Postbag X3010,

"I want to know if I should adjust my thinking." He sauntered closer. "I've been picturing your delectable body covered only by a pink silk sheet."

Lacey forced herself not to move away, although she couldn't help tensing. "The guest room is done in blue. Your decorator wouldn't make such a glaring error."

"That doesn't answer my question," he said softly.

She did move away then. Raoul was only trying to get a rise out of her. It amused him to see her blush. But situations such as this had a way of escalating.

"If you expect to eat any time in the near future, you'd better stop harassing the cook," she answered tartly.

"Man doesn't live by bread alone," he murmured.

He was being purposely annoying, and she was tired of being on the defensive. Lacey decided to turn the tables. Lowering her lashes, she gave him a Mona Lisa smile. "Or women, either. Why don't you pick out a nice bottle of wine while I slip into something more comfortable."

The surprised look on his face was very gratifying. Lacey suppressed her glee as she slanted a suggestive glance over her shoulder before drifting out of the kitchen.

Her languorous movements speeded up in the bedroom. In a matter of minutes she'd changed to jeans and a shapeless navy sweatshirt that reached the top of her thighs.

Instead of rejoining Raoul immediately, she let the suspense build. If he expected her to return in a sheer negligee—or possibly less than that—she might as well give him time to enjoy the anticipation.

When it occurred to her that he might think she was waiting for him in the bedroom, Lacey hurriedly made her entrance. He was standing at the bar with his back to her.

"Did I take too long?" she murmured in a seductive voice.

Raoul's original response had been rewarding, but his reaction now was disappointing. When he turned and saw her, he merely nodded approvingly.

"That looks comfortable, all right."

Lacey frowned. "This wasn't what you were expecting. Admit it!"

He smiled. "I wasn't sure of the precise color, but I knew it would be something like that."

"You did not," she replied indignantly. "When a woman says she's going to slip into something comfortable, this isn't what she means."

"It is if you're the woman." His eyes danced with merriment. "A kitten doesn't turn into a tiger."

"In other words, I'm tame and predictable."

"The female of the species is never predictable."

"Thanks for small favors." She stalked into the kitchen.

He followed her, holding a bottle of wine. "I can't seem to please you. When I become too personal you're annoyed, and when I accept your terms you're still not satisfied."

"You don't have to be insulting," she muttered, banging a large frying pan down on the stove. "No woman likes to be told she's about as interesting as a house cat."

"Is that what you got out of it?" His voice was warm and teasing. "I thought I'd made my feelings clearer than that."

"Your feelings are a complete mystery to me. I never know what to expect from you." Frustration overwhelmed her as she placed pieces of chicken in the sputtering pan.

Raoul's amusement waned when he saw she was serious. "I hope you know you can trust me," he said quietly.

"Yes, but that's *all* I know. You're like a mountain lake, smooth and inviting on the surface, but with incredible depth."

He smiled wryly. "I'm not sure if that's a compliment or an insult."

"Neither, just a statement of fact. You're as much a stranger as you were when we met."

"You can't feel that way," he protested.

"I do! Everything I know about you I've learned from your sister. And *that* isn't much."

His warmth cooled. "I'm surprised Rosa would indulge in gossip."

"She didn't—and I didn't encourage her to. All I meant was that you're a very private person."

"Many people are," he answered evenly.

"But they don't have such wild mood swings. I was honestly flabbergasted when you called this morning."

Surprise registered on his face. "Why would you be?"

"After the mood you were in when you took me home from Elena's, I didn't expect to see you again."

"I apologize if my manners were faulty," he said distantly.

"They weren't—except maybe when you told me to mind my own business."

"I don't recall being that discourteous."

"You didn't say it in so many words, but your meaning was clear. I realized you were upset, but I didn't have any idea why."

Her inadvertent use of the past tense was revealing. She held her breath, but Raoul was too intent to notice.

"I'd prefer to forget the whole evening, if you don't mind," he said tautly.

Lacey knew she should let the matter drop, but she wanted to hear Raoul's version. After the thoughtful, generous companion he'd been all day, she couldn't believe he'd done any of those underhanded things Carlos had accused him of. He couldn't have told her the whole story.

"It was very unpleasant," she said haltingly.

"Then why pursue it?"

"Because you changed so drastically. You're changing right now. How can I feel comfortable with you if I have to be constantly afraid of saying the wrong thing?"

Warring emotions chased each other across his stern face. Finally he said, "I'm truly sorry I let that spectacle the other night affect me so obviously. Any rudeness I showed you was unintentional."

"I understood that," she said earnestly. "I know you must have had a good reason."

"There's never a good reason for venting your anger on an innocent party."

Lacey's hopes of getting him to confide in her were waning. Raoul didn't feel the need to justify himself as Carlos had. She persisted anyway. "If I don't know what upsets you, how can I be sure I won't touch on the subject again?"

"That isn't likely," he replied curtly. "It doesn't concern you."

"There, you've done it again! Those were the exact words you used that night."

His voice softened. "I merely meant this was something between Carlos and me. A long-standing...disagreement."

"He wants to make up, though. Wouldn't you be happier if you put it all behind you?"

"No." The word was bitten off.

Lacey chose her own words carefully. "Sometimes both sides are guilty of...errors in judgment."

"My only mistake was in being too civilized," he replied savagely. "I shouldn't have been content with merely letting him sink into the gutter."

Her heart plunged. His admission seemed to confirm Carlos's accusations. A glance at Raoul's harsh face reinforced the impression. His thirst for revenge was as powerful now as it had ever been—indicating that Raoul was indeed an implacable enemy.

He stared moodily at her bent head. "Will you agree it's a subject we'd do well to avoid?"

She nodded silently.

"Here's the wine you requested. Can I pour you a glass?" he asked formally.

"No, I don't care for any. I really wanted it for the chicken."

He put the bottle on the counter. "Then if you'll excuse me, I'll go make myself a real drink."

Lacey turned the chicken in the pan automatically. She peeled some small onions and scrubbed a handful of mushrooms with the same lack of attention. Why had she rushed in where angels feared to tread when she'd known better? It hadn't even gotten her anywhere. She had just spoiled this last evening with Raoul. Dinner was going to be torture. They'd both sit there trying to make conversation. She almost wished he'd leave. Almost.

How could she still find him attractive when she knew what he was really like? That calculated cruelty went against all her principles. If people couldn't forgive each other it would be a pretty rotten world.

But Raoul wasn't all bad. The suffering he'd been through had warped him, yet he was still capable of great kindness. She was proof of that. It wasn't up to her to judge. If there was any way to salvage the evening, she was going to try.

When the chicken was simmering, and the lettuce for the salad had been washed and put in the refrigerator to crisp, Lacey went into the living room.

"Could you tell me where the pads are for the dining room table?" she asked diffidently.

"Why don't we eat in the kitchen? Wouldn't that be easier?"

She couldn't help smiling. "Have you ever had even a cup of coffee in there?"

He returned her smile. "Are you going to start that again?"

"No, I just thought you'd be more comfortable in the dining room. I'm trying to get back in your good graces."

He came over and put his hands on her shoulders. "I'm the one who should be trying to make amends. Can you forgive me for being an insensitive clod?"

Lacey eagerly accepted the proffered olive branch. "Why don't we declare a truce? From now on the most controversial thing we'll talk about is the weather."

"You're on." He grinned. "What do you think of our climate?"

"I think you ought to do something about your smog."

"If you have any suggestions, the government would be delighted to hear them."

"I'll leave that to Rosa. Did you know she's already working for Manuel Salizar?"

"No, but I'm not surprised. She'll get you involved next." He laughed. "You only think you're going home."

"It wouldn't take much to get me to stay."

"Do you mean that?" His eyes narrowed with sudden speculation.

She'd spoken without thinking. "Only if I could live in the lap of luxury like this." Her tone was purposely light. "But that isn't likely."

"It might be arranged," he murmured.

Lacey didn't want an "arrangement." "I pay my own way," she stated crisply. "And I can't afford the high-rent district." She stood up. "I'd better check on dinner."

"Can I help?"

"Do you know how to do anything useful?"

He chuckled. "You're always feeding me these straight lines."

"This time I'm calling your bluff. You can set the table. It will be interesting to see if you know where the dishes are."

"That's not much of a challenge. How many places could they be?"

"You honestly don't know where they're kept?"

"I don't eat at home very often."

"Well, in case there's a general strike that closes all the restaurants, I'll give you a crash course in survival. The plates are here, and the silverware is there." She indicated cupboards and drawers.

"What good would that do if you're not here to cook for me?"

"You'd find someone," she said cynically.

"Not anyone as decorative."

"You'll just have to decide which of your senses you want to gratify. Set the table," she ordered before he could respond.

The lighthearted mood between them was a delight after their close brush with disaster. Lacey was determined to keep it that way, too. Nothing was going to mar their last evening together if she could help it.

"This chicken is great!" Raoul exclaimed. "You're a fantastic cook."

"Would you say that if you'd had lunch?" She laughed. "The secret of success is to wait until your customers are so hungry they're beyond criticism."

"You're being too modest. I've never tasted better coq au vin. You could make a fortune by opening a restaurant."

"It sounds like a rather limited menu."

"Is that all you can cook?" he teased. "I knew you were too good to be true."

"I'd show you the range of my talents if we had more time."

His laughter died as he gazed at her lovely face. "I never knew time could pass so swiftly."

"I didn't either," she agreed. "I can't believe it's been almost a week."

"It won't be the same around here without you."

Her smile was a little forced. "Look at it this way: you aren't losing a boarder, you're gaining your home back."

"I like having you in it," he said softly.

Lacey was determined not to let the conversation become personal. There was no future in it, and the evening could easily be ruined.

"I've gotten dreadfully spoiled here," she remarked casually. "My apartment's going to feel like a closet."

"Why don't you stay longer?"

She shook her head. "I can't."

"Isn't a vacation usually two weeks?"

"Yes, but I left myself a few days to take clothes to the cleaners and do a lot of little errands."

"That doesn't sound too time consuming."

"You'd be surprised."

"You could manage a couple of more days," he coaxed.

Lacey was tempted, but a few more days wouldn't change anything between herself and Raoul. He wasn't going to let her get any closer to him—except physically. That was a possibility that presented itself every time they were together. Under the circumstances, it was better to leave now before they did something they'd both regret.

"Maybe some day you'll visit me in San Diego," she said. "It isn't as glamorous as Mexico City, but we do have our attractions."

"You're enough attraction for me," he answered huskily.

"You'll forget about me the day after I leave." She sighed unconsciously.

He covered her hand with his. "I don't forget that easily."

That was true. He was still mourning his lost love after five years. Lacey slid her hand away. "I'll get dessert."

After they'd finished dinner, Raoul carried the coffee service into the living room while Lacey put the dishes in the dishwasher.

She joined him on the couch afterward, and they enjoyed the pleasant relaxation.

"I love this view," she remarked, gazing out at the lights of the vast city. "I've always wanted one."

"You don't have a view?"

She smiled. "Sure. Of the building across the street."

"What's your apartment like?"

"Undistinguished."

"You can do better than that."

"Why do you want to know?"

He twined his fingers with hers. "I need a background to place you in so I'll have a mental picture when I think about you."

She turned her head to look at his compelling face. "Will you really think about me?" she asked wistfully.

"You'd better believe it." His fingers tightened. "Tell me all the details. What color is your bedroom?"

"I might have known that was the room you were interested in," she answered dryly.

He laughed. "I'll admit it's the one that's apt to predominate in my imagination, but I really do want to hear about the rest of the place."

"There isn't that much to tell. It's a typical, moderately priced apartment. I've brightened it up a bit with a row of violets on the kitchen windowsill and some colorful pillows in the living room, but it won't ever make the pages of *Elegant Homes and Gardens*."

"How is it furnished?"

"In early thrift shop, except for a few pieces that belonged to my parents. Most of their furnishings were sold with the house, but I kept a few things—my dad's big leather chair and my mother's writing desk. I don't really have room in the apartment, but I couldn't bear to part with them. Those were two things they used regularly."

"It must have been terrible to lose both your parents at once." Raoul's voice was warm with sympathy.

"It was." Her eyes were shadowed, remembering. "After the grief came the terror, the realization that I was all alone in the world with no one to love, or anyone who loved me."

He put his arm around her, drawing her close in an instinctive attempt to give comfort. "You must have a lot of friends who love you."

"It isn't the same." She put her head on his shoulder. "You have a big family, so you can't know the loneliness."

"The loss of any loved one is devastating, no matter how many are left."

Lacey was too caught up in her own tragedy to catch the odd note in his voice. "We were so close. I didn't know what to do without them. And then to make matters worse, I had to deal with business problems that were a complete mystery."

"Poor little Lacey." He smoothed her hair gently. "Wasn't there anyone to help you?"

"People tried, but ultimately I had to make the decisions. I grew up in a hurry."

"Your parents would be proud of you," he said softly.

"I like to think they know I can take care of myself now, that I have confidence in my own ability. I used to be as helpless as I was when you found me in the park. I'm truly ashamed of the panic I displayed. I never fall apart like that anymore."

"It was perfectly understandable," he soothed. "I'm just glad I was there to help."

"I really reverted," she said thoughtfully. "I've let you take care of me all this time as though I were a child again." Her brow creased. "That isn't healthy."

He smilingly smoothed away her frown with a long forefinger. "Are you trying to tell me you regard me as a father figure?"

She stared at him, not actually listening. "Could that be why I don't want to go home? Because I feel so safe and protected here?"

He cupped her cheek in his hand, gazing deeply into her eyes. "I want you to feel cared for, but I hope that's not the reason you'd like to stay."

Lacey snapped out of her introspective mood, finally becoming aware of him. Raoul's dark eyes were compelling, searching for the answer he wanted. She was conscious of everything about him, his chiseled features, his angular body cradling hers, the musky scent of his aftershave. At least one question was answered. Raoul was no father figure!

"Tell me I've contributed to your pleasure just a little bit," he coaxed.

"More than a little," she whispered.

"My sweet, adorable Lacey." His voice throbbed as he drew her close.

She closed her eyes when his mouth covered hers, giving in to the inevitable. It was no longer possible to deny the truth. She had fallen deeply, irrevocably in love with this man in spite of all her efforts.

Sadly, this was the end instead of the beginning, but wasn't it better to experience one perfect moment of ecstasy rather than regret the lost opportunity for the rest of her life?

When his hands moved caressingly over her body, conscious thought deserted her and pure sensation took over. She quivered as he reached under her sweatshirt and stroked her midriff with agonizing deliberation. Her breasts tingled in anticipation, impatient for his touch.

"You have the softest skin, *cara*." His warm breath tantalized her ear. "I love to touch you."

The tip of his tongue explored the contours of her ear as his hands moved up to cup her breasts. A small sound of enjoyment escaped her when his thumbs rotated gently over her sensitive nipples, which pressed against her delicate bra.

"You're so warm, so responsive," he murmured huskily.

"I've never felt like this before." She wound her arms around his neck and kissed the hollow in his throat.

He pulled her closer, burying his face in her hair. "Do you know what that means to me? I want to bring you more pleasure than you've ever known."

"You do, Raoul," she answered softly.

"You're like a fever in my blood. I've never wanted any woman this much." In a sudden movement he stripped off her sweatshirt. "I need to see all of you."

He unclasped her bra and removed it in an equally swift motion. Her exposed nipples were like coral rosettes before his ardent eyes. Ripples of excitement shivered through her when he bent his head and took one taut nipple in his mouth. Lacey caught her breath as his tongue circled around it, his lips gently sucking. She clenched her fingers in his dark hair as wave after wave of sensation swept through her taut body.

"I need you so," she gasped.

"And I need you, *querida*. Don't leave me," he said urgently.

"I won't." Lacey wasn't even conscious of what she was saying. She would have promised anything at that moment.

"Do you really mean it?" His mouth continued its devastation.

"Yes, oh, yes!" she breathed.

"I'll be so good to you, *mi amor*. You can have anything you want."

His fevered words dimly penetrated her consciousness, but she tried to ignore them. "You don't have to make any promises, Raoul. Just love me," she begged.

He framed her face in his hands then, gazing at her with molten desire. "You're too generous, *mi ángel*, but I won't take advantage of you. I'll treat you like a little princess. This will be your castle."

The hot tide of Lacey's passion ebbed. "Are you asking me to live with you?"

"I'll make you so happy." He strung a line of burning kisses up her neck, unaware of her sudden stillness. "I'll take such good care of you."

She sat up and reached for her sweatshirt. Without bothering with her bra, she pulled the jersey over her head.

He looked at her in bewilderment. "What are you doing? What's wrong?"

"We should know better by now, shouldn't we?" she asked, unable to look at him.

He jerked her chin up. "I won't let you do this again!"

"You have no choice. I don't think you'd resort to rape."

His face was hard. "Some say that's what a tease deserves, but I won't descend to your level. Just tell me this. Does it give you pleasure to turn men on?"

"You know better than that, Raoul. I wanted you every bit as much as you wanted me."

"Then what made you change your mind?"

"I thought we were equal partners, but I was mistaken. I was offering you...affection. You were offering me advantages."

"You thought I was trying to buy you?" he asked slowly.

"Not exactly, but you did think your money would be a factor."

"I didn't, Lacey, I swear it! I only wanted to give you all the things you deserve."

"We're on different wavelengths, Raoul. I was saying goodbye."

"I can't believe that. What happened to all those principles about casual sex versus commitment?"

She decided to be honest. He deserved as much. "I know there's no future for us, but I still feel something more than mere sexual attraction toward you. It wouldn't have been a brief encounter for me. It would have been a memory to treasure." Her smile was twisted. "I have a feeling you would have made it that. Unfortunately, you spoiled it."

"I don't know what to say," he said helplessly.

"Nothing is required. Just don't remember me too harshly."

He stared at her for a long moment before touching her cheek gently. "That goes without saying."

She stood and smiled gallantly. "Have a good time at your ranch."

"I will. And you have a good flight home."

Lacey nodded. "I'll leave the key with the doorman."

She followed him to the door, prepared for the final handshake, the last glimpse of the man she wished she could have spent the rest of her life with. He must never know that, though.

Raoul hesitated in the entry. "How much longer will you be here?"

"My flight leaves on Tuesday."

"Do you have enough money to last you?"

"More than enough," she assured him. "I'll leave what I have left over and send you a check for the rest."

"That isn't necessary."

"It is to me," she answered firmly.

"I'll be back before you leave," he said indecisively.

Lacey ducked her head. "Maybe it would be better if we said goodbye now."

"Better for whom?" He grasped her hands impulsively. "How would you like to come to the ranch with me tomorrow?"

She looked at him blankly. "You don't mean that."

"I do!" His hands tightened. "Will you come?"

It was so unexpected that she didn't know what to say. After resigning herself to never seeing him again, this was a tantalizing offer. Accepting it would only postpone the eventual misery of parting, yet how could she turn down a chance to solve the mystery that was Raoul? If she knew why he was the way he was, maybe it would lessen the pain.

"If you're sure you want me, I'd be happy to go with you," she said slowly.

His tense expression dissolved in a smile. "The one thing I'm sure of is that I want you."

Chapter Seven

After Raoul left, Lacey decided she must have been in shock to accept his invitation. *He* certainly had been after he'd extended it. The surprised look on his face was proof of that. Why had he asked her? All indications were that Raoul never let anyone near his daughter. That would seem to make this visit significant.

Lacey was afraid to attach too much importance to it, yet she sensed that she'd been accorded a rare privilege. Excitement fizzed inside her like a Fourth of July sparkler. He must find something special about her.

The telephone dampened her euphoria when it rang a short time later. She knew instinctively that it was Raoul. He'd had second thoughts and was calling to get out of the invitation. Lacey braced herself for disappointment as she reached for the phone.

"I hope you hadn't gone to bed yet." Raoul's expected voice greeted her.

"No, I was just getting ready to."

"I thought it might be better to call tonight instead of waiting till morning."

"Yes, I'd rather know now," she answered dully.

Unexpectedly, he laughed. "I've learned from Rosa that women are like that."

"What do you mean?" Lacey's brow furrowed.

"You were probably wondering what kind of clothes you'll need. Right?"

"Well, I . . . I hadn't thought about it."

"We're very casual at the ranch. Bring things you'll be comfortable in."

Her heart bounded back to its rightful place. "You still want me to come?"

"You haven't changed your mind?" Disappointment colored his voice.

"No, I thought *you* had."

He sighed. "Dear little Lacey, do you think we'll ever understand each other?"

"I'm certainly counting on it," she answered softly.

Lacey felt a little diffident with Raoul the next morning, remembering the mixed traumas of the evening before. His completely relaxed manner put her at ease, however. They were soon laughing and joking as they did at the best of times.

While they were driving he remarked, "You look lovely as always, but I hope you brought something more serviceable than that."

Her white linen slacks were topped by a black and white print blouse. "You said to be comfortable, and this is comfortable."

"I had something more rugged in mind. We usually go horseback riding. You do ride, don't you?"

"I learned when I was ten," she assured him. "What else do you do?"

"Not much." He frowned slightly. "I hope you won't be bored."

"Don't worry about entertaining me. I can be perfectly happy sitting under a tree reading a book."

"I can provide a little more activity than that. I just meant there isn't much nightlife. The nearest town is about thirty miles away, and that's only a village."

"I didn't realize your ranch was so isolated."

"Are you sorry you agreed to come?"

"Not at all. I was just wondering..."

Lacey was thinking about Raoul's daughter. It seemed cruel to plunk a child down in the middle of nowhere, with little human contact. That was more than protective, it bordered on paranoia.

"What were you wondering?" he prompted.

"It must be lonely for...the people who live there all the time."

"You're referring to my daughter," he said quietly.

"Well, I...Rosa mentioned that she lives there. It just happened to come up in the conversation," she added hastily.

Anything to do with his child was potentially dangerous, but the subject couldn't be avoided forever. She'd be meeting her shortly. Why hadn't Raoul mentioned Carlotta until she'd practically forced him into it? Lacey felt a chill of apprehension. Was there something wrong with the little girl?

"I think you'll find she's happy and well adjusted," he said evenly.

"I'm sure she is," Lacey murmured.

Their conversation faltered for the first time. Raoul seemed slightly withdrawn until they turned onto a dirt road fenced on both sides by barbed wire.

"Welcome to Tierra del Campo," he said. "We're here."

In spite of his announcement, no signs of habitation were visible. They drove for what seemed like miles through flat countryside broken by clumps of trees. Cattle were everywhere. Some clustered in the shade, while others wandered aimlessly through the lush pastureland.

"I had no idea your ranch was this big," Lacey remarked. "Are there people in the vicinity, or did they all perish trying to find their way back to civilization?"

Raoul grinned. "Actually they rather enjoy roughing it—since they learned how to make a fire by rubbing two sticks together."

The road curved through a grove of trees whose tops formed a natural arch. When they emerged it was as though they had entered a different country.

A rambling one-story ranch house was surrounded by a green lawn bordered by brilliant flower beds. The setting might have been Beverly Hills or any one of a dozen other plush neighborhoods. An oval swimming pool provided another spot of glowing color beyond the house, and the edge of a tennis court was visible.

An older man came out to greet them. *"Hola, Señor Ruiz."* His weathered face split in a wide smile.

"Hola, Jorge. How's your back? Have you been taking it easy like I told you?"

"You know how it is, *señor*. That Carmen, she is a slave driver."

"Women are both a duty and a delight." Raoul gave Lacey an amused glance.

"I know about the duty," the older man grumbled. "But when I try to have the delight, Carmen always catches me."

"Life is hard." Raoul chuckled. "This is *Señorita* Scott, Jorge. She'll be staying with us this weekend. Put her things in the guest room, *por favor*."

"Sí, señor." The man slanted an interested look at Lacey as he picked up her suitcase.

"Jorge is the general factotum around here," Raoul told her after the servant had gone. "His wife, Carmen, is the cook. He runs the house, and she runs him."

"I thought Spanish men were supposed to be the bosses."

"The word hasn't filtered down to Carmen. And after twenty years of marriage, I doubt if she'd believe it."

A little girl shot around the corner of the house and launched herself into Raoul's arms. "Papa, I've been waiting for you!"

He kissed her tenderly. "I'm here, *mi amor*."

Lacey's qualms about Carlotta being handicapped in some way were groundless. She was an enchanting child with a limber body and beautiful features. Intelligence shone out of her face as she chattered on, telling her father all the momentous things that had happened during the week.

Her dark, lustrous eyes resembled his, and the same high cheekbones and fine bone structure had to have been inherited from his family genes. No doubt remained in Lacey's mind that Carlotta was Raoul's child.

A plump, motherly woman came out of the house. She looked as startled as Jorge had on seeing Lacey, but after the initial surprise her smile was warm.

"Hello, I'm Margaret Waverly," she said.

Raoul's attention was diverted from the child in his arms. "Mrs. Waverly is our governess. And this is my daughter, Carlotta," he said proudly. "I'd like you to meet Miss Scott, *cara*."

"How do you do." The little girl's polite response was accompanied by a frank appraisal. She wasn't the slightest bit shy.

"I'm so happy to meet you, Carlotta," Lacey said sincerely.

"Miss Scott is going to spend the weekend with us," Raoul said. "Won't that be nice?"

Carlotta wanted to be sure before she agreed. "Can you swim and ride a horse?"

Lacey was aware of being put on trial. "I'm a good swimmer, but my riding might be a trifle rusty. Maybe you can help me."

"Okay. You can ride my pony. She's very gentle."

Lacey had a feeling of elation that she'd passed muster.

"Can we go riding this afternoon, Papa?" Carlotta begged.

"As soon as Miss Scott gets unpacked and I show her around," Raoul promised, setting her down.

Two young boys and a girl came down a path leading to some more modest houses in the distance. Beyond them were stables and a cluster of low buildings where men were working on various equipment. The compound was like a small village.

"Come on, Lotta, we're waiting for you," one of the little boys called impatiently.

"I have to go now," she told her father importantly. "We're playing spaceship."

"Head the ship home in an hour," he said fondly.

"Okay. Save my present till I get back," she called over her shoulder.

From the stricken look on his face, Mrs. Waverly correctly guessed that Raoul didn't have anything for his daughter. "You don't have to bring her a present every week," she said.

"I always do. How could I have forgotten?"

"Carlotta has everything she could possibly want," the older woman soothed.

"That's not the point." He sighed. "Well, I suppose it can't be helped. I'll show you to your room," he told Lacey.

A spacious living room was visible to the right of the entry. It was comfortably furnished with big couches and chairs covered in a cheerful yellow and white print. A doll was perched on the arm of a sofa, and some knitting sat on the coffee table. All the furnishings were top quality, yet not imposing. The room was meant to be used.

As they walked down the hall to the bedroom wing, Lacey said, "Carlotta is adorable."

"Yes, she's a wonderful child," he answered softly.

"She really *is* happy and well adjusted. Now I know why you've made this her home."

"I'll have to bring her back to the city when she gets old enough for school, but she has a much better quality of life here for the present."

"Where did all the children come from?"

"They live here, too. Their parents are ranch hands."

Raoul led her into a large airy bedroom with a four-poster bed. Crisp white organdy curtains were criss-crossed over the windows, and the dark, polished floor was accented by fluffy white throw rugs.

"If you need anything, my room is next to yours," he said.

It didn't take long to unpack the few things she'd brought. At the bottom of the suitcase was a small wrapped package, a present for Carlotta. Lacey suddenly realized it was the answer to Raoul's problem.

She went into the hall and knocked on his door.

"Come in," he called.

When she saw he was barefoot and had removed his shirt, she started to leave. "I'm sorry. I'll come back later."

"You don't have to run away. I was just changing to something more comfortable," he answered mischievously, reminding her of her own failed joke of the night before. "This is your chance to find out if I wear polka-dot shorts."

"When you're through clowning around I want to talk to you," she said impatiently.

"What can I do for you, *cara*?"

She held out the package. "I have something you can give Carlotta. She won't have to know you forgot to bring her a present."

"What's this?"

"A little doll. I don't know how lavish your gifts usually are, but this will do in a pinch."

He continued to look puzzled. "How could you produce a doll out of thin air?"

"I got up early this morning and ran over to the museum. They have these dressed in different native costumes. I noticed them in the gift shop when I was there that first day."

Raoul gazed at her tenderly. "That was very thoughtful of you."

Lacey smiled. "You have to bring a present when you visit a child. It's in Miss Manners's book of etiquette."

"Then you must give it to her yourself."

"I was only joking. Take it, Raoul. It's more important for it to come from you."

He put his hands on her shoulders, gazing deeply into her eyes. "You're a very beautiful person."

"It's the least I can do after all you've done for me," she mumbled.

He drew her closer. "You don't owe me anything. I'm in *your* debt."

"Not for a little thing like this," she protested.

"No, for much more."

The pressure of his hands increased until their bodies were only inches apart. His dark head was poised over her, his pupils dilated with emotion.

"For making my heart sing when I thought it had forgotten how," he murmured. "For making every day a special occasion."

"That's lovely." She felt a lump in her throat.

"And so are you."

As his arms slipped around her waist and his mouth was only a breath from hers, footsteps sounded in the hall.

"*Señor* Ruiz." Jorge's voice preceded him. "Carmen wants to know if you wish lunch."

Raoul made a sound of annoyance as Lacey slipped hastily out of his arms. He was composed, however, when the servant appeared. "Tell her we've already eaten."

"*Sí, señor.*" Jorge's tone of voice couldn't be faulted, but his eyes betrayed lively curiosity.

"I hope he didn't get the wrong impression," Lacey said after he'd left.

"Don't worry about it."

"But I do! And you should, too."

"I'm more concerned with his bad timing," Raoul answered wryly.

"Be serious! It must have looked somewhat suggestive, finding me in your room while you were getting undressed."

"Jorge isn't the house detective. Now if it had been Carmen, that's another story."

"I'm glad *somebody* around here keeps you in line." Lacey took refuge in tartness because she was still glowing from Raoul's stirring words.

He combed his fingers through her long pale hair. "Don't count on it, *cara*."

"I'd better go," she said hastily.

"I suppose so," he agreed reluctantly. "We'll go riding when Carlotta returns. Come out to the terrace when you're ready."

After she'd changed into jeans and a plaid cotton shirt, Lacey went looking for the terrace. A long walled patio ran the length of her bedroom, Raoul's and the room next to his, but he wasn't out there.

She found him at the back of the house, sitting in a chair at an umbrella table. He was sipping a tall drink while scanning a large ledger intently. Mirrored sunglasses gave him a remote look. Since he seemed to be working she hesitated to disturb him, but he glanced up.

"If you're busy I can wander around the grounds," she said. "This place is magnificent."

The lawns and flower beds around the pool were carefully tended, but in the distance were paths and wildflowers that invited a closer look.

Raoul closed the ledger and stood up. "I was just going over some accounts, but they can wait. Would you like me to show you around?"

By the time they returned, Carlotta was waiting impatiently.

"I told Tomas to have the horses ready," she announced.

"Then what are we waiting for? Run in and ask Carmen for our refreshments."

Raoul's horse was a big black stallion that might have been his alter ego. It was handsome, spirited and skittish. A much tamer horse was provided for Lacey after she declined Carlotta's offer of her pony.

"This is wonderful!" Lacey was exhilarated as they trotted through the beautiful countryside. "I haven't ridden in ages, but evidently you never forget."

"How long has it been?" Raoul asked.

"Years!"

"We'd better not stay out too long, then."

"That's ridiculous. I used to ride for hours."

"Okay, but don't blame me if you have to eat dinner standing up," he said dryly.

"What do you think I am, a tenderfoot?" she scoffed.

"That isn't the part of your anatomy I'm worried about." He grinned.

"Come on, let's have a race," Lacey suggested. "Carlotta gets a head start. We'll race to that farthest oak tree."

"What are the stakes?" Raoul asked.

"Make it a dollar." She knew they'd both let the little girl win.

"How about the loser?"

"Losers don't get a prize."

"But they should pay a forfeit."

"Something tells me you're turning this race to your advantage," she said suspiciously.

"It was your suggestion. Ready, set, go!" he called to his daughter who had positioned her pony ahead of them.

They merely cantered until the little girl was sure of coming in first. Then Lacey spurred her horse to a gallop. Raoul kept pace at first, but halfway to the finish line he gave the powerful stallion his head. The horse surged forward in an effortless burst of speed that was beautiful to watch. Lacey came in a breathless third.

"I won, I won!" Carlotta shouted.

"Yes, you did, *mi amor*. Fair and square." He grinned at Lacey.

"Only *one* of us won fairly," she grumbled. "That animal of yours didn't run, he flew!"

"Next time you'll think twice about issuing a challenge."

"Haven't you ever been beaten?"

She'd meant the question to be a joking one, but his very invincibility was awesome. Did Raoul need to win because he couldn't handle defeat? Her face sobered as she remembered Carlos.

"When do I get my prize?" Carlotta demanded.

"As soon as we get to the picnic spot," her father promised.

Lacey's momentary somberness vanished after they reached a grassy knoll shaded by tall trees. They all dismounted, and Raoul helped his daughter take a thermos bottle and cookies out of a woven knapsack he'd carried on his saddle.

As she watched the loving way he acted toward the child, Lacey's dark speculation seemed absurd. That gentleness couldn't hide a cruel streak.

"This is our picnic spot," Carlotta told her. "Papa and I have our lunch here sometimes, but today we're having lemonade and cookies."

"They look delicious," Lacey said.

The cold lemonade was refreshing, and the cookies were as good as they looked. She was filled to the brim with quiet contentment. Carlotta, however, was filled with the restless energy of a four-year-old.

"What can we do now?" she asked.

"Why don't we all close our eyes and think beautiful thoughts?" Raoul teased.

"Papa!"

"I have an idea," Lacey intervened. "Let's make a garland of flowers for your hair. I used to do that when I was your age."

"I don't know how."

"I'll show you. First we pick a lot of clover blossoms with long stems."

The little girl eagerly began to gather the fragrant purple and white flowers that studded the thick grass. When they had a small pile of them, Lacey showed her how to twine the stems together to form a wreath.

Carlotta broke off quite a few heads in the process, but Lacey praised her efforts and she enjoyed herself tremendously. Raoul watched them both from a vantage point under a tree, his expression unreadable.

Carlotta was entranced by the finished product Lacey put on her hair. "Let me see how I look." She climbed into her father's lap and tried to see herself in his mirrored sunglasses.

"Like a little queen," he proclaimed. "Isn't Miss Scott clever?"

"Oh, yes! Do you know how to make anything else?"

"Well, let me see. It's been a long time since I was a little girl," Lacey commented.

"Don't you have any little girls of your own?"

"No, honey, I'd like to, but I'm not married."

"Juan's sister isn't married, and she has a baby girl."

"Oh. Well . . . uh . . . sometimes that happens."

"How does it happen?" Carlotta looked at her with wide, unblinking eyes.

Lacey was aware of Raoul's suppressed mirth. She shot him a glare of annoyance. Why didn't he field some of these questions?

"Carmen says you get babies at a department store, but I didn't see any when I went shopping with Tia Rosa."

"That's because she didn't take you to the baby department." Raoul's voice was choked with laughter.

"I'm too old for that," Carlotta remarked complacently. "I'm going to start school next year," she told Lacey.

"About time, too," Lacey muttered. "Your father and Carmen have you living in fantasy land."

"Would you like to enlighten her?" he asked.

"No, I would not! That's a job for—" Lacey stopped abruptly. It was a mother's job, but Carlotta didn't have a mother.

"Exactly," Raoul said quietly.

"Can we ride some more?" Carlotta asked, her attention veering again. "I want to show Miss Scott the brook." She took her hand as they walked over to the horses.

They rode over hills and through valleys. The ranch covered a vast area. At one point a small stream cut through a meadow, bubbling between the shallow banks with a pleasing murmur. They dismounted and dabbled their fingers in the cool water.

When Raoul picked up a flat rock and skimmed it over the surface, Lacey said, "We used to look for rocks like that on the beach at home."

"You Americans have strange customs." He laughed. "*We* used to look for girls."

"That's the difference between boys and girls."

"I think I'd better have a little talk with *you*," he murmured.

She ignored him, picking up an oval rock and drying it between her palms. "We'd paint funny faces on these and use them for paperweights."

"I have some paints. Will you show me how?" Carlotta asked excitedly.

"Whenever you like," Lacey promised.

"I never suspected you had so many hidden talents," Raoul remarked as the little girl ran off to look for stones.

She gave him a seductive look from under lowered lashes. "I have even more that you don't know about."

"That's what I always suspected." His voice deepened.

"I can sing 'The Star Spangled Banner' on key."

"Do I have to salute?"

"It would be a nice tribute."

"I know something that would be nicer."

He traced the shape of her mouth with his forefinger, making the small gesture an act of love. Lacey could almost feel his lips moving over hers. Her body quickened with desire for more than that feathery touch.

"I got a whole bunch," Carlotta said, joining them with her hands full of dripping rocks. "Will you carry them for me, Papa?"

"Of course, *mi amor*." He stuffed them into his pockets and swung her onto the pony before turning back to Lacey. "I owe you a tribute, and you owe me a forfeit."

It was late afternoon before they returned to the house. Although she'd spent hours in the saddle, Lacey wasn't conscious of any soreness…until she dismounted. Then every bone and muscle in her body ached. She wasn't about to admit it to Raoul, though.

"Are you okay?" he asked as she winced involuntarily.

"Just great!" She smiled brightly.

"I'll have to agree with that," he said, returning her smile. His, however, was genuine.

"Let's go paint my rocks," Carlotta urged.

"Give our guest a break, *cara*," her father said. "Why don't we all go for a nice, invigorating swim first?"

Lacey suppressed a groan. "I think perhaps I'll take a shower instead."

Raoul raised one eyebrow. "Beginning to stiffen up a little?"

"Certainly not." She was stiffening up a *lot*! "I just feel grubby. I'd like to get cleaned up."

"I suppose we could all do with a shower." He swung Carlotta onto his shoulders. "Drinks on the terrace in an hour."

Lacey followed at a snail's pace. Where did Raoul get all his energy? The only thing she wanted to do was lie down—on her stomach.

She was approaching her bedroom when Raoul came back from delivering Carlotta to the governess. Giving him a weak smile, she continued into the bedroom.

He followed her and closed the door. "I believe you owe me something."

"Not now," she pleaded.

"Yes, now," he answered firmly. "When you lose you have to pay up."

"Okay," she sighed. "What do you want—as if I didn't know."

"I'll try to make it as painless as possible," he said mockingly.

He took her in his arms and touched his lips gently to hers. Lacey submitted passively, knowing it was just a joke. She relaxed against him, enjoying the tactile pleasure of his mouth.

But when he parted her lips and probed with sensuous deliberation, her inertia fled. At first she tensed, uttering a tiny protest that went unheeded as he continued to cradle her tenderly. The intimate contact weakened her defenses. Gradually her body became fluid, conforming to his. She wound her arms around his neck and returned his kiss, rather than merely accepting it.

A groan of satisfaction sounded deep in his throat. His tongue moved more quickly and he strained her closer, making her aware of his desire. Her own desire flared into an aching need. When his hands trailed down her back she arched her body. But when his fingers gripped her buttocks, urging her against his taut loins, she let out a loud yelp.

"What is it, *mi amor*?" He looked at her in amazement. "Did I hurt you? How?"

Lacey had forgotten her stiffness in the heat of Raoul's lovemaking. But his fingers digging into her sore muscles had brought a sharp jolt of pain. It effectively cooled her ardor.

"It wasn't your fault," she mumbled. "I...uh...I guess I'm a little tender after all."

His concerned expression cleared. "I didn't know what I'd done."

"Go ahead and say I told you so." She sighed.

"I'll do something more constructive. Take off your jeans."

"Raoul!"

He chuckled. "Don't worry. I realize you're in no condition to make love. I intend to give you a massage, and then you're going to take a hot bath."

"The bath will be quite enough."

"Must you argue about everything?" he asked impatiently, reaching for the snap at her waist. "Do you want to hobble around all day tomorrow?"

She grabbed for his hand. "A massage would hurt more than it helped."

"I'll be very gentle," he promised, leading her toward the bed when he saw she was wavering.

But when he tried once more to unsnap her jeans, Lacey stopped him again. "All right, if you think it will do any good. But I'll put on a robe," she said firmly.

Without waiting for him to object she limped into the bathroom and closed the door. After removing her jeans and shirt, she put on a filmy pink caftan over her panties and bra.

Raoul eyed the voluminous garment with dissatisfaction when she returned. "I'll have to use braille to find you in that thing."

"This was your idea. I'll be glad to call it off."

"Lie down," he ordered.

Lacey lowered herself gingerly onto her stomach. She tensed automatically when Raoul sat down next to her, but his touch was gentle, as he'd promised. First he massaged the tight muscles in her neck and shoulders, then progressed down her back. The soothing strokes brought a feeling of well-being.

"Mm, that feels wonderful," she murmured.

"I told you it would," he said confidently.

Next he skipped to her calves. She winced slightly, yet as he worked on the tight tendons, she could feel the knots loosening. The same was true with her thighs, and she truly began to relax—until he spread her legs slightly to reach the point where they joined her torso.

Raoul's behaviour couldn't be faulted. He was as adept and impersonal as a professional masseur. It was her own reaction that was causing the trouble. His hands were lighting tiny fires the length of her body. When he began to stroke her bottom very gently, she made an involuntary sound.

"You really are tender, aren't you?" he exclaimed. "I'm barely touching you." He turned her on her side, supporting her with an arm around her waist. "I'll never forgive myself for not taking better care of you."

"It wasn't your fault. Besides, the massage really helped. You can go back to your own room now."

"I suppose I'd better before I try to make love to you," he said ruefully. "That negligee is actually quite provocative."

"It's a caftan, and I have clothes on underneath."

"Yes, I can see. An enchanting pink lace bra." He traced the outline through her sheer robe.

His trailing fingers were almost unbearably arousing. Her nipples formed rose-colored peaks, visible through the thin layers. When he touched one gently, Lacey's breathing quickened.

"We're going to make love. You know that, don't you, *cara*?"

"Yes," she whispered, unable to deny it at that point.

He bent his head and took one hardened little rosette in his mouth while he rotated the other with his thumb. The veiled contact was more erotic somehow than if she'd been nude. She moaned softly, threading her fingers through his hair. As he reached under the caftan to stroke her bare thighs, a knock sounded at the door.

"Are you ready, Miss Scott?" Carlotta's sweet little voice called.

Lacey and Raoul both froze for a second. Then she scrambled off the bed. "I . . . just a minute," she called back.

"I'm sorry, *querida*." He stood up and cupped her cheek tenderly. "This isn't our day."

"She mustn't find you here," Lacey said distractedly.

"She won't." He kissed her briefly before leaving by the door to the patio.

"You're not dressed yet." Disappointment showed on the small girl's face when Lacey opened the door a moment later.

"No, I . . . I'm afraid not."

"I took *my* bath already."

"Carlotta." Raoul's voice sounded from the room next door. "Come here, my love. I have something for you."

Lacey was grateful to him. She couldn't face a four-year-old's pointed questions at that moment. Not while she was still vibrating from Raoul's caresses.

Was he right? she asked herself as she soaked in the tub. Were they destined to make love? That was almost a foregone conclusion, but not here. Not with distractions at every turn. When it happened she wanted it to be memorable, not hurried and furtive. An experience to treasure forever, because it was all she would ever have of Raoul.

He and Carlotta were on the patio when she joined them a short time later.

The child ran over and threw her arms around Lacey's neck. "Thank you for my doll."

Before Lacey could deny the gift, Raoul said, "I told her you picked it out just for her."

"You didn't have to do that," she murmured.

"It wouldn't be honorable to take credit for such a thoughtful act," he answered softly.

"I'm going to call my dolly 'Miss Scott,'" Carlotta declared.

"That sounds so formal. Wouldn't you rather call her Lacey? And me, too?"

"Oh, yes, I'd like that! Then you'd be my friend like you are Papa's." She skipped away to show her doll to the governess, who had come onto the terrace.

Raoul smiled. "You've captivated the whole family."

Mrs. Waverly joined them after admiring the doll. "Perhaps I'll eat dinner with Carlotta tonight. The two of you don't need an extra person around."

The shade of wistfulness in her voice told Lacey the governess probably took her meals with Raoul when he was there. She undoubtedly looked forward to those evenings of adult companionship.

Raoul's hesitation was imperceptible. "You mustn't disappoint us. We're looking forward to having you join us for dinner." He turned to Lacey. "We usually dine after Carlotta's in bed, if that's all right with you."

"It sounds fine," she answered.

Mrs. Waverly brightened. "Well, if you're sure I won't be in the way."

After assurances from both of them, she took Carlotta inside.

When they were alone, Lacey said to Raoul, "You're really a very nice person."

"I've been trying to convince you of that. What was the deciding factor?"

"No one thing." She smiled. "I just like you, that's all."

"*Querida,*" he said deeply, taking both her hands.

She withdrew them after a moment. "I think we'd better keep our distance."

"You're right, *mi amor*. Things tend to get out of hand when I touch you, but I didn't bring you up here for that purpose."

"I'm glad you did bring me," she answered softly. "Seeing you with Carlotta has given me a whole new perspective."

"She's been my life up till now," he said slowly.

"I can understand why. She's utterly adorable. You've done a marvelous job of raising her by yourself."

"I've tried." His eyes were enigmatic as he stared at her.

Dinner was a relaxed affair, due to Mrs. Waverly's presence. She was very well-read, and the conversation was interesting. Lacey wondered how she had come to live on a comparatively isolated ranch, far from friends and relatives. She put the question tactfully.

"My husband and I retired to Mexico many years ago," the older woman explained. "After he passed away there was no reason to return to the States, since neither of us had any family left. I love children and I was lonely, so the logical step was to become a governess."

"Fortunately for us," Raoul commented.

"You don't find it a little quiet living here year round?" Lacey asked delicately.

"Next year when Carlotta's ready for school, we'll all be together in the city," Raoul said.

"For a while, anyway," Mrs. Waverly remarked.

"You're not planning on leaving us?" he asked in alarm.

"No, but you'll be getting married sooner or later." She smiled at Lacey. "I've had a longer stay than I ever expected."

The woman didn't know it, but she had a job for life, Lacey reflected sadly.

As though to underscore the fact Raoul said, "You'll be part of our household for as long as you desire."

After they'd finished dinner he said to Lacey, "I'm afraid I can't offer you much in the way of entertainment."

"I don't need any. It's late and I'd just like to go to bed and read for a while."

When she returned to her room Lacey put on her nightgown, intending to do just that. But when she opened the French doors to the patio, it was such a lovely night that she went outside for a moment. A quarter moon silvered the landscape, and the air was scented with the perfume of flowers. As she was inhaling deeply, Raoul stepped out of his room.

"Are you intentionally trying to drive me out of my mind?" His voice was deep and husky.

"What do you mean? I just came outside for a minute because it's so beautiful tonight."

"And so are you." His eyes glowed as they traveled over her from head to toe.

Lacey was belatedly aware of how sheer her nightgown was. With the moonlight shining through it she might as well have been naked.

Raoul walked slowly toward her. "Have you any idea how much I want you?"

Dawning excitement shivered through her. "I thought we agreed," she said weakly.

"We agreed that we were going to make love."

As he drew her against his hard body, Lacey surrendered with a sigh. How could she wait any longer for the man she loved? When his hands caressed her through the thin gown, she reached up and pulled his head down to hers.

They were lost in each other, fused by a common need that was rapidly spiraling out of control. Lacey dug her fingers into his straining back muscles while they both made incoherent little sounds of pleasure.

A loud crash from the bedroom next to Raoul's was followed by an exclamation of dismay from Mrs. Waverly. Lacey jumped like a startled doe and Raoul swore savagely under his breath.

"This place has all the privacy of a soccer match," he muttered.

She smothered nervous laughter. "We certainly aren't scoring, are we?"

"Let's go inside, *cara*."

"No, Raoul, not now." When the tide of passion receded, resignation took its place. "With our kind of luck, a herd of cattle would stampede through the room."

"It's the only thing that hasn't happened." He sighed. "You're right, my darling." He brought her hand to his mouth and kissed the palm. "But make no mistake, our time will come."

Chapter Eight

Lacey's sore muscles felt much better the next day. Any lingering stiffness was worked out in the pool. They spent the afternoon lying in the sun and playing games with Carlotta.

The little girl divided her attention equally between Lacey and her father. At first Lacey was a little apprehensive. Raoul was so possessive of his daughter; he might resent sharing her affection. But, although he was a little thoughtful, he didn't seem displeased.

They stayed until it was time for Carlotta to go to bed. She hugged and kissed her father and then threw her arms around Lacey's neck.

"Will you come back and see me again next week?" she asked.

Lacey held her close. "I wish I could, honey, but I have to go home on Tuesday."

"Won't I ever see you again?"

"I certainly hope so. Maybe your daddy will bring you to visit me in California some day."

"Can we, Papa? Can we?" Carlotta asked excitedly.

"We'll see." He lifted her in his arms. "Be a good girl this week. I'll be back on Saturday, *querida*."

In the car going home, Raoul said, "You made quite a hit with my daughter."

"She's a darling child."

"I've never seen her form such an instant attachment to anyone," he remarked.

Lacey slanted a wary glance at him, but his impassive face told her nothing. "I was just a novelty," she said dismissively. "She probably doesn't meet many strangers."

"I don't keep her isolated in the country," Raoul answered dryly. "Mrs. Waverly brings her into the city regularly."

"How does Carlotta like apartment living after the freedom of the ranch?"

"She's remarkably adaptable. I don't anticipate any problems when she starts school."

"It will be a whole new life for you, too."

"Yes, a whole new life," he repeated, staring at the road with narrowed eyes.

They drove in silence for a short time before Raoul suggested stopping for dinner. Lacey agreed, although she wasn't hungry. Excitement kept building inside her as they drew nearer to the city.

The sexual tension between Raoul and herself had been just under the surface all day. It had flared in the pool during a game of keep-away with Carlotta when he wound his legs around hers to prevent her from jumping for the ball.

It was present when he smoothed suntan lotion over her body as they reclined on mats afterward. Nothing was deliberate, but every touch generated electricity between them. Lacey could tell by the awareness in Raoul's eyes that he was affected by it, too.

If his prediction was true, they would make love tonight. Only one more night remained. She was going home on Tuesday. The subject came up during dinner.

"This has been a wonderful weekend," she said softly. "The ideal ending to my trip."

"You're not really leaving Tuesday?"

"I have to."

"No, you don't. You could stay until Sunday, at least."

"I have my ticket already," she said hesitantly.

"That's no problem. I'll change it." He gripped her hand across the table. "Don't go, Lacey."

"These two days have been so perfect," she answered slowly. "Maybe we should just leave it at that."

"I need more time!" he said urgently. "We could have a wonderful week together," he added when she looked at him questioningly.

"We already have."

"Not like it could be," he murmured.

Lacey's pulse quickened as she imagined the ways. Wouldn't that make it harder to part from him? But why would a week be worse than a night? Her heart would break when the time came anyway. At least she'd have more memories to store up.

"All right. If you really want me to, I'll stay until Sunday," she said quietly.

His hand tightened. "I'll see that you don't regret it, *cara.*"

Lacey shivered slightly, partly from excitement, but also from an unaccountable feeling that the coming week would change her life. But for better, or worse?

She was so absorbed in her own thoughts that she didn't realize Raoul was also withdrawn. Even if she had noticed, his expression was unreadable in the dim light from the dashboard.

As they rode up in the elevator to his apartment he said, "I have some customers flying in from South America tomorrow. Unfortunately our business will probably last through dinner, but I'll make it up to you on Tuesday. We'll spend the whole day doing whatever you like."

"I don't expect you to devote all your time to me," she protested.

"Why do you think I asked you to stay?"

She smiled. "Possibly because everyone waits on you hand and foot at Rosa's, and you don't want to come back here and be alone."

They had reached the apartment door. Instead of taking the key Lacey held out, he stared at her searchingly.

"You may be partially right," he replied finally.

Raoul was wearing the remote look that always spelled trouble. He was erecting the familiar wall around himself. What had she done to trigger this reaction?

"Well, I . . . I guess we might as well go inside." She opened the door herself.

Instead of following her, he cupped her face between his palms and looked at her features almost clinically. "You're hauntingly beautiful." It was a statement of fact rather than a passionate declaration. His voice was curiously devoid of emotion.

"That's...uh...very flattering." She laughed self-consciously.

"A man could easily lose his head over you and confuse—" He stopped abruptly.

"What are you trying to say, Raoul?" she asked when he didn't continue.

His hands dropped to his sides. "You were right about these last days being perfect. Carlotta adored you."

So he *did* mind! "She was just excited about having a woman around—someone younger than Mrs. Waverly," Lacey explained earnestly. "It could have been any woman you brought."

"No, *querida*, it was you," he said tenderly.

She was thoroughly confused by his suddenly softened expression. Would she ever understand this man? His next actions astonished her even more.

He bent his head and kissed her gently. "Sleep well, *mi amor*. I'll see you on Tuesday."

Lacey stared after him, speechless, as he disappeared into the waiting elevator.

What did it all mean? She paced the living-room floor looking for answers. At the ranch, Raoul had tried to make love to her at every opportunity. He'd been wild with frustration at all the interruptions. Yet now that they were alone, he'd walked away without a backward glance. *Why?*

It must have something to do with Carlotta's attachment to her. Did he think she'd deliberately played up to the child? Perhaps other women had tried that to snare him. Yet that couldn't be the reason. For one thing, he never took women to the ranch. For another thing, if she was angling for a relationship, why would she turn down an invitation to live with him?

Lacey finally gave up and went to bed, but sleep was impossible. The unanswered questions kept running through her mind, along with some others.

Should she leave as originally planned? Maybe Raoul regretted urging her to stay. That day-long business appointment tomorrow was a little suspect. But he did ask her to spend the whole day with him on Tuesday. That had to mean he wanted to be with her.

Finally she decided just to play it by ear. If relations seemed strained between them she could always take a plane on Wednesday.

When the phone rang the following morning Lacey was wide awake instantly. Maybe Raoul's meeting had been called off. Her eagerness faded when Rosa's voice greeted her.

"Where have you been?" the other woman demanded. "I've been calling you for two days."

"Didn't Raoul tell you? We went to the ranch."

A short silence fell. Then Rosa said incredulously, "Was Carlotta there?"

"Of course. We had such a good time together. She's a little doll."

"Do you realize you're the first woman he's ever taken up there?"

"I sort of gathered as much," Lacey admitted.

Rosa's voice held suppressed excitement. "This must mean Raoul is really serious about you."

If he'd been leaning in that direction, he wasn't anymore. Carlotta had come between them, not brought them together.

Lacey reluctantly set her straight. "You're way off base."

"I know my brother," Rosa answered confidently. "I think we've found you a rich husband."

Lacey could have told her that matrimony wasn't what he had in mind, but she put it a different way. "Raoul isn't about to get married. He told Mrs. Waverly she has a job for as long as she wants it."

"Well, naturally you'll need a governess. Oh, Lacey, this is the greatest news!"

"You're making a big deal over nothing," Lacey protested.

"Aren't you interested in him? I got the impression from seeing you together that you were . . . very compatible."

"Your brother is a charming man. Any woman would be flattered by his attention," Lacey explained carefully. "But I don't delude myself that he's serious about me."

"You *are* attracted to him," Rosa said triumphantly.

"A lot of good it's going to do me." Lacey sighed, giving up the pretense. "Becoming friends with Carlotta was the worst thing I could have done. Raoul was very withdrawn on the way home last night. I think he resented the fact that we hit it off so well."

"He wouldn't have taken you there if he hadn't wanted that to happen."

"Then why did he—" Lacey stopped before revealing too much.

"Why did he what?"

"Oh, nothing. He just said some sort of cryptic things and then he . . . he left rather abruptly."

Rosa laughed unexpectedly. "That's my brother. Raoul thought he had his future all mapped out. He's used to being in charge. When you came along and changed the whole pattern of his life, he needed some time alone to analyze the situation."

"If you say so," Lacey replied neutrally. It was her private opinion that Rosa was living in a dream world.

"Take my word for it. You're practically in the family."

"Well, just in case I'm not, let's keep in touch after I go home."

"You're not still leaving tomorrow?"

"No, I decided to stay on for a day or two anyway," Lacey said cautiously.

"Wonderful! Can you sneak away from Raoul for a few hours? That's really why I called. I'm planning a luncheon and fashion show to raise funds for Salizar. I'd like you to help me pick out some clothes for the models to wear."

Lacey laughed. "You certainly jumped in with both feet."

"I haven't had such a feeling of purpose in a long time. Will you help me?"

"I'd be glad to, but you probably know more about fashion than I do."

"No, I need some professional input. When are you free?"

"All day today. Raoul said he'd be tied up on business."

"Marvelous! How soon can you meet me?"

Lacey spent an enjoyable day going to the best dress shops with Rosa. It was fun to pick out glamorous clothes without looking at price tags. Rosa handled the business details, getting the stores to loan the gowns at no charge. She was a completely new person in her professional guise. Lacey got a lot of personal satisfaction out of seeing how the other woman was blossoming. At least something good had come out of this surreal trip to Mexico City.

She wasn't sure anything else had. Her exhilaration vanished when she returned to the silent apartment in the late afternoon. Was Raoul really tied up with customers? It seemed strange that he'd be unavailable day *and* night.

Her gloom vanished when the telephone rang. She simply had to stop doubting him! But Lacey was plagued by disappointment that day. It was Carlos on the phone, not Raoul.

"You're very hard to get ahold of," he complained. "Where were you all weekend?"

"I was at Raoul's ranch." She saw no reason to lie about her whereabouts.

Carlos's reaction was the same as Rosa's. "You saw Carlotta?"

"Yes."

"How did Raoul explain you?"

"That's a strange question. He said I was a guest. Which I was."

"A very honored one. Who does Carlotta—no, you must tell me everything in person. Will you have dinner with me tonight?"

Lacey's first impulse was an automatic refusal. Then she reconsidered. What was the point in sitting at home by herself? She'd just spend the night trying to analyze Raoul, and wind up a bundle of nerves.

"I'd be delighted to have dinner with you," she told Carlos.

"Fantastico!" His elation was a balm to her drooping spirits.

Her acceptance proved to be the high point of the evening, however. Carlos wasn't any more stimulating. His conversation still centered around Raoul, the last person she wished to discuss.

When he wasn't harping on the injustices done him, he asked a lot of questions about Carlotta, which Lacey found equally unacceptable. Carlos had no interest in the child. He was simply gathering information because he knew Carlotta was Raoul's one weak spot. Did he think Lacey was too stupid to realize that?

"If you intend to get back at Raoul through his daughter, you'd be safer taking a stroll through a mine field," she said finally.

"I'm not the one seeking revenge," he replied with outraged innocence.

"Then why all the questions about Carlotta?"

"Just normal curiosity."

"You really care what she looks like?" Lacey asked skeptically.

His face wore a strange expression. "It would be interesting to find out."

Which parent she resembled? Carlos knew who the child's mother was, but it would be useless to ask him again. He wouldn't tell her—not the truth anyway.

"You can stop wondering," she said crisply. "Carlotta is a feminine edition of Raoul."

"I'm glad," he said unexpectedly.

The softened tone of his voice confused Lacey even further. Maybe she was wrong about his motives. Carlos was a whiner and a bore, yet he wasn't all bad, evidently.

He wanted to go dancing after dinner, but she pleaded fatigue. Her new insight made her more tolerant, but she'd had enough of his company.

When the taxi drew up in front of the apartment building, Lacey told him not to dismiss it.

"A gentleman escorts a lady to her door." He gave the cab driver a bill.

"That really isn't—"

She never got to finish the sentence. Suddenly Raoul was towering over her, his face contorted with rage.

"Is this what you do when I'm not around?" he demanded.

She looked at him in bewilderment. "What are you talking about? All I did was go out to dinner."

"If you had to have a date you could have found a better one at an all-night mission."

"What's the matter, Raoul? Are you afraid of a little competition?" Carlos smiled triumphantly.

"Not from you." Raoul's voice dripped contempt.

"Maybe you should reconsider. The lady did accept my invitation."

"This was your first and last date," Raoul stated ominously.

"That's another of your mistakes. We've been out together before."

Raoul looked at Lacey incredulously. "Is that true?"

"No! At least not the way it sounds," she amended.

"You've been seeing him behind my back?"

"We just had a drink together. It wasn't a date. Tell it like it is, Carlos."

"Of course, *cara*. Whatever you say." His tone of voice guaranteed disbelief.

"It's the *truth*!" she practically shouted. "We met at a bar the other day and talked for an hour. That's all there was to it."

"But you didn't think to mention it?" Raoul stared at her with narrowed eyes.

Lacey's own anger started to rise. He was treating her like a criminal when she hadn't done anything wrong.

Lifting her chin she said, "No, I didn't consider it an obligation."

Carlos looked at Raoul with a sneer. "You always were a little too sure of yourself."

Raoul grabbed his shirtfront and yanked him close. Raw hatred shone out of his eyes. "Stay away from her. Do you hear me?"

Carlos was shaken, but he tried not to show it. "That's up to the lady."

Raoul's hand tightened. "I'm warning you. If I hear of you coming near her again, I'll personally see to it that you don't ruin any more lives."

"You can't threaten me," Carlos blustered weakly.

"It isn't a threat." Raoul's voice was all the more lethal for being so soft. "It's a promise."

"What are you going to do that you haven't already done?" Carlos taunted. "Kill me?"

"Killing is too good for you. You need to be altered, like any other tomcat."

His threat couldn't be taken seriously, but Carlos paled. He pulled away and smoothed his crumpled shirt, trying to regain some dignity.

Turning to Lacey, he said, "I'm sorry you were subjected to this unpleasantness. Please remember *one* of us tried to be a gentleman."

Raoul watched his speedy departure with smoldering eyes.

"Well, I hope you're proud of yourself," Lacey exploded when they were alone. "Do you intend to threaten *me* next?"

A muscle twitched in his tight jaw. Without a word, he took her arm in a punishing grip and jerked her inside.

"Let go of me!" She struggled to free herself as he shoved her inside the elevator and pushed the top button. "You have no right to treat me like this. I can go out with whomever I please!"

"Not with Carlos," he grated, propelling her down the hall and into the apartment. "Not if I can prevent it."

Lacey finally shook off his hand. "You might be the last word in your own family, but you can't tell *me* what to do."

"I didn't realize he meant that much to you," he said icily.

"He doesn't! That's not the point."

"If you don't care about him, why all the indignation because I ended your date?"

"That has nothing to do with it. The evening was over anyway. He was just bringing me home."

"To *my* home! Were you going to let him make love to you here?"

They faced each other furiously. But under Lacey's anger was a sick feeling. How could Raoul even imagine such a thing? She turned away so he wouldn't see her pain.

"Think whatever you like," she muttered.

He yanked her back to face him. "Answer my question!"

"You won't believe me anyway. You've let your jealousy of Carlos warp your whole life."

"Jealousy?" He stared at her incredulously. "Why would I be jealous of him?"

Lacey's anger faded when he tried to cover up. Raoul had good reason to regard Carlos as an enemy. She hated to wound his pride by revealing her knowledge, but he mustn't think she'd defected to Carlos, too.

"You don't have to pretend with me," she said quietly. "I know the whole story."

He looked at her warily. "What do you mean?"

"Carlos told me. That's why I agreed to meet him for a drink. It was the day after Elena's party. I'm not proud of myself for asking questions, but I had to know why you were so upset. I thought maybe it was something I'd done," she concluded haltingly.

"What did he tell you?" Raoul's expressionless voice didn't reveal much.

"About the girl you were both in love with. The one who ran away on your..." Lacey flinched from putting it into words.

"Let me get this straight. I was in love with a girl who ran away with Carlos? Is that what you're saying?"

"You don't have to talk about it. I realize you're still in love with her," she said sadly.

"That lying *murrano*!" Raoul ground out.

Lacey didn't recognize the word, but his tone of voice and the fury on his face gave her the general idea.

"You believed him?" he demanded.

"I had no reason not to," she answered hesitantly. "It would explain the way you felt about him. I can see how you'd blame him for the girl's death."

"I think it's time I heard exactly what Carlos told you."

She repeated the painful story reluctantly. Raoul listened without interrupting, his face like a stone mask. Lacey suffered for this proud man who clung to a past that was ruining his life. She ached to show him how glorious the present could be. But he didn't want her love.

"Are you all finished?" he asked at the conclusion of her story. When she nodded, he pointed to the couch. "Sit down. You're about to hear the truth."

"I didn't mean to open up old wounds," she protested. "Maybe we should just drop the subject, now that you know my only interest in Carlos was you."

He began as though she hadn't spoken. "There was a girl, all right, but only one of us loved her. Her name was Angela, and she was very young...only eighteen." Raoul paused as pain gripped him. "She'd been away at a girls' school, sheltered from the real world. Carlos had known her as a little girl, but during those years away from home she turned into a beauty."

Lacey's heart twisted at the tortured remembrance on his face. How could any woman replace a lovely ghost who never aged?

"He was captivated by her," Raoul continued. "He took her to the kind of glamorous places she'd never been. He bought her gifts and showered attention on her. Naturally her head was turned. She fell in love with him, and assumed he was in love with her."

So far it was essentially the story Carlos had told Lacey. She waited, dreading to hear Raoul's entry into it.

"It was easy for him to seduce her," he said grimly. "She must have thought he was going to marry her. She certainly expected him to after she became pregnant."

"Oh, no!" Lacey exclaimed involuntarily.

"When he refused, she was like a wounded little doe. All the gaiety and spirit drained out of her."

Lacey was beginning to have a glimmering of the outcome. "She had the baby?"

"She insisted on it, even though there were complications and the doctors warned against it. She even made me promise on her deathbed that I'd name the child Carlotta if it was a girl. She never stopped loving that—" A nerve throbbed at his temple.

"You were with her at the end?"

He nodded, his eyes bleak. "Angela was my little sister."

The revelation was shocking. Tears clogged Lacey's throat. "I'm so sorry," she whispered. "I didn't realize."

"It isn't something you talk about."

"It's difficult to conceive of anyone that heartless," she said helplessly.

"Carlos thrives on innocents like you," he answered bitterly. "Now you know why I told him to stay away from you. He's unclean. He fouls everything he touches."

Lacey experienced a rush of unexpected vindictiveness. "You had every right to drive him out of town," she declared.

Raoul laughed mirthlessly. "Is that what he told you?"

"That isn't true either?"

"I wish I could take the credit, but Carlos left because he was shunned by every decent person who knew him. He didn't have a friend in the world here. Even his family wouldn't have anything to do with him."

"You didn't ruin him in business?"

"I didn't have to. The family company was headed for bankruptcy until his younger brother came to me for help."

"*He* came to *you*? Carlos said it was the other way around."

"That's typical. Actually, the family was desperate. They were all working frantically, while Carlos was siphoning off the profits."

"So you gave them money if they'd get rid of him?"

"They had already kicked him out, but Carlos had almost drained the firm dry. His brother approached me to buy what few assets were left. He wanted to raise enough money so at least their mother would be taken care of."

"But Carlos indicated the business continued without him."

"It did—a lot more profitably."

"How could that be? If the machinery was outdated and they didn't have any working capital, how could they stay afloat?"

"I gave them a loan and sent some of my technicians in to show them how to operate more efficiently." Raoul admitted his generosity reluctantly.

"You did that for the family of a man who treated yours the way he did?"

"It wasn't their fault. They've suffered, too. Just being related to Carlos is a stigma that's hard to live with."

"Does Carlotta know you're not her real father?" Lacey asked hesitantly.

"I *am* her father. I adopted her legally."

"I see," she murmured noncommittally.

"Perhaps you're wondering why I didn't let Rosa adopt her instead."

"Well, yes, it did occur to me. She has children of her own."

"That's exactly the reason. Rosa loves Carlotta, but her affections would have to be divided. I was determined that Angela's child would have all the love she's entitled to."

Lacey finally understood Raoul's decision not to become deeply involved with anyone else. He didn't want Carlotta to feel slighted in any way.

Her smile was wistful. "You've certainly accomplished your purpose. She's a very happy little girl."

He looked at her moodily. "Most of the time, anyway. Sometimes I think she minds not having a mother."

"That's only natural. Most of her playmates have two parents."

He ruffled his thick dark hair. "I know what you're thinking. I could provide her with that, too. But I've never let myself become attached to any woman."

"I know," Lacey answered ironically.

He slanted a quick glance at her. "It hasn't been a hardship."

"I realize what you're saying." She didn't think he'd been celibate all those years.

"No, I don't think you do. I mean I've never fallen in love."

"You've never allowed yourself to."

"Falling in love isn't a matter of choice."

Lacey sighed. "You don't have to explain yourself to me, Raoul. I understand everything now, and I really admire you."

"For adopting Carlotta? That wasn't a burden. She's brought me great joy."

"I'm sure it's been mutual, but that wasn't what I meant. I admire you for playing fair with me. I'll admit I was a little…puzzled when you left me at the door last night." Color stained her fair skin. "I realize now you were telling me that anything between us would be a casual affair."

"Is that what you thought?"

"I'd told you it had to be something more for me." Her long hair swept forward, veiling her face as she bent her head. "It was good of you not to lead me on. You could very easily have stayed."

"Darling Lacey." He tipped her chin up, gazing at her with deep feeling. "You don't know how hard it was to leave you. But I had to sort out my emotions—away from your magic. When I'm around you I can't think straight. I've never felt like this about a woman before.''

''You mean more than just sex?'' she asked slowly.

''So much more. That's what scared me.''

''You thought I was a threat to Carlotta?''

''No, *cara*. Nothing could affect the love I have for my daughter. That's a different kind of love. My feelings about you were what I had to examine.''

''You were afraid you were beginning to...to care for me?'' She shied away from using the word love.

He nodded. ''You're so exquisite. It would be easy to confuse desire with something more meaningful. The attraction between us is very potent.''

''I know,'' she murmured.

''It's always been enough before, but not with you. I had to decide what to do about it.''

''And what did you decide?''

He smiled for the first time. ''Does it give you a clue that I came back?''

Tremendous joy flooded her as she returned his smile tremulously. ''It doesn't really prove anything. You might just have needed a clean shirt.''

''I need something more important than that,'' he said deeply, folding her in his arms.

Their kiss expressed all the longing and frustration each had felt. Lacey held him as tightly as he held her, uttering tiny sounds of satisfaction.

When Raoul finally released her mouth she gazed at him earnestly. ''Let's not ever argue again.''

''Even though making up is so enjoyable?''

She ignored his teasing tone. ''I don't ever want to see you that angry again. You were almost frightening.''

His face sobered. ''You can't imagine how I felt when I found you with Carlos. I raced through my business to get here so we could spend at least a short time together, but you'd gone out with that piece of filth."

"How could you think it was anything more than a simple date?"

"Because I know Carlos," he answered grimly.

"You know me, too—or you should."

He smoothed the silky hair away from her face and gazed at her tenderly. "I don't yet, *mi amor*, but I want to. I need to know everything about you."

She was faintly troubled by what seemed like reservations. "A good relationship is based on trust, Raoul."

"It's Carlos I don't trust," he said somberly. "He didn't return to make amends. He wants something, and it wouldn't surprise me if he tried to get it through you."

"I did get the impression that he wanted me to intercede with you on his behalf. I wasn't interested even before I knew what a worthless creep he is," she said contemptuously.

Raoul's frown didn't disappear. "Just be on your guard, *querida*. Carlos can make a lie sound more plausible than the truth."

"He won't get a chance." She smoothed away the frown lines. "Especially if you're around a lot."

"How about night and day?" Raoul asked huskily.

"Are you trying to compromise me?" she teased. "What would Rosa think if your bed wasn't slept in?"

He strung a line of burning little kisses over her face. "She doesn't make the bed."

Lacey laughed breathlessly. "That doesn't solve the problem. What would the maid think?"

"Do you really care?"

As they gazed into each other's eyes, Lacey felt her whole body heat with anticipation. "No," she answered softly.

Raoul lifted her in his arms and started down the hall. He passed the guest room and continued to his own bedroom. It was dimly lit by moonlight and the thousands of city lights visible through the picture windows.

He placed her gently on the bed and leaned over her. "Not many men have their dreams come true. Mine have, and I hope I can fulfill yours, *mi amor*," he said tenderly.

"You already have," she answered in a muted voice.

Lacey trembled as he lifted her slightly to slide down the zipper of her dress. This moment was the culmination of all her fantasies. This man was the only one who could fulfill them.

"Don't be afraid of me, *ángel*," he murmured, kissing her eyelids. "I want to bring you only joy."

"You do, Raoul," she whispered.

His eyes blazed as he looked at her drugged face. "You're a gift from heaven, *querida*."

Lacey felt as though she'd entered its portals when Raoul began to undress her. He removed each garment slowly, caressing her with his fingertips until she was on fire with longing. Her breasts swelled as he stroked them erotically. When he bent his head to roll one sensitive nipple between his lips, she clutched his hair in a desperate grip.

"Do you like that, *cara*?" His tongue made devastating circles, tasting, teasing, fueling the raging flames inside her.

"You're driving me out of my mind," she gasped, reaching up to unbutton his shirt with shaking fingers.

"I lost mine over you long ago," he answered huskily.

When his shirt was open to the waist he knelt over her and lowered his torso. The curling mat of dark hair on his chest felt soft against her breasts, in contrast to the taut muscles under her restless hands.

She dug her fingers into his shoulders, his hard forearms, arching her body in a need for closer contact with his. When he finally clasped her tightly, the sensation was exquisite.

As her desire mounted he pulled her to a sitting position and locked his legs around her while he shrugged off his shirt. Their mouths remained joined as Lacey unbuckled his belt with frantic haste. Raoul's darting tongue was creating an ache that was almost unbearable. Then he broke off the kiss to finish undressing hastily.

His own passion was visible when he returned from flinging off his clothes. He stood by the bed and gazed down at her, his smoldering eyes ranging over her bare body.

"I knew you'd be this beautiful." His palms glided over her breasts, her flat stomach, down to her quivering thighs. "Your skin is like warm satin," he murmured.

Lacey reached out for him blindly, wanting to experience the same tactile pleasure. When she stroked his loins he uttered a strangled exclamation and captured her hand.

"You don't know what that does to me, little one," he groaned.

"Let me touch you, Raoul," she said softly. "It gives me pleasure, too."

He gathered her fiercely in his arms. "I want to give you more than pleasure, *mi amor*. I want to bring you ecstasy."

His entry did exactly that. Lacey's heart beat in a wild rhythm that matched her frenzied movements. Raoul's driving force was the center of her universe. She was joined with him in unbelievable rapture.

The throbbing sensation went on and on, intensifying until every muscle was taut. Release came in a sudden burst of power that swept through her body in recurring spasms.

She could feel the same vibrations in Raoul as fulfillment overtook them both. He held her close while they descended from the heights to warm contentment.

"My darling love," he murmured against her damp skin. "I knew it would be like this."

"I never knew it *could* be," she whispered.

"There's so much more I want to do for you. This is only the beginning for us." Raoul's arms tightened as he kissed her tenderly.

Chapter Nine

Raoul woke Lacey in the most satisfactory way the next morning, with a kiss. The sun was just coming up, gilding the city with gold.

She was confused for a moment by the strange surroundings. Then memory rushed back and her body reminded her of the thrilling events of the night before.

Raoul stood by the bed, smiling mischievously. He was holding a tray containing a bottle of champagne and two glasses. "I thought after last night you might reconsider your prejudice against champagne for breakfast."

Lacey's happiness dimmed as she remembered this was a practice of his. Had the previous night been just one in a long procession, too?

His merriment vanished when he observed her clouded expression. "You don't have to drink it, *cara*. What would you prefer? I'll bring you anything you want."

"No, champagne sounds very festive." She managed a smile. He had given her a night to remember. Raoul mustn't know she wanted it to be special for him, too.

He set the tray on the nightstand and sat down beside her. "What's wrong, Lacey? Are you regretting last night?"

"You must know better than that." She gazed at his strong face, memorizing every feature.

"Then what's bothering you?"

"Nothing," she insisted.

"You wouldn't try to fool a guy, would you?"

"A woman has to have *some* secrets," she answered lightly.

His eyes narrowed. "I didn't think you were the kind of woman who played games. One of the reasons I fell in love with you was because you were so honest and genuine."

Lacey's mouth dropped open. "You love me?"

"What do you think I was telling you last night?" he demanded.

"You were very...tender," she said hesitantly.

"But you thought it was just satisfying sex?"

"You never said you loved me," she faltered.

"I thought I was showing you." He took her in his arms. "Darling Lacey, I didn't know women like you existed. You're the most wonderful thing that ever happened to me."

Her eyes were like stars as she flung her arms around his neck. "Oh, Raoul, I can hardly believe it!"

"Then perhaps I'd better show you again," he murmured as he slid into bed next to her.

His kisses began with her lips and trailed down her body, pausing at each vulnerable spot. His mouth and tongue tantalized her until she arched her body demandingly.

When her passion was completely unbridled, Raoul completed their union. Pleasure splintered through Lacey's body in shock waves that built in intensity, then burst in a giant crest.

At the very peak he breathed against her lips, "I love you, my darling."

It was nearly noon before they arose, showered together and dressed. Lacey had never dreamed she could be this happy. Their only disagreement was over Raoul moving back to the apartment.

"I want to find you in my arms when I wake up in the morning," he stated firmly.

"Can't you see how embarrassing it would be for me? What would Rosa and Edouard think?"

He grinned. "I can speak for Edouard. He'd be envious."

"Please be serious, Raoul. We've known each other such a short time. They'd never believe we fell in love."

"They're going to see it in living color from now on."

Lacey's heart swelled in her breast. Did that mean what she hoped it did? Raoul hadn't asked her to marry him, but he might be taking it for granted. He'd also assumed that she knew he loved her.

"Why do you worry so much about what people think?" he complained.

"Because I admire your sister and brother-in-law, and I value their respect."

"My sweet, adorable Lacey," he said, sighing. "Your modesty is going to frustrate me no end, but it's one of the things I love about you."

She was making breakfast when the telephone rang. Raoul started to answer it, but Lacey stopped him.

"Let me get it," she said. "It's probably Rosa."

He chuckled. "She knows right where to find me. Doesn't that tell you something?"

Lacey's heart sank when she heard the male voice on the phone. Raoul would go up in smoke!

"I hope I'm not calling too early," Carlos said solicitously.

"No, I'm in the kitchen." She cast a wary eye at Raoul, who smiled indulgently.

"I wanted to apologize for that disgraceful scene last night, although you could see I wasn't the aggressor."

"It's all over and done with," she answered without emotion.

"You mean you don't blame me?"

"That's not what I meant at all." Lacey was very aware of Raoul listening to the conversation. She tried to keep her side of it as cryptic as possible, so he wouldn't know who she was talking to.

"Surely you don't consider me a coward because I let Raoul bully me? I was trying to act civilized for your sake."

"I didn't realize you could be that thoughtful." She couldn't quite disguise her irony.

"You've been listening to my enemies," Carlos said sadly.

"It would be difficult not to. You have so many."

"I can tell Raoul has filled your head with lies about me. How can you believe a man who would callously destroy other people's lives?"

Lacey suddenly saw red. She had recently met the fruit of *his* callousness. Discretion was forgotten in the need to lash out at this man who was beneath contempt.

"Raoul showed a lot more restraint than you deserved," she flared. "People like you should be made to pay for the suffering they cause."

Raoul had been puzzled at first by her tone of voice. As suspicion dawned, he pushed his chair back violently.

"Give me the phone," he demanded.

Lacey backed away instead. "Don't ever call me again," she told Carlos. "Your whining is almost as unpalatable as your lies." She hung up before Raoul could take the phone.

"That was Carlos, wasn't it? Why didn't you let me talk to him?" His whole body was rigid.

"Because it wasn't necessary. He got the message."

"I knew he wouldn't give up!"

"He will now," she soothed.

"I'm not so sure," Raoul answered darkly.

"Trust me, darling." She put her arms around his neck.

He was too furious to respond in kind. "I would have put the fear of God in that gutless wonder if you'd only let me talk to him."

Lacey sighed. "Look what you're letting him do to you. Carlos would be delighted to know he spoiled our day."

Raoul stared at her for a tense moment. Then his anger faded and he wrapped his arms around her. "Nothing could spoil what we have together."

"Just remember that," she said softly.

"Refresh my memory," he answered in a husky voice.

She framed his face in her palms and kissed him with all the love she felt. Raoul crushed her tightly against his hard body and deepened the kiss. They were enveloped in the familiar magic, oblivious to the world around them. Until an acrid smell finally penetrated their consciousness.

Lacey was the first to realize what it was. "The bacon!" She snatched the smoking pan off the fire.

"I'd better open a window," Raoul said.

"And I'll turn on the fan."

The smoke started to dissipate, although the odor lingered. When he returned she was wiping the grease-spattered stove with a sponge.

"That was the last of the bacon, but at least the toast didn't burn," she told him.

"How did that escape?" he teased.

"I forgot to put it in the toaster."

He began to laugh. "I can see we'll have to hire a cook."

Lacey's pulse started to race. "You mean you're going to change your ways and start eating at home?" she asked casually.

He smoothed her hair tenderly. "*You've* changed my ways."

Was he being purposely dense? She was tempted to come right out and ask if she figured in his plans for the future, but a proposal shouldn't have to be extracted like a tooth. Lacey forced down her disappointment. Their love was only consummated last night. It was probably natural that Raoul needed a little time to get used to the idea of marriage. He knew she would leave on Sunday if he didn't say anything, so what was she worried about? Let the dear man have his last illusion of freedom.

She smiled enchantingly and kissed his chin. "I'll try to make the changes as painless as possible."

The small mishap with the bacon drove Carlos out of their minds, but Raoul's intuition about him was closer to the mark than Lacey's. Rage and frustration consumed Carlos after she hung up on him. He dialed another number, still fuming.

Delores sounded drowsy when she answered the phone. "I'll call you back after I've had coffee. I'm still half asleep."

"My news will wake you up," he snarled. "Your great scheme for getting revenge on Raoul and his girlfriend just laid an egg."

"What happened?" she asked sharply.

"Let's just say she doesn't believe in fairy tales anymore," he replied derisively.

"I might have known you'd botch it up!" Delores was wide awake now.

"Don't try to put the blame on me. The whole idea of seducing her was stupid in the first place."

"That's true," she answered sarcastically. "What woman would ever prefer you over Raoul?"

"Pull in your claws, baby. You're not at the top of *his* hit parade, either."

Delores drew in her breath with an angry hiss. "Raoul isn't in love with that stupid blonde! She's just a novelty. Once she's out of the picture he'll come back to me."

"That's another of your misconceptions," Carlos mocked.

"Raoul is mine!" she insisted heatedly. "No cheap little opportunist is going to walk off with him."

"Well, you'll have to find another way to stop her. And don't blame me. How could I compete against Raoul's money?" he asked bitterly.

"You couldn't beat him in a fixed fight." Contempt laced her voice. "You always were a quitter, Carlos. I thought you wanted to get even with Raoul."

"I do, but Lacey's not as dumb as you think she is. And knock off the name-calling. I can think of a few choice ones for you."

"Okay, you're right, we won't get anywhere fighting each other. Luckily I have an alternative that's a lot better than the first plan."

"She won't listen to any more tall stories," he warned.

"You won't need to say a word to her."

"What crazy plot are you dreaming up now?"

Delores laughed unpleasantly. "One that will utilize your greatest talent."

The next few days were idyllic for Lacey and Raoul. He arrived at the apartment early in the morning, and didn't leave her till late at night. If he'd asked again to stay she couldn't have refused him, but Raoul assumed that her decision was unchanged. Especially since Rosa kept in constant touch. She called regularly with bulletins on her candidate's progress, or to ask Lacey's advice. Raoul seemed pleased by the growing friendship between the two.

One morning Lacey was still asleep when Raoul arrived. He woke her by breathing into her ear.

When her eyelids fluttered open he pretended surprise. "Did I wake you?"

She smiled. "Wasn't that what you had in mind?"

"Plus a few other things," he murmured, caressing her body, which was still warm from sleep.

Much later, when they were lying in each other's arms, Lacey gave Raoul a puzzled look. "How did you get into the apartment?"

"The door wasn't bolted. Don't you use the chain anymore?"

She gazed at him through long lashes. "Not since I learned to like champagne for breakfast."

"You mean I could have used my key any of those nights when I couldn't sleep for wanting you?"

"You told me you didn't have another key."

"I meant in my possession at the moment. I had a spare in my dresser drawer."

"Which you pocketed at the first opportunity!" she said indignantly.

Raoul chuckled. "It seemed more convenient than having to pull Manuel off his post every time I wanted something out of my closet."

"You're a very devious man," she scolded.

"But truthful. I didn't lie to you, admit it."

"You sound like a politician. From now on I'm not taking anything you say at face value," she grumbled.

"One thing you can be sure of." He bent his head to kiss her bare breasts. "Always believe that I love you."

As he twined his legs around hers and her body responded to his warmth, Raoul could have convinced her of anything.

Rosa telephoned while they were deciding what to do that day. She wanted Lacey to assist again with her fashion show.

"But we already picked out all the clothes," Lacey objected.

"Now I need help with the models. They walk like puppets."

"Aren't you using professionals?"

"No, I tried to keep expenses down by asking my friends to model. That's the problem. After they volunteered their time, I can scarcely tell them they move like a bunch of robots."

"So you want me to be the heavy." Lacey laughed.

"I'd appreciate it if you'd show them how to walk. It looks so easy when you're sitting in the audience at a fashion show, but there's evidently a lot more to it."

"They'll loosen up. They're probably just a little self-conscious."

"It's more than that, believe me. Will you come over?"

"I don't know what Raoul has planned," Lacey said doubtfully.

"Go ahead," he told her when she consulted him. "I really should put in an appearance at the office. I haven't been there all week."

Lacey spent a busy afternoon whipping Rosa's raw recruits into shape. Initially they were as stiff as Rosa had described them, but Lacey soon had the willing neophytes performing like pros.

First she turned on the stereo in the den, then led the group into the long hall that bisected Rosa's big house.

"Listen to the music and move with it as you would on a dance floor," she instructed.

They watched as she glided gracefully to demonstrate, pausing, turning.

"Look at the audience, smile as though you're enjoying yourself," she said. "The day of the bored mannequin is over."

By the end of the afternoon everyone was enthusiastic. "You ought to open a modeling school," Elena told her. "You could start a whole new career."

Lacey smiled. "It wouldn't be very profitable. You've all graduated in one day."

"It's something to keep in mind in case you get bored after a while," Rosa remarked thoughtfully. "I'm sure Raoul would back you."

Elena looked from one to the other with delighted speculation. "Does that mean what I think it does?"

"No, certainly not," Lacey said hurriedly. "I couldn't accept anything more from Raoul."

"My brother's a rarity among Latin men, but don't be *too* independent," Rosa warned.

Elena laughed. "That's right. Let him think he's the boss, even if he isn't."

"You're both talking nonsense," Lacey said coolly. "Raoul and I are just friends."

The last thing she wanted was for gossip to spring up. What if Raoul thought she'd instigated it to force his hand? Things were at a delicate stage between them, and they'd had misunderstandings before.

The other two women exchanged knowing glances, but they dropped the subject after a look at Lacey's perturbed face.

After everyone else had gone, Rosa and Lacey relaxed over a glass of sherry, discussing the upcoming fashion show. When Raoul telephoned as Lacey was getting ready to leave, Rosa tactfully left the room.

"How did it go?" he asked. "Did you give the ladies their marching orders?"

"They were very apt pupils," she answered. "They did exactly what I showed them."

"I'd follow the teacher's instructions, too." His voice deepened.

"You don't need lessons," she replied softly.

Raoul groaned. "You're making this very difficult. I called to tell you I can't see you this evening."

"Oh. Well . . . that's all right."

"No, it isn't, it's frustrating. But I have to work to-night. I haven't been to the office all week, and some rather serious foul-ups occurred."

"You shouldn't have been neglecting your business for me."

"I can't think of a better reason," he said warmly. "I'll try to stop by the apartment when I'm through, but it might be quite late."

"Don't do that. You'll be tired after such a long day."

"Never too tired for you, *querida*."

Lacey tingled at the tone of his voice, but she resisted temptation. "Nevertheless, you need your sleep." She laughed breathlessly. "Tomorrow might turn out to be quite strenuous."

"That's a sure bet," he replied with conviction.

Raoul's phone rang shortly after his conversation with Lacey. He picked it up absently, already immersed in paperwork. Delores's voice at the other end was an unpleasant surprise.

"You're a hard man to get in touch with," she said. "I've been calling your office for days."

"I've been out a lot. What do you want, Delores?" His tone was steely.

"To apologize," she said penitently.

"For which transgression?"

"I guess I deserve that. I've been a terrible shrew, and I'm sorry."

"That's supposed to make everything all right?"

"I'm trying to make amends. Can't you find it in your heart to forgive me?"

"I've put up with your tantrums and your rudeness for years, but there's a limit," he said grimly. "Any further relationship between us is impossible."

"Please, Raoul. I only want to be friends again, nothing more, I swear. I can't bear it when you hate me."

He sighed. "I don't hate you, Delores. I'm simply...tired. Tired of the scenes and recriminations, the general nastiness."

"There won't be any more, I promise! Just don't put me out of your life completely. We had some laughs together. Try to remember those times," she coaxed. "Is that too much to ask?"

"I suppose not," he replied grudgingly.

"I'm right around the corner from your office. Will you have a drink with me to show there are no hard feelings?"

"I really can't. I'm knee-deep in work."

"In an hour, then. I'm in no hurry."

"Sorry. I'm going to be slaving until all hours."

"You're not seeing Lacey tonight?" Her voice held an odd note.

"No, but don't get any ideas about telling her I had a date with you," he warned.

"Do you think I'd do a thing like that?"

"It's exactly the sort of stunt you'd pull. But I already told Lacey I was tied up here, and she knows I wouldn't lie to her."

"Do you have the same confidence in her?"

"Yes," he answered curtly.

Delores sighed. "Well, I guess I can't compete against a relationship like that. Good luck, *mi amor*. I hope you two have all the happiness you deserve."

Raoul was frowning when he put down the receiver. He didn't trust Delores's metamorphosis. It wasn't like her either to forgive or forget. But perhaps the ostracism she'd received since Elena's party had made her realize there were limits to what people would tolerate.

Rosa had told him Delores was cut off everyone's guest list. That must have shaken her confidence. It also made getting back in his good graces essential, he thought cynically.

Raoul dismissed Delores from his mind. She was a royal pain, but at least it seemed her claws had finally been filed down.

Lacey went back to the apartment after declining Rosa's invitation to stay for dinner. She had a lot of little things to do that she hadn't had time for lately. Almost every moment had been spent with Raoul.

After rinsing out her lingerie and washing her hair, she put on a fresh nightgown. Her soft mouth curved in a smile. That was something else she hadn't done lately.

The book she intended to read was engrossing, but Lacey's eyelids started to droop. The past few days had been very eventful, to say the least.

Finally she turned out the lamp and gazed contentedly at the sparkling lights of the city. In a few moments she was asleep.

Hours later, the traffic along Paseo de la Reforma slowed as most people in the vast metropolis slumbered. Lacey was in a deep sleep, but she wouldn't have heard the front door open anyway. The intruder had picked the lock with practiced silence.

Once inside the apartment he merged with the darkness and became just a shadowy figure. After he removed his clothes he was slightly more visible, yet not really distinct. No one could actually have identified the blur as a naked man.

Raoul was asleep, too. After a twelve-hour day he had come home exhausted and fallen into bed. When the telephone woke him, he scowled ferociously. A glance at the clock made him even angrier. It was almost three in the morning.

"Do you know what time it is?" he demanded without asking who was calling.

"You've got to come quickly. There's someone in the apartment!" The panicky words were delivered in a whisper.

"Lacey? Is that you?"

"Oh, please, Raoul. I'm terrified!"

"Lock the bedroom door and call the police," he ordered. "I'm on my way."

He was dressed and out of the house in a matter of minutes. The distance to the apartment was covered in a similarly brief time. Adrenaline was pumping through his arteries as he dashed into the building and took the waiting elevator. It seemed to take forever to get to his floor. Raoul's whole body was taut as he started down the corridor.

The shadowy figure inside the front door was equally tense. He had been listening for the sound of the elevator. When the doors opened with a muted clang he ran swiftly down the hall to the master bedroom.

Lacey stirred when he got into bed and took her in his arms. Her lashes fluttered and she smiled.

"I knew you wouldn't be able to stay away," she murmured.

Raoul's urgent voice sounded from the hall. "Lacey, are you all right? I'm here, darling."

Her eyes flew open and she stared into Carlos's triumphant face. "What are *you* doing here?"

"Giving your boyfriend a jolt." His eyes glittered with excitement as he cut off her furious words by plastering his mouth against hers.

Lacey made muffled sounds of outrage as she struggled frantically, but Carlos was too strong for her. His arms and legs were wrapped tightly around her. The contact with his nude body was nauseating as they thrashed around in the bed.

Suddenly the room was flooded with light. She said a silent prayer at her deliverance, but it seemed like an eternity before Carlos was yanked off of her.

If Raoul had been in shock for an instant, he was making up for it now. His hands were like steel bands around Carlos's throat.

"You unspeakable piece of filth!" he snarled. "This time I'm going to kill you."

Carlos clawed at his hands, gasping for breath. "It's not my fault. She was the one who asked me to come over."

"Liar!" Raoul's hands tightened.

Carlos gagged, but he managed to get out a strangled protest. "It's the truth. She said you were working and she was bored."

"So you decided to move in like the stinking jackal you are."

"You don't believe him?" Lacey exclaimed.

Both men ignored her. "I thought it was a good chance to get her on my side," Carlos panted. "Have her put in a word so you'd lighten up on me."

"And as an added inducement you made love to her," Raoul sneered.

"No! I mean it wasn't my idea. I only came over to talk, I swear it on my father's grave! *She* was the one. After a while she said she wanted to slip into something comfortable."

Raoul turned his head to stare incredulously at Lacey.

"Can't you see he's lying?" she pleaded.

"She came back in a nightgown," Carlos hurried on as Raoul's grip slackened slightly. "I was turned on, naturally, but I told her you'd skin me alive if you caught us together. She said there was no danger of that as long as I left before morning."

"You know that's not true. Why are you doing this to me?" Lacey whispered.

"I'm sorry, baby, but I'm not taking the rap. We both wanted it, and we got caught. Those are the breaks."

"Don't listen to him! He attacked me," she said distractedly to Raoul. "I was sound asleep, then all of a sudden he was in bed with me."

"How did I get in if you didn't invite me?" Carlos challenged.

"You're probably as good at breaking in as you are at lying," she answered bitterly.

"Nice try, kid, but it won't wash. Those sweet little sounds you were making weren't cries for help. They showed how much you liked it."

Raoul hit him then, a vicious uppercut that snapped Carlos's head back and sent him sprawling. Lacey was frightened by the demonic expression on Raoul's face as he jerked Carlos to his feet and prepared to hit him again.

She sprang forward and grabbed Raoul's arms. "No, don't!" In his wild state, she was afraid he might kill Carlos.

Raoul stared at her as Carlos sagged to his knees. He released him abruptly and gazed down at the prone man with smoldering eyes. "It seems I underestimated you."

"I'm just trying to stop you from doing something you'll regret," Lacey explained earnestly.

"It's a little late for that." Raoul's smile was a travesty.

"Don't you see what Carlos is doing? This is exactly what he hoped would happen. That you'd think we were making love."

"Are you asking me to deny what I saw with my own eyes?"

"It wasn't what it looked like," she insisted.

He might not have heard her. "I would have expected it from him, but not from you," Raoul said somberly. He nudged the cringing man with his foot. "Get out of here before I change my mind and do the world a favor."

Carlos gathered up his clothes and crawled out of reach before daring to stand up. He made a rush for the door, not quite certain he was actually free to go, but Raoul's attention was centered on Lacey.

"Now I understand why you didn't want me to come over tonight. At the time I was quite pleased by your concern for my welfare. I didn't know you just wanted a free night to find out if Carlos was the great lover he's touted to be."

"You can't believe that," she whispered.

"How long are you going to keep up the pretense? At least *he* didn't try to insult my intelligence," Raoul said contemptuously.

She looked at him with great, hurt eyes. "You don't know me at all, do you?"

"That's pretty evident."

"Our relationship meant nothing to you. I was just another warm body in your bed. You only said you loved me because you knew that's what I wanted to hear," she said sadly.

"I wouldn't talk about love if I were you. Not after the disgusting little scene I just witnessed."

"You honestly think I could let another man make love to me after what we've been to each other?"

A muscle jerked in Raoul's square jaw. "Quit while you're ahead, Lacey. Right now I'm fighting the urge to break your beautiful, cheating body in two."

Her slender shoulders drooped. "Go ahead if it will make you feel any better."

"You're finally ready to admit you betrayed me with Carlos—*Carlos* of all people!"

"That's all that's really bothering you, isn't it?" she flared. "Not my supposed infidelity, just my choice of partners."

"I'll have to admit I'm disappointed in your taste." His eyes roamed insolently over her body. "Or do you prefer men who play rough?"

She wasn't aware until then that her nightgown was ripped. That should have corroborated her story, but Raoul was so blinded by jealousy that he saw it as evidence of kinky sex play. She covered her bare breasts silently.

"You should have told me what you wanted," he continued mockingly. "I don't get my kicks that way, but we might have worked something out."

Lacey was too sick at heart to lash back. "This isn't getting us anywhere. You'd better leave."

"This happens to be *my* apartment."

"All right," she said tonelessly. "I'll go to the guest room."

He caught her arm as she started past him. "No maidenly protests about what my sister will think if I stay all night?"

"No." What difference did it make now?

"That was a great act you put on. Your modesty was refreshing." His hand tightened as he looked at her bowed head. "I almost wish you'd been more discreet."

"Let me go, Raoul," she murmured.

He jerked her chin up instead, his face contorted. "How could you do it?"

Lacey's eyes shimmered with tears, but she refused to let them spill over. "Keep asking yourself that question. Maybe you'll finally arrive at the answer."

He stared at her, tumultuous emotions warring on his strong face. Then he turned abruptly and left the room. The front door slammed, putting an end to Lacey's dreams.

Chapter Ten

Lacey awoke early the next morning after only a few hours of fitful sleep. It was an effort to drag herself out of bed. She tried to concentrate on getting dressed and packing, but the fateful events of the night before made that impossible. She spent long moments staring into space, wondering what she could have done differently.

When the phone rang her heart began to hammer alarmingly. Had Raoul finally realized she was blameless?

Rosa's cheery voice greeted her. "Sorry if I woke you. Raoul's going to have a fit, but his office called. They need to get in touch with him."

Lacey's disappointment was so great that she couldn't speak for a moment. Her voice was muted when she finally said, "He isn't here."

Rosa hesitated. "I didn't mean to embarrass you, but it really sounded important. Tell Raoul to check in."

"He isn't here, honestly."

"Then where is he? He isn't here, either."

"I wouldn't know," Lacey answered tonelessly.

"I admire you for keeping up appearances, but it isn't necessary. I've been wanting to tell you that for days. It's craziness for Raoul to come back here to sleep for a few hours. We understand that you two want to be together." Rosa laughed. "Edouard and I remember how it was before *we* were married."

Every word was a knife in Lacey's heart. "I tried to tell you that you were jumping to conclusions. I'm going home this morning."

"You're joking! Why?"

"It's a long story. I'll let Raoul tell you."

"Don't do anything hasty," Rosa implored. "Every couple has lovers' quarrels."

"I wish that's all this was," Lacey answered somberly.

"Come over for lunch, and we'll talk about it. Everything seems worse when you're alone."

"I realize you're trying to be helpful, but it's no use, Rosa. Just try not to believe everything you hear about me."

"Don't worry. No one had better say anything about you to me!"

Lacey's throat felt tight. "You're a good friend. I only wish things had turned out differently."

"I don't know what's going on, but I'm sure it isn't as serious as you think. Raoul loves you. That's all that matters."

"I thought so, too, but you and I both believed what we wanted to believe," Lacey said forlornly. "I'll always remember how kind you were to me."

"Stop talking as though this were the end of the line."

"It is."

"I won't let you just drop out of our lives," Rosa exclaimed. "If you insist on leaving instead of working things out, Raoul will come after you."

Lacey knew that wasn't so, but she didn't want to discuss the reasons. "Goodbye, Rosa, I'll write to you."

She realized she wouldn't do that, either. The only bearable course would be to cut all ties to Raoul.

Lacey arrived home on Friday afternoon. Her apartment smelled musty from being closed up so long; there was a film of dust over everything, and her African violets were drooping. They accurately mirrored her mood.

Refusing to give in to despair, she opened all the windows and then unpacked. After everything was put away she changed to old clothes and cleaned the apartment thoroughly.

The next morning Lacey went to the supermarket. She'd opened a can of soup for dinner the night before, not really wanting even that, but she had to start eating. Life went on even when it didn't seem worthwhile.

She was wheeling her cart down one of the long aisles when someone called her name. It was Margot Willey, a friend from work.

"We've all been wondering what happened to you," she exclaimed. "When did you get back?"

"Just yesterday."

"Did you have a marvelous time?"

"It was very nice. What's new around here?" Lacey changed the subject.

Margot shrugged. "Same old thing. Except that Mary Beth is back from her honeymoon."

"How did she like Acapulco?"

"I don't think she saw much of it." Margot grinned.

Lacey returned her smile. "That must mean the honeymoon was a success."

"She's on cloud nine."

"I'm so happy for her," Lacey said sincerely. "Have you met her husband?"

"No one has yet. They're having a big party tonight so everybody can meet him at once. I'm sure Mary Beth's been trying to get you. Call her right away. She'll be glad you got back in time."

"I'll phone her as soon as I get home," Lacey promised.

"It was lucky I ran into you this morning. Although I'm surprised you didn't get in touch with her as soon as you returned. You two are so close."

"She's still on her honeymoon. I didn't want to intrude."

The truth was that Lacey hadn't wanted to face probing questions. Mary Beth would be sure to ask for a detailed account of her trip. Lacey wasn't good at lying, and the real story was too heartbreaking to relate.

"She certainly sounds happy," Margot said. "I just hope she stays that way."

"Why would you have any doubts?"

"They only went together for a couple of weeks before deciding to get married. You don't really get to know a person in that short a time."

"Do you ever truly know somebody?" Lacey asked somberly.

"Not while the bloom is still on the rose, anyway. It's easy to think you're in love when the other person is new and exciting. But what if all you have in common is great sex?"

"People don't decide to get married for that reason alone—especially men," Lacey said woodenly. Raoul had certainly never brought up the subject. Which should have given her a clue.

"I guess you're right. Sex is no problem nowadays. People can go from one affair to another if they don't feel any commitment."

"Exactly. Well, I'd better check out before my frozen food defrosts," Lacey remarked. The conversation was proving painful.

"Okay, I'll see you tonight." Margot pushed her cart in the opposite direction.

Lacey called Mary Beth after she'd put away the groceries. Her friend sounded even more effervescent than usual.

"It's about time you got home! I was about to send out a Saint Bernard with a keg of brandy around its neck."

"They're only good at finding people buried in avalanches."

"For all I knew you might have been," Mary Beth scolded.

"In Mexico?"

"Don't try to weasel out of it. You could at least have sent a postcard."

"They always arrive a month after you're home. How was Acapulco?"

"Divine! Oh, Lacey, you have to go there. It's the most romantic spot in the world."

"Even if you're not on your honeymoon?" Lacey teased.

"Well, of course that helps," Mary Beth admitted. "But it truly is beautiful. We stayed at this really plush hotel. Would you believe we had our own private swimming pool?"

"That does sound smashing."

"It was. I got a glimpse of how the very rich live." Mary Beth sighed. "It wouldn't be hard to get used to their life-style."

"It's a different world," Lacey said soberly.

"I suppose so. They're probably too jaded to have any fun." Mary Beth giggled. "I'll bet they don't go skinny-dipping."

"I gather *you* did."

"At two in the morning. And then we had champagne and looked out at the stars." Mary Beth's bubbly laugh sounded again. "That's another thing I could get used to—champagne."

Lacey hadn't realized so many things were going to be hurtful reminders. She forced a light tone. "You certainly went all out."

"Why not? That's what a honeymoon is all about. You simply must stay at this hotel when you're ready to take the big step."

"Did they put you on their payroll?" Lacey joked weakly.

"They didn't have to. I just want everybody in the world to be as happy as I am!"

"That would be nice." Lacey's voice was wistful.

"I plan to start with you. My next project is finding you a man as wonderful as Scott."

"Are you admitting anyone could be?"

"No, but when you fall in love, you'll feel the same way."

"Do we have to keep talking about love?" When Lacey realized how sharp her voice had been she modified it hurriedly. "I want to hear about Acapulco."

"It's heavenly."

Mary Beth described the beaches, the snorkeling she and Scott had done, the discos, and the moonlight cruise they'd taken. Lacey only half listened, making occasional sounds of approval. Her thoughts were turned inward, on another visit to Eden. But hers had turned into Paradise Lost.

Mary Beth finally came to a breathless halt. "Why didn't you stop me? I've been doing all the talking. I haven't let you get in a word about your own trip."

"That's okay. It couldn't compare to yours."

The other woman laughed. "A honeymoon is in a class by itself, but I'll bet you had a great time."

"Yes, Mexico City is very interesting, but it isn't a resort like Acapulco. Do they still have those men diving off a cliff?"

"Why do I get the feeling you're trying to change the subject?"

"Why would I do that?" Lacey pretended innocence.

"I don't know, but you're the only person I ever heard of who didn't jump at the chance to talk on and on about her own vacation."

"Then count your blessings."

Mary Beth refused to be diverted. "Where did you go?"

"Everyplace." Lacey smothered a sigh. This was what she knew would happen. "I saw all the points of interest, including the pyramids. They were unbelievable."

"Did you go around by yourself all the time?"

"Not exactly. One day I took a bus tour."

"Did you meet anyone on the tour?" Mary Beth persisted.

"A lady from New York who believed in redistributing the wealth."

Mary Beth made an exasperated sound. "From listening to you I'd say your trip was a complete washout. But you'd scarcely have stayed longer than you intended if that were the case."

"It isn't! I was only joking. Everything was terrific. I went to the museums and to wonderful restaurants, and I—"

"What's his name?" Mary Beth asked.

"I don't know what you're talking about."

"You can't fool your best friend. What's his name?"

Lacey gave up the pretense. "Raoul Ruiz," she said quietly.

"How did you meet him?"

"You wouldn't believe me if I told you."

"Try me."

"I can't." Lacey's voice broke. "Maybe some day, but not now."

"Are you okay?" Mary Beth asked anxiously.

"Not yet, but I will be."

"I've never known a man to get to you like this," her friend said slowly. "He must be something special."

"He is."

"I don't mean to pour salt in the wound, but are you sure it's all over?"

"Very sure."

"Well...there are other fish in the sea," Mary Beth observed with false cheerfulness.

"Sure. I can always change my bait and try again." Lacey's attempt at laughter was a dismal failure.

"I can't bear to see you this unhappy!" Mary Beth couldn't keep up her end of the charade. "You have to tell me what happened. Did you find out something terrible about him? Did the rat forget to mention that he was already married? What?"

"None of those things. We just...had an argument."

"Good Lord, is that all? I thought he must be a bigamist at the very least."

"No, marriage isn't his forte," Lacey remarked bitterly.

"That's what most men think until a woman changes their minds. Don't worry, your dream prince will be burning up the telephone wires as soon as he cools off."

"He doesn't even have my phone number," Lacey said sadly.

"I presume he knows how to dial information. You'd scarcely fall in love with a man who had to have his meat cut up for him."

"Raoul doesn't need *anything* done for him," Lacey said somberly. "That's the trouble."

"Those strong silent types can fool you. Why don't you call and leave your number on his answering machine. It couldn't hurt."

Lacey smiled slightly for the first time. "You're not the right type to play Cupid. He was a fat little boy with a bow and arrow."

"You've already been struck," Mary Beth said impatiently. "Now do something about it. Call him!"

"I'll think about it." Before her friend could press the point, Lacey said, "Can I bring anything for the party tonight?"

"How did you find out about the party?"

"I met Margot in the market. Didn't you intend to invite me?" Lacey teased.

"I felt terrible when I thought you were going to miss it. Come early so we can talk some more."

After she hung up, Lacey wandered around the apartment restlessly. Mary Beth's advice was well-meant, but flawed. Raoul wouldn't listen to reason any more now than he had that awful night. If he was ever going to, he would have called the next day.

Besides, why should she be the one to try to make up? He owed *her* an apology! If he was too pigheaded to realize it, she was well rid of him. It would hail in hell before she'd call him!

She might phone Rosa, though. Just to say thanks for all her hospitality. Lacey ignored her earlier resolution to make the break final—and the fact that a written note would convey her gratitude just as well.

Excitement and nerves raced through her veins as she dialed Rosa's number. What if Raoul answered? It was a possibility, although rather a remote one. He'd surely have moved back to his own apartment by now. Her heart was beating rapidly, however, as she listened to the measured rings.

When a servant answered, she was almost relieved.

Rosa was cordial, yet surprised when she came to the phone. "I didn't expect to hear from you so soon."

"Well, I...uh...I wanted to thank you for making my visit so enjoyable."

"That wasn't necessary, although I'm delighted to hear from you. I'm the one who's indebted to *you*."

"You'll have to let me know how the election turns out," Lacey said, knowing what Rosa was referring to.

"We'll win," Rosa answered confidently.

"That's the old spirit. How is Edouard taking your new career?"

Rosa laughed. "He's adjusting slowly. It helps to have Raoul on my side. They get along like brothers rather than in-laws."

"How is Raoul?" Lacey asked casually, although it was an effort.

Rosa's voice sobered. "Haven't you heard from him?"

"No, I didn't expect to."

"I thought that might be why you called. To tell me you'd made up."

"Raoul would have told you that."

"I haven't seen him. He went up to the ranch as usual this weekend. When I phoned to talk to Carlotta, he sounded so hap—I mean he seemed perfectly normal. I just assumed you had patched up whatever went wrong."

"It wasn't anything important." Lacey was suddenly eager to get away. "Take care, Rosa. I'll be in touch."

Lacey thought she'd hit bottom before, but she reached new depths after talking to Rosa. So much for Mary Beth's good advice. If she'd let well enough alone she could at least have imagined that Raoul was suffering, too. It hurt almost unbearably to find out he was completely unaffected.

All he'd felt was anger—and he'd gotten over that rapidly. Rosa's slip of the tongue was very revealing. She'd almost said Raoul sounded *happy* at the ranch! He'd had no trouble at all putting her out of his mind.

Lacey squared her shoulders. It was time she cut her own losses. No more pining, no more false hope. From now on, Mexico City was just a place on the map.

Mary Beth's small apartment was already crowded when Lacey arrived at the party that evening. The noise level was high. Music from the stereo added volume to the laughter and conversation of the guests.

The hostess and a tall, blond man were standing in the middle of the room with their arms around each other's waists. Mary Beth waved and brought her husband over to be introduced.

"Isn't he everything I said he was?" she asked proudly.

Scott gave her a fond smile. "Why do I feel like a stud being offered for inspection?"

"I just like to show you off. Your stud days are over, pal," she warned.

"I'm henpecked already," he told Lacey.

"Don't listen to him," Mary Beth advised. "He adores being married. Don't you, darling?"

"I think you have a right to a lawyer being present before you answer that," Lacey joked.

"I thought you were supposed to be my best friend," Mary Beth complained.

Scott grinned. "Since this is a community-property state, does that mean I inherit half of her?"

"Are you lusting after another woman before the honeymoon is even over?" His wife pretended indignation.

"Our honeymoon will never be over," he answered deeply.

The way they looked at each other brought a lump to Lacey's throat.

She enjoyed the party through a conscious effort. The most difficult part was when friends asked about her trip, raising unwanted memories. It was surprising how many things recalled the past two weeks.

"These are delicious," Margot remarked, biting into a small quiche.

"You buy them in the frozen-food section, but don't tell a soul." Mary Beth laughed. "I want everybody to think I slaved for hours over a hot stove."

"You mean the servants were off today?" Margot drawled in an affected voice.

"Yes, the help situation is impossible. I had to do everything myself."

"Don't we all?" Margot dropped her stilted tone.

"Not the people in the society section," one of the other women in the group observed. "You're always reading about them having a hundred or so people to a cocktail party. How would you like to cook for a crowd like that?"

"I'd just buy more toothpicks and cut the hot dogs in smaller pieces," Mary Beth joked.

Lacey's smile was fixed as she visualized Elena's elegant party with uniformed maids passing out delicacies.

The early part of that evening had been such fun—before she'd seen Raoul's dark side.

Margot nudged her, jolting Lacey out of her absorption. "Wow! Look what just walked in. I wonder who he is."

Mary Beth glanced over at the tall, handsome man in the entry. "That's Barry Tyson. He's an old friend of Scott's."

"Please don't tell me he's here alone because his wife is in the hospital having a baby," Margot pleaded.

"You can start putting live chickens in your trap. He's single."

"I'll flip you for him," Margot said to Lacey.

"You can have him." Lacey smiled.

Mary Beth looked at her disapprovingly as Margot left with a gleam in her eyes. "You shouldn't have been so hasty. Barry is awfully nice."

"I'm sure he is."

"Let me take you over and introduce you," Mary Beth coaxed.

"No, thanks."

"Don't be stubborn. Barry is exactly what you need, someone new and different."

"What I need right now is another drink," Lacey said lightly before walking away. It was easier than arguing.

She was in the kitchen a little later, filling the ice bucket for Scott, when Barry joined her. She found it mildly amusing to see him alone. He'd been surrounded by eager women since he arrived.

"You're the only one here I haven't met. Are you avoiding me?" he asked.

"No, I'm just not very competitive."

"I doubt if you've ever had to be." He gazed at her admiringly. "You must have to beat men off with a stick."

"Only when they become too persistent." She gave him a perfunctory smile and started for the living room, but he blocked her path.

"It can't be anything I said, because we haven't spoken. Is it my hair? My tie? Tell me, and I'll change it."

"Judging by the attention you've been receiving, I wouldn't change a thing if I were you."

"I assume you're referring to the charming ladies here. They were just being friendly to a stranger," he protested.

"And they're waiting to be even more friendly," Lacey remarked dryly. "I suggest we go in and join them."

"Wait! I'm really a very nice fellow when you get to know me." He smiled engagingly. "I've never been arrested, I eat red meat sparingly, and my dog loves me."

"Thanks for the résumé. I'll keep it on file and call you if I need anyone." She smiled to take away the sting of rejection.

"Can you give me any idea of when that will be? I have a tennis game scheduled for one o'clock tomorrow, but I can cancel it."

"It won't be tomorrow," she assured him.

"I have an idea. Why don't we go out for a drink after the party so we can discuss your requirements? It will save you a phone call."

"You're really wasting your time. Any of the women in there would be more...cooperative."

Barry's playful manner vanished. "I know that," he said quietly. "But I'm in here...with you."

"Your timing is a little off," she answered ruefully. "Why don't you call me in a couple of months?"

He gazed into her wide, wistful blue eyes for a long moment. "I think you need me now."

Maybe he and Mary Beth were right. Perhaps a new interest would at least ease the pain of disillusionment, if nothing else.

She forced a smile. "Okay, we'll have one drink. But you'd better not be lying about your dog's affection."

As it turned out, their drink had to be postponed till the next night. The party didn't break up until late, and Lacey offered to stay and help clean up.

Barry volunteered his services, too, but his contribution was minimal. When Mary Beth told him to put away the dip and potato chips, he put the entire tray in the refrigerator.

"You don't put potato chips in the refrigerator," she told him disgustedly.

"Where do you put them?"

"Back in the bag."

"That doesn't make sense. You'll just have to take them out again the next time you serve the goop. My way avoids wasted motion."

"If you like soggy potato chips."

"That's the one angle I haven't figured out," Barry answered reflectively.

"Work on it," Mary Beth advised.

After she'd sent him into the living room to help Scott put the furniture back in place, Mary Beth said to Lacey, "Can you imagine any man being that helpless in a kitchen?"

Lacey's head was bent over an olive jar, concealing her expression. "I've known one or two."

"Really? Well, I suppose it's something you can overlook if they have other redeeming features."

The bars were closed by the time they finished cleaning up the apartment.

"We could go to your place for a nightcap," Barry suggested when he walked Lacey out to her car.

"Not unless you're into vanilla extract."

"I have a well-stocked bar at my place," he mentioned casually.

"Somehow I knew you would."

"I'm not propositioning you," he protested. "I just don't want the evening to end."

"Everything comes to an end," she replied somberly.

"Not before it even gets started." He smoothed her pale gold hair. "Give me a chance, and I'll make you forget all about that other guy."

"I never said—"

"You didn't have to." His voice was gentle. "How about tomorrow night? We'll do the town."

"If you're sure you want to," she said doubtfully.

"Well, I'd really rather go skydiving, but my parachute's at the cleaners." He kissed her cheek. "I'll pick you up at eight."

The weekend passed more pleasantly than Lacey had anticipated. Mary Beth's party helped, as did the date with Barry. He was easy to be with, and his open admiration was soothing.

No sparks flew between them—at least not from her side—but Lacey wasn't looking for romance. It was just comforting to be with someone who considered her a nice person. Raoul's shocking accusations had cut her deeply.

She looked forward to going back to work on Monday morning. Maybe once her life settled into its old pattern she'd stop dreaming of Raoul.

It would have been painful, yet preferable, if sleep had brought solely images of their last terrible scene. But in her dreams he was always the tender lover whose greatest delight was bringing her pleasure. She melted in his arms as he covered her body with kisses, and they merged together in the darkness. It was almost unbearable when she awoke and found it was just a dream.

"Thank heaven you're back!" Ingrid Brenner exclaimed when Lacey reported for work. Ingrid was the head of the fashion department.

"Gee, boss, I didn't know I was indispensable. Does this mean I get a raise?"

"It means you're going to work your little buns off for the next ten days. The fall fashion show has been moved up, and I'm going crazy!"

"What's the big deal?"

"We're shorthanded. Catherine is on vacation, and Sylvia broke her ankle waterskiing."

"Can't you hire some models from an agency?"

"That's what I did, but it won't be the same as having our own team. I have to switch everything around, too. Sylvia was supposed to wear the bridal gown. You'll have to take over for her."

"No!" Lacey exclaimed, feeling the knife twist. When Ingrid stared at her in surprise, she stammered, "I . . . I think it would look better on a brunette."

"Nonsense. You'll look like an absolute dream. Bring me the bridal gown," Ingrid instructed one of the seamstresses. "You might as well try it on now so we can take up the hem if necessary. All I need is for the bride to trip and fall off the runway," she muttered.

"I'll try not to ruin your day by breaking my leg," Lacey said bleakly.

The dress was everything a bride could have wished for, which deepened Lacey's gloom. Her eyes darkened as she looked at herself in the mirror.

"That pearl beading is divine!" Ingrid clasped her hands prayerfully as she gazed at Lacey.

The entire bodice was covered by tiny seed pearls embroidered in an intricate design. The dropped waist ended in points decorated with larger pearls.

"Every one of those beads was sewn on by hand," the seamstress remarked. She was on her knees arranging the billowing satin skirt over layers of lace-trimmed crinoline petticoats. "That's what makes it so expensive."

"You could buy a car for what that gown cost," Ingrid commented. "I'll be happy to make the sale, but can you imagine anyone spending that kind of money for something she'll only wear once?"

"It would be worth it," Lacey murmured.

"Don't get any ideas. You couldn't afford this dress even at a discount."

"I wouldn't have any use for it anyway." Lacey tried to smile.

Getting back into her old routine didn't provide quite the cure she'd hoped for, but most of the time she was too busy to think. Days at the store were hectic, and Barry monopolized her nights. Too much so. He was beginning to want more than she could give.

The first time he kissed her she had tried very hard to be receptive. He was physically attractive, thoughtful, kind. The sort of man most women yearned for. Yet she didn't feel anything but friendship toward him. Lacey was disturbed when he seemed to be getting serious.

She tried to warn him off. "You shouldn't be spending all your time with me, Barry."

"I'm simply following my mother's advice. She said to find a nice girl and settle down."

"But that's just the point. You haven't found her."

"You're not a nice girl?" He gave her a mock leer. "Then what are we waiting for? Let's fool around."

He continued to turn aside her concern with jokes, until the night before the fashion show. Things came to a head when he brought her home from a date and wanted to stay.

"You must know by now how I feel. I love you, Lacey."

"You're attracted to me, that's all. We've known each other just a little over a week."

"It doesn't take long to fall in love."

Lacey silently agreed. How long had it taken her to fall in love with Raoul? A lot shorter time than it would take to forget him. She didn't want Barry to be hurt the way she had been.

"I'm very fond of you," she explained carefully. "You're a wonderful person. You deserve someone who feels as deeply as you do."

He cupped her cheek in his palm. "I'm a very patient man."

"I wish I could tell you it would pay off," she answered sadly.

"It would if you'd give yourself a chance. I can't believe any man would walk out on you, but if he did, he doesn't deserve you."

"I've told myself that, but it doesn't help," she said forlornly.

"What does he have that I don't?"

"Nothing. It's no reflection on you. I only wish I *could* feel the same about you."

"I can make you forget the guy," Barry said confidently.

When he put his arms around her, Lacey submitted passively. It was useless to try to churn up emotions that simply weren't there. She had tried that, and it hadn't been successful. Barry would have to accept the fact.

His embrace wasn't unpleasant. In a way, it was like receiving comfort from a friend. But when he cupped her breast, Lacey flinched. Although Barry must have felt her reaction he intensified his efforts, pressing her body tightly against his while he kissed her with a passion he hadn't allowed himself to show before.

She felt only distaste at his arousal. It rippled down her spine and she became rigid in his arms. He tried kisses and caresses, extravagant words of love. Until it became apparent that she wasn't responding.

"It isn't going to work, is it?" His breathing was ragged when he finally released her.

"I'm sorry," she whispered.

"Me, too." His eyes held sadness as he gazed at her lovely face. "It would have been wonderful."

"Are we still friends?"

"Always." He took both her hands and held them in a strong grip. "I'll never forget you."

"Won't I see you again?"

He shook his head. "If I try hard, I'll get over you in time. But if I stick around on the fringes deluding myself, I'll wind up as hooked as you are."

Lacey nodded wordlessly.

She felt utterly deserted after he left, yet she knew Barry had made the right decision. Nobody should go through what she was suffering if he had a chance of saving himself. It didn't bode well for the future, though. Was she doomed to walk through the rest of her life alone?

Chapter Eleven

A restless night's sleep did nothing to dispel Lacey's depression. She wanted to stay in bed and pull the covers over her head. Why did the fashion show have to be that day when her energy level was so low?

As she expected, everything was frantic in her department. Items were misplaced and then located, but not without a lot of frayed nerves.

The show would be staged in the department-store restaurant, where customers could have lunch while reviewing the new fall fashions. A temporary runway had been erected down the middle of the large room, with a stage leading onto it.

The models changed in an impromptu dressing room set up backstage where long racks held the clothes that were to be worn, each with proper accessories.

As soon as a model left the runway, someone would be waiting to help her out of one outfit and into another. A hairdresser also stood by to smooth ruffled coiffures swiftly. The atmosphere was always one of controlled chaos.

The show was scheduled for noon, which meant a very early lunch or none at all for the participants. A lot of people were grumbling about it, but Lacey wasn't one of them. She drifted through the pandemonium in a withdrawn state.

"How can you be so calm?" Ingrid demanded. "Do you realize the Trevani collection just arrived, and every single garment has to be pressed?"

Lacey shrugged. "There's plenty of time."

"We start off with his gray pantsuit!"

"So switch the starting order."

"Next time I want sympathy I'll go to a grief counselor," Ingrid answered indignantly.

Lacey's friend Margot had been recruited from the lingerie department to help backstage. She finished zipping Lacey into a red leather miniskirt and stood back to view the result. A cashmere sweater went over the skirt, and the outfit was completed by a bulky, white leather jacket.

"You certainly have the legs for the new minis," she remarked enviously. "If it was up to me I'd have ankle-length hems mandated by law."

"You can wear whatever you like. Women aren't slaves to fashion anymore."

Margot sighed. "That's the consolation prize. I'd rather have the kind of figure men drop dead over."

"Today's woman doesn't need a man to make her happy," Lacey said disapprovingly.

"I've tried joining a ladies' bowling team, but it doesn't give the same feeling of togetherness," Margot observed dryly. "Let's face it, men are like house pets.

They're a lot of trouble, but when they curl up next to you it's all worthwhile.''

"If you're only interested in sex. In a real relationship a man has to admire more than your body. He has to respect your intelligence.''

"Sure, but what good is it if he doesn't stick around long enough to discover you have any? Barry Tyson zeroed in on you at the party last week, and it wasn't because you were quoting Shakespeare. Mary Beth says you're practically going steady.''

"Not any more.''

"What happened? Mary Beth says he's crazy about you.''

"Will you stop quoting her as though she were the oracle at Delphi!''

Margot wasn't intimidated by Lacey's sharp tone. "Don't tell me you dumped him! What's the matter with you? If Barry couldn't turn you on, *no* man can.''

Lacey was relieved when Ingrid interrupted their conversation, although her behavior was puzzling. Instead of issuing her usual crisp, last-minute instructions, the older woman showed a most uncharacteristic softness.

"You look adorable,'' she said gently.

"This is a stunning outfit,'' Lacey answered uncertainly.

"It ought to be at that price,'' Margot remarked.

"Leather is very durable.'' Lacey smoothed one supple sleeve. "You could wear this jacket for years.''

"How about the skirt?'' Margot grinned. "What would you use it for when styles change, a wide belt?''

Ingrid appeared not to have been listening. "You've been an asset to the store,'' she said to Lacey.

"Are you trying to tell me something?'' Lacey frowned.

"What do you mean?''

"It sounds as though I'm being fired."

"Don't be silly. I was merely paying you a compliment." Ingrid turned to a group of models standing nearby. "Fasten that top button, and straighten your collar, Charlene."

Lacey stared after her as she walked away. "What did you make out of that? Ingrid doesn't pay compliments—especially right before a show."

"You put in a lot of extra work on this one. Maybe she's trying to show her appreciation."

"Maybe," Lacey repeated skeptically.

She might not have thought any more about it if something else strange hadn't occurred. Walter Livingstone, the store manager, put in an unexpected appearance, apparently to see her.

"Is everyone decent?" He stuck his head in the door tentatively.

"Come right in," Ingrid said. "We're almost ready to start the show."

He handed Ingrid a large box. "I know you're probably busy with last-minute details so I'll be out of here in a minute. I just wanted to see our beautiful bride," he said jovially.

Lacey walked toward him slowly. "I don't wear the bridal gown until the finale. Did you want to see the dress?"

"No, I'll be watching from the audience. I only stopped by to...uh...drop off the bouquet." He continued to look at her with a smile on his face. "You're certainly going to be a gorgeous bride."

"Can I speak to you privately for a moment?" Ingrid's voice held a strange note.

Lacey watched with a puzzled air as she led him away. "What's going on around here? Mr. Livingstone never comes backstage before a show."

"He said he came to deliver the bouquet," Margot said.

"And you believed him? He doesn't even get his own coffee!"

"It is a little out of character." Margot looked thoughtful. "It was almost as though he came expressly to see you."

"Why would he do that?"

"Maybe the old boy has the hots for you."

"Don't be ridiculous. Mr. Livingstone has three children!"

"What's that got to do with it?" Margot laughed. "He doesn't want to adopt you."

"We're both making a big deal out of nothing," Lacey said firmly.

"Okay, then you tell me why he had a grin from ear to ear. When those old guys start sowing their wild oats they can act pretty silly."

The music began, signaling the end of their brief lull. The show was about to start. Lacey had taken part in dozens of fashion shows, but this time her nerves were jangling as she prepared to go on.

Could Margot possibly be right? Mr. Livingstone's behavior *had* been unusual. And what about Ingrid's? She'd certainly hustled him away in a hurry. Was she trying to head off trouble before it developed? And did that include going so far as to remove temptation from his vicinity?

Lacey's stomach tightened as she glided down the runway, opening her jacket to display the scarlet lining, her smooth face showing none of the turmoil raging inside. Was she really in danger of being fired? The job wasn't that great, but this was no time to be out of work, even for a short period. Not when she'd borrowed money from Mary Beth to repay Raoul.

Writing a note to accompany it had been the difficult part. How did one politely thank a man for his hospitality when it had included sharing his bed?

The audience was a faceless blur as Lacey twirled and postured, her thoughts turned inward on a darkened room where moonlight illuminated a man's lean body.

She started disrobing as soon as she was out of sight of the audience. Margot took the clothes she discarded and handed her a black wool jumpsuit. A lizard belt with intricate gold medallions cinched her small waist. While Lacey was fastening the buckle, Margot slipped a heavy gold chain around her neck. They worked together smoothly. Lacey changed shoes and started back to the runway without having to think about what she was doing.

The next hour brought a number of similar changes. She progressed from sportswear to clothes suitable for luncheons at a restaurant or country club, soft prints and dressy knits. Evening wear came next.

A murmur of approval greeted Lacey as she appeared in a strapless pink taffeta bubble dress with a huge bow on one hip. Her long legs showed to advantage as she pirouetted in spike-heel silver sandals.

As she was sliding down the back zipper afterward, Margot said, "Did you know you have a secret admirer out there?"

"What are you talking about?"

"I've been peeking through the curtain. There's a dreamy man sitting alone at a table in the back."

"So?"

"So every time you come out in a different outfit he writes something down."

"What does that prove?" Lacey stepped carefully out of the pink gown and reached for her next change.

"I don't know, but he doesn't do it with the other girls."

"Maybe he's buying a wardrobe for his wife or girl-friend, and I'm her size," Lacey said indifferently.

"You're all the same size," Margot pointed out.

"Then it doesn't have anything to do with any of us. He's probably bored out of his skull and is doodling on his program."

There were always a scattering of men in the audience, usually tourists whose wives had dragged them there. The rest were either salesmen or scouts from other stores.

"I'm telling you, you're the only one he's interested in," Margot insisted.

Lacey sighed. "I wish I were the femme fatale you think I am."

"You haven't done so badly."

Margot zipped her into another strapless gown even more eye-catching than the pink. This one was black tulle flecked with red velvet dots. The bodice was shirred, and the short skirt was a froth of layered ruffles.

"Watch him and see if I'm not right," Margot said. "He's sitting on the left side way in the back."

"Stop dawdling, you two," Ingrid said sharply, appearing beside them. "You can talk later."

Lacey kicked off her silver sandals and stepped into black satin ones. Margot's words were echoing in her ears as she walked onstage. If I haven't done so badly, why am I alone? she asked herself bitterly. What good did it do to attract men if she couldn't hold on to them?

"Did you see him?" Margot asked eagerly when she returned. "Wasn't I right? I'll bet he checked off *that* gown in his program, didn't he?"

"I don't know. I forgot to look for him."

"You are the absolute limit!" Margot exclaimed disgustedly. "It wouldn't hurt you to smile in his direction. Who knows what it could lead to? He might turn out to be a millionaire playboy."

"Leave me alone, Margot!" Lacey said sharply.

"Well, aren't we temperamental all of a sudden!"

Margot's hurt feelings kept her quiet for a while. She didn't relent until the show was winding to a close. The volume of noise had risen as everyone geared up for the finale.

"Keep it down, ladies," Ingrid ordered. "We aren't through yet. Get into your bridesmaids' gowns on the double."

This was the part Lacey had been dreading, although she told herself not to be foolish. It was one last number in just another show. She'd modeled bridal gowns before. It was simply the timing that was getting her down. The fact that she had hoped to be a bride herself.

But she'd never anticipated wearing a dress like this. Margot was holding it almost reverently. The sheer opulence of the fragile garment overcame her earlier pique.

"You're going to knock them dead out there in this little number."

"If your mystery man makes a note in his program, we'll know he's a bachelor, anyway." Lacey smiled to atone for her earlier shrillness.

"And that his intentions are honorable," Margot agreed, accepting the tacit apology. "Wouldn't that be something if it was love at first sight?"

"Do you mind if I take a look at him before we get married?" Lacey teased.

"It would be much more romantic if you met at the altar."

"What if I married the best man by mistake?"

"You have a point there." Margot grinned. "Okay, let's go peek through the curtain. I'll show you where he's sitting."

"Lacey! Where do you think you're going?" Ingrid called. "You aren't on yet. You aren't even ready!" she added distractedly.

"Yes I am, except for the veil."

"Did you plan to stick it on the back of your head as you were walking onstage?" Ingrid demanded. "It has to be arranged properly. Where's the bridal veil, for heaven's sake? Do I have to be responsible for everything around here?"

As she stalked off, Margot raised her eyebrows. "What's she so hysterical about? She's more nervous at the end of the show than she was in the beginning."

"Maybe something went wrong that we didn't notice."

"What could happen at a fashion show? One of the models turned left when she should have turned right?"

"Who knows? I just wish it were over," Lacey said.

"Me, too," Margot agreed, putting her hand to her waist. "All this high fashion is giving me a low backache."

Ingrid returned with the bridal veil, a fluff of tulle attached to a satin band decorated with orange blossoms. After carefully placing the circlet on Lacey's crown she beckoned to the hairdresser, who recombed Lacey's hair so that it flowed over her shoulders like a golden stream.

Finally both women stood back and looked at her critically, but with approval. A froth of white framed her face, then billowed out in back like a wispy cloud.

"I like the style," Ingrid declared.

"So much more sensible than the ones that cover up the face," the other woman agreed. "People want to see the bride's happy expression."

They were due for a disappointment, Lacey thought bleakly. She'd lost that look of breathless anticipation permanently.

Soft strains of music started in the outer room, signaling the resumption of the show. In spite of Ingrid's fit of nerves, all the models were ready and waiting to go on. They carried bouquets of pink and lilac flowers that complemented their bridesmaids' gowns of mauve taffeta.

As they filed out, Ingrid handed Lacey the bridal bouquet. It was an exquisite arrangement of white orchids surrounded by stephanotis, fragrant star-shaped blossoms.

Lacey took the flowers matter-of-factly, before noticing that Ingrid's eyes were glistening suspiciously. Surely those couldn't be tears! What did *she* have to cry about?

"Are you all right?" she asked the older woman uncertainly.

"Don't look so surprised." Ingrid laughed self-consciously. "Doesn't everyone cry at weddings?"

The wedding march sounded before Lacey could make sense out of that. It didn't matter anyway. All that mattered was getting through this charade. She walked onto the stage in a numbed state.

Lacey blocked out the audience. She paced to the end of the runway, following the measured beat of the music, willing herself to think of nothing else.

As she turned to retrace her path up the aisle, she saw a man facing her. He had on a white vestment of some sort, and he was holding a book. The models in their bridesmaids' outfits were arranged on either side of him.

Lacey frowned as she realized the man was supposed to represent a minister. They had never been this realistic before. Why now, of all times? She proceeded up the walkway with reluctant steps.

When she approached the group, a man walked out of the wings. Her steps faltered as she thought for a moment it was Raoul. What was happening to her? Had she lost complete touch with reality?

The unreal feeling deepened as he closed the short distance between them and took her hand, drawing her forward. He was smiling the way he had in the dreams that plagued her, which seemed to prove she was hallucinating.

But Raoul's remembered touch was real. The fine golden down on her arm prickled as his warm hand firmly enclosed her icy fingers. However he'd gotten here, for whatever reason, Raoul was no figment of her imagination.

A murmur ran through the audience as he led her to the center of the stage without taking his eyes from hers. Lacey followed him in a trance. A million questions hammered at the back of her mind, but she was afraid to break the spell. All that really mattered was having Raoul back.

She was dimly aware of the models standing in a semi-circle, waiting to bring the show to a close. Lacey vaguely realized that Raoul shouldn't be there. Ingrid would be furious. It seemed supremely unimportant at the moment.

But when the man in the white vestment began the wedding ceremony, Lacey came out of her trance. How could they expect her to go through such a cruel hoax? She didn't know how Raoul had managed it, but his purpose was clear. He wanted to humiliate her with this mock marriage, knowing she'd hoped for a real one.

She snatched her hand out of his. "What does it take to satisfy you?" she asked in a low, trembling voice.

"You must know the answer to that." His eyes were unfathomable.

"Haven't you punished me enough?"

"I've punished both of us, and I'll never forgive myself. I'll spend the rest of my life making it up to you, if you'll let me."

The minister coughed discreetly.

Raoul flashed him a lilting smile. "We'll be with you in a moment." He took Lacey's hands and held them tightly. "I love you, *querida*. Will you marry me?"

She stared at him in a daze, certain that she must be dreaming after all.

When she didn't answer, his grip tightened. "Won't you give me another chance? I'm begging you, *cara*."

It was so unlike this proud man to beg. The desolation in his eyes touched Lacey deeply. She'd felt the same pain. It was washed away by a flood of happiness that almost drowned her.

"I'd be very proud to marry you," she said softly.

Raoul had to exert a visible effort to keep from sweeping her into his arms. "We'd better get on with the wedding. I can't wait much longer to kiss the bride."

"You mean he's a real minister?" Nothing surprised Lacey at that point.

The solemn rites sounded like poetry to her ears. They held hands and exchanged the vows that would bind them together for life. When the ceremony was over, Raoul took her in his arms and kissed her with a tenderness that expressed his love more clearly than words could ever do.

Then everyone crowded around with enthusiastic congratulations. Even members of the audience joined in the general excitement. This fashion show would be talked about for a long time.

Raoul stood by, smiling indulgently at the commotion. After a suitable time he took Lacey's arm and gently eased her away.

As they started down the aisle several voices called, "Throw the bouquet!"

Ingrid stood at the edge of the group, smiling through sentimental tears. Lacey didn't know the whole story yet, but she realized that the older woman had been instrumental in her present joy. In the midst of all the uproar she threw the beautiful bouquet directly into Ingrid's arms.

A long white limousine was waiting outside at the curb. People passing by eyed it curiously, then stopped to stare as Lacey and Raoul emerged from the store.

"I never rode in a stretch limo before," Lacey commented happily as she spread out her skirt in the roomy back seat.

"You can have one for every day of the week if you like."

"I didn't marry you for your money, Raoul," she said quietly.

"I know that, my love." His fingertips stroked her cheek. "I still can't get over the miracle that you did marry me."

His husky voice and feather touch were creating a storm inside her. Lacey wanted to throw herself into his arms, but she couldn't help being conscious of the driver. The man was very correct, watching the road without expression, yet his presence was inhibiting. She tried to lighten the charged atmosphere.

"What would you have done with this fancy car if I'd turned you down?"

"I'd have told the chauffeur to run over me."

"That would have ruined your suit." She smiled.

He didn't match her light tone. "My whole life would have been in ruins if I'd lost you." Raoul's voice throbbed with remembered torment. "Promise you'll never leave me."

Reality suddenly intruded into Lacey's fairy-tale romance. "I didn't leave you, Raoul," she said haltingly. "You left me. Why did you come back?"

"Because I found out I can't live without you. Not a night went by that I didn't reach out for you in my sleep."

A little chill crept up her spine. "Sex isn't enough to base a marriage on."

He framed her face in his palms and gazed deeply into her eyes. "Is that all you think I want? Darling Lacey, you mean so much more to me. I want to share my life with you. I want to father your children. You're everything I could ever hope for."

Emotion tightened her throat. Before she could respond, they pulled up in front of San Diego's finest hotel.

Lacey attracted a great deal of attention in her bridal gown. People in the lobby smiled, and the manager greeted them warmly.

A bellman led them down a corridor to the bridal suite, which was the ultimate in opulence. Flowers filled the large living room, where a bottle of champagne was cooling in a silver ice bucket. Although it was the middle of the afternoon, the bellman drew the drapes and tuned in soft music on the radio. By the time he departed with a large tip and a broad smile, Lacey was having trouble controlling her mirth.

"If it weren't for this bridal gown, I'd swear he was setting the scene for a seduction."

Raoul linked his arms around her waist. "Let's not disappoint him."

Lacey thrilled as his hot mouth devoured hers with pent-up longing. Her own desire rushed to meet his. She was tempted to let all her questions wait, but some important ones demanded immediate answers.

"We have to talk first, Raoul," she said firmly.

"Now?" He blew gently into her ear.

"Yes, now."

He released her reluctantly. "Whatever you say, *cara*. From this moment on I'm your slave."

Lacey laughed. "I'll settle for equal partners."

"Always, my darling. That's what I want more than anything."

Her face clouded. "Partners trust each other."

"I'll never need to be reminded of that again."

"What changed your mind? Did Carlos tell you the truth?" She could scarcely conceive of that. Unless Raoul had beaten it out of him.

"I'm through listening to Carlos," he answered contemptuously.

"That's a relatively new decision." Lacey couldn't keep the cynicism out of her voice. "You felt differently the last time I saw you."

"I was crazed with jealousy. It's the only excuse I can offer. When I saw you two in bed together—" His voice broke off hoarsely.

"I tried to explain what happened, but you wouldn't listen."

"I know," he said soberly.

"It hurt so much that you believed Carlos instead of me."

"I wasn't thinking straight, obviously. I've been half out of my mind these past two weeks."

She looked at him doubtfully. "We have to be honest with each other, Raoul."

"I've never been anything else, *cara*. Every day without you has been a living hell."

"Even the next day at the ranch?"

"*Especially* at the ranch."

"That's not what Rosa said."

He frowned. "How would she know? She wasn't with me. When did she say that?"

"I called her after I returned home." Lacey stared down at her twisting fingers. "She said you weren't there, but she'd spoken to you on the phone, and you sounded very happy."

Raoul laughed harshly. "Is that what she thought? I was dying slowly inside, but I had to keep up appearances for my daughter's sake. To make matters worse, Carlotta talked about you constantly. For the first time, I couldn't wait to get away. I had to go someplace that didn't hold memories of you."

"Where did you go?"

"To one of our mines in the mountains. I lived in the camp with the men, and worked alongside them. During the day I was able to block you out of my mind, and at night I was tired enough to fall asleep."

"You were more fortunate than I," Lacey said bleakly.

"I'm sorry, *querida*." His voice was muted. "I've put us both through such a bad time."

"What finally made you see the light?"

"I was living in a vacuum, trying to blot you out of my consciousness, but it didn't work for very long. I couldn't get you out of my mind. Every glorious moment we'd shared came back to haunt me. I remembered the love we shared, the way you gave yourself to me without holding anything back."

"You were all I ever wanted," she whispered.

He crushed her fiercely in his arms. "I finally realized that, *mi amor*. When I started to think clearly, I figured out what had happened. Carlos and Delores had done a neat job on us."

Lacey drew back to look at him incredulously. "Delores was in on it?"

"She was the one who phoned me that night, pretending to be you. She was always a very clever mimic," he said bitterly. "The phone call alone should have tipped me off. You'd scarcely have urged me to come over if you'd been entertaining Carlos."

"Couldn't she have done it out of spite, without his knowledge?" Lacey hated to raise doubts in Raoul's mind, but it was better than having them surface later.

He shook his head. "Everything was too pat. You'd told Carlos off and hung up on him, telling him not to bother you again. Most men would have been pretty annoyed. But instead of getting angry, Carlos waited by the phone on the one night we weren't going to be together—a free night you didn't even know about until five o'clock. Delores knew you'd be alone because I told her. But how could she know you'd be with Carlos unless she sent him?"

"It would have involved a lot of coincidences, wouldn't it?"

"Too many. But you were the biggest flaw in their plan."

"I don't understand."

He smoothed her hair tenderly. "We were as close as a man and a woman can get. You'd never given me any reason to doubt you before. I finally realized that you weren't capable of that kind of deception."

"That's the best reason for coming back," she said softly.

His eyes darkened to ebony. "I was terrified that it might be too late."

"Why didn't you phone me when you'd worked it all out?"

"I was afraid to. It's so easy to hang up on someone, and you certainly had reason to. I had to make my apology in person, and hope you'd give me another chance."

"You were sure of it," she scolded gently.

"No, darling, I was never so scared in my life."

"But you had the minister waiting. How did you arrange a real wedding?"

"Originally, I planned to show up where you worked. I figured you couldn't run away from me there. When I called the store to find out your schedule, they told me about the fashion show." He smiled. "It seemed like a sign from heaven. I gambled that if I proposed and rushed you into marriage before you had time to think about it, you'd be too confused to object."

"You'd have been pretty embarrassed in front of all those people if I had."

"It wouldn't have mattered." His smile faded as he gazed at her. "Nothing in life was important without you."

"I felt the same way," she whispered. "I merely went through the motions—especially today. I was miserable when I had to wear the bridal gown."

Raoul traced the neckline lingeringly. "You made a beautiful bride."

"Everybody knew about your plan, didn't they?" Ingrid's behavior made sense now.

"Only the store manager and your department head were in on it. They were very cooperative."

Lacey began to laugh. "Mr. Livingstone was so nice to me that my friend thought his intentions were dishonorable."

"How can I blame him?" He unfastened one of the tiny buttons at her bodice. "Mine are."

"Yours can't be," she murmured as her skin started to tingle. "We're married."

"For now and forever," he said fervently.

Raoul's kiss contained all the pent-up yearning that separation had brought. While his tongue plundered the moist depths of her mouth, he uttered little groans of hunger and love.

Lacey was equally impassioned. Her hands glided over his wide shoulders, his back, tracing the taut muscles. She raked her fingers through his crisp hair, wanting to experience every part of him.

As their passion rose, Raoul reached again for the tiny buttons on the front of her gown. When they proved difficult to unfasten he tugged at them. Lacey reluctantly stopped him.

"You'd better let me do it."

"I want to undress you," he protested.

"I want you to, my love, but this dress has to go back to the store. It costs a small fortune."

He looked at her searchingly as she stood up and completed what he'd started. "Do you like it, Lacey? Is it what you would have chosen if you'd known it was to be your own wedding gown?"

"It's the most beautiful dress in the world." She stepped out of the voluminous folds of satin and held the gown against her breast. "I only hope it brings as much happiness to the next bride as it has brought to me."

Raoul's face cleared. "I do, too, since that will be Carlotta."

Lacey stared at him in bewilderment. "Carlotta?"

"Isn't it traditional for a daughter to wear her mother's wedding gown?"

It suddenly struck Lacey that she had not only gained a husband, but an adorable daughter as well. After being all alone in the world, she now had a family.

Raoul watched her uncertainly. "You don't mind about Carlotta, do you?"

"Mind? I love her almost as much as I love you!" She flung herself on top of him.

After a startled moment his arms closed around her. "She's the only person I'd share you with," he said deeply.

He crossed his legs around hers, imprisoning her against him. Lacey was a willing captive. She pressed her body against his and lowered her head to drop breathless little kisses over his face.

Raoul gripped her head in both hands so his mouth could join with hers. She thrust her tongue in his mouth, delighting in her dominant position. Suddenly she was the aggressor. She'd always let him take the lead in their lovemaking. Now she discovered the joy of taking what she wanted.

Raoul indulged her fantasy, letting her set the pace. She shifted slightly to remove his tie and unbutton his shirt without relinquishing possession of his mouth. Realizing her pleasure in exploring his body, he quivered but remained passive when she ran her palms over his flat nipples.

Lacey drew out the pleasure, raking her nails through the mat of dark hair that covered his broad chest, then tracing the diminishing triangle down to his waist. But when her exploration went deeper, Raoul grabbed her hand.

"Are you trying to make me lose all control?" he demanded.

Her smile was pure enchantment. "You do it to me all the time."

She wiggled her fingers free and continued down to her objective. Grasping his pulsing manhood, she uttered a tiny sound of satisfaction.

In a lightning move he rolled over, covering her body with his. "You beautiful little siren, you enjoy driving me over the edge, don't you?"

She trailed a teasing finger down his spine. "I just love to touch you. Don't you like me to?"

He stared at her with glittering eyes. "Shall I show you how much?"

Instead of answering, she smiled and moved against him in mute invitation. Raoul parted her legs and slid his hands under her hips, lifting her body. Lacey received him with deep satisfaction that mounted to a kind of frenzy as his driving passion carried her higher and higher. She was racked by almost unbearable ecstasy. The climax came in a burst of power that rocketed through their bodies simultaneously.

Raoul cradled her in his arms afterward, caressing her with sated appreciation. No words were necessary. They were content to bask in the afterglow of their love.

Much later he said, "Where would you like to go on your honeymoon?"

Lacey sighed contentedly. "I'm perfectly happy right here."

He rubbed his cheek against hers. "So am I, *mi amor*, but there must be someplace you'd like to go."

"As a matter of fact, Acapulco was recommended highly to me."

"We'll leave in the morning," he promised.

"You'd better make that afternoon. I have to go home first and pack."

"All you need is a bathing suit, and you can get that in Acapulco. We'll pick up the rest of your clothes at the store on the way to the airport."

"Did you actually buy all those things I modeled?" she asked. "I thought Margot was just fantasizing about a mystery man."

"Every bride needs a trousseau."

"But she's supposed to provide her own. You're always doing nice things for me."

Raoul's eyes kindled as he looked at her lovely face. Twining his legs around hers, he murmured, "If you really feel obligated, you can do something for *me*."

Lacey smiled bewitchingly. "That won't be an obligation. It will be a pure pleasure."

* * * * *

FEBRUARY TITLES

CHAMPAGNE FOR BREAKFAST
Tracy Sinclair

THE PLAYBOY AND THE WIDOW
Debbie Macomber

WENDY WYOMING
Myrna Temte

EDGE OF FOREVER
Sherryl Woods

THE BARGAIN
Patricia Coughlin

BOTH SIDES NOW
Brooke Hastings

Silhouette
WINTER
COMPETITION

How would you like a year's supply of
Silhouette Desire Romances ABSOLUTELY FREE?
Well, you can win them! All you have to do is complete the word
puzzle below and send it into us by 30th June 1989.
The first five correct entries picked out of the bag after that date
will each win a year's supply of Silhouette Desire Romances (Six
books every month - **worth over £90!**) What could be easier?

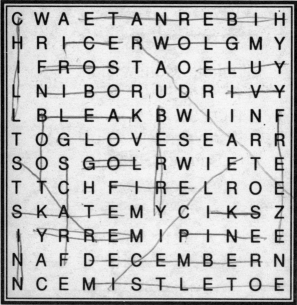

```
C W A E T A N R E B I H
H R I C E R W O L G M Y
I F R O S T A O E L U Y
L N I B O R U D R I V Y
L B L E A K B W I I N F
T O G L O V E S E A R R
S O S G O L R W I E T E
T T C H F I R E L R O E
S K A T E M Y C I K S Z
I Y R R E M I P I N E E
N A F D E C E M B E R N
N C E M I S T L E T O E
```

Ivy	Radiate	December	Star	Merry
Frost	Chill	Skate	Ski	Pine
Bleak	Glow	Mistletoe	Inn	
Boot	Ice	Fire		
Robin	Hibernate	Log	**PLEASE TURN**
Yule	Icicle	Scarf	**OVER FOR**
Freeze	Gloves	Berry	**DETAILS ON HOW TO ENTER**

How to enter

All the words listed overleaf, below the word puzzle, are hidden in the grid. You can find them by reading the letters forwards, backwards, up or down, or diagonally. When you find a word, circle it, or put a line through it. After you have found all the words the remaining letters (which you can read from left to right, from the top of the puzzle through to the bottom) will spell a secret message.

Don't forget to fill in your name and address in the space provided and pop this page in an envelope (you don't need a stamp) and post it today. Hurry - competition ends 30th June 1989

Only one entry per household please.

Silhouette Competition,
FREEPOST,
P.O.236,
Croydon,
Surrey CR9 9EL

Secret message _____

_____

Name _____

Address _____

_____

_____

_____ Postcode _____

SCOMF